THE
RIVER PATH

THE
RIVER PATH

A Novel

JENNIE HANSEN

Covenant Communications, Inc.

Cover image © PhotoDisc, Inc.

Published by Covenant Communications, Inc.
American Fork, Utah

Printed in the United States of America
First Printing: March 2000

07 06 05 04 03 02 01 00   10 9 8 7 6 5 4 3 2

ISBN 1-57734-620-3

I was the second of three daughters born to Jed and Mary Smith. We three girls were sandwiched between three older and two younger brothers in a family that moved frequently. Consequently, we learned to depend on each other in a way many sisters never do. My sisters were my best friends, and still are. This book is for them—my sisters, MarJean Henson and Vada Little. I love you both.

CHAPTER ONE

"Dana!"

Something in Matt's voice sent a chill up her spine. Hastily setting the salad bowl she'd been carrying on the counter, she hurried to their son's bedroom, where Matt had gone to get Josh up from his nap. Josh's whimpering cry reached her as she hurried down the short hallway.

"What's wrong . . . ?" Her question ended in a gasp. Matt stood in the middle of the room with Josh in his arms. Blood spurted from the child's nose, red smears covered one end of his crib, and red droplets stained the blue rug beside the crib. The baby's cries sounded weak and scared.

"Ma-ma." He held out his arms to her.

"Joshua!" she called as she rushed forward to take her baby from her husband's arms. Matt stood shock still, a look of horror on his face to match the one in her heart. She couldn't bear the pain and fear in her baby's cry. He'd attempted to climb out of his crib numerous times, and she'd meant to talk to Matt about getting him a bed, but Matt was gone so much, and for the past month Josh had seemed content to stay in the crib when she put him there. She should have found an opportunity to speak to him. She couldn't blame Matt now if he was angry because she'd neglected to tell him Josh had outgrown his crib.

"Get cold, wet cloths from the bathroom!" She lifted her eyes from Josh long enough to urge her husband into action. She tried to speak calmly and remember everything she knew about nosebleeds. Her brother had had frequent nosebleeds while they were growing up, and she'd learned to deal with them. Wet compresses held to Rick's nose had usually stemmed the flow of blood in a few minutes. She glanced quickly toward Matt again, pleading with her eyes for him to hurry. He looked back at her oddly, but rushed to do her bidding.

When he returned with the cold compress, she held it to the baby's nose and whispered words meant to sooth and comfort. Settling in an old rocking chair with the child in her arms, she rocked him while Matt changed the crib sheet and sponged the rug. It seemed to take much longer for the flow to stop than it ever had for Rick, Dana thought, but her brother had been older when she first started sneaking into his room to help him. She didn't know if Rick's nosebleeds had started when he was Josh's age, and if they had, how long they had lasted. Some of the old anger swept through her. Rick's nosebleeds hadn't been the result of playing too hard or childish falls.

Finally the bleeding slowed, then appeared to stop. Josh lay limply in her arms as she washed his face and hands. Dark circles under his eyes and an air of exhaustion brought a worried frown to her face. He looked so small and vulnerable, she wanted to weep. She shouldn't have left him this afternoon, and she should have talked to Matt about getting Joshua a bed.

Josh had been quiet, almost listless for several days. She'd worried that he might be coming down with a cold and had wondered earlier this afternoon if she should change her plans. But she had promised to help with the older Primary girls' activity, and Matt had a rare afternoon off and could watch Josh, so she had gone.

"Do you think we should call Dr. Young?" she looked up to ask Matt. It seemed to her that Josh had lost an excessive amount of blood for a two-year-old.

Matt nodded his head and looked as though he might cry. He couldn't quite meet her eyes, and her heart went out to him. Josh's nosebleed must have frightened him more than she realized. She knew he was tender-hearted and that he loved their two-year-old son with all his being. Still, he'd grown up with three brothers; surely he knew little boys sometimes got nosebleeds. He didn't speak for several minutes, but seemed to be struggling with some deep emotion.

"Dr. Young will want to see him . . . he'll ask about the bruises," he said flatly, but with a kind of determination.

"Bruises?" Her heart beat with fear. Had Josh sustained more serious injuries than just a bloody nose? How far had he fallen?

"Yes, bruises. Mother was here this afternoon while you were gone. Josh woke up and needed to be changed. She wanted to do it, but when she removed his diaper she got upset and called me. We both saw black marks on the backs of his legs. There's also a big one on his buttock, almost at the base of his spine."

Dana stared back at her husband, her mind registering his words but unable to make any sense of them. She'd noticed dark smudges on Josh's arms and legs several times during the past few weeks, but they weren't dark enough to really be bruises. He was an active, busy two-year-old who tripped over toys, climbed where he shouldn't, and refused to stay in his crib. But there hadn't been any serious falls. Slowly she stood with Josh in her arms. She carried him to the changing table and methodically stripped away his clothes.

Her eyes widened in horror. The bruises were exactly where Matt said they were. There was also one on his small chest and the smudges on his arms had darkened. The hollows beneath his eyes also looked more sunken and darker than usual. Slowly she lifted her eyes to meet her husband's. In their depths she saw fear and misery—and accusation. She had trouble absorbing the implication that stared her in the face. He blamed her. She hadn't watched Josh closely enough.

———•———

Matt didn't know what he thought, only that Joshua had been hurt. His heart said no, Dana couldn't possibly be responsible for the bruises. Not once had he seen her so much as spank Josh. Besides she was kind and loving, not the kind of monster who would leave bruises on a baby. But there wasn't anyone else; Dana never allowed anyone else near Josh. She irritated his family endlessly with her jealous possessiveness toward the baby.

He'd been angry when his mother first suggested Dana might be punishing Josh too severely. He'd never doubted that her love for their baby was as real as his. Now this. There had been nothing normal about the blood streaming from Josh's nose. He'd had a few nosebleeds himself as a kid—so had his brothers—but never like this. Bruises didn't appear without cause and blood didn't flow for no reason.

Doubt crept in as he remembered coming home from work one day last week to find Dana cranky and out of sorts. She'd told him Josh had fussed and whined all day, insisting she hold him. A small easel lay tipped on its side on the table and spatters of paint accented the table top. She'd complained she'd gotten nothing done all day but hold Joshua and clean up messes. She'd attributed his fussiness to teething, and when Matt had leaned over the rails of his sleeping child's crib, he'd noticed a dark spot of paint—or was it blood?—at the corner of his mouth. Dana had wondered aloud why these little molars were causing so much more difficulty than Josh's other teeth had.

Moments ago, he'd felt sick when he'd seen his son's bared body, even though he'd seen the bruises several hours earlier. He couldn't erase from his mind the gush of blood that streamed from the baby's small nose when he'd leaned over to lift him from the side of his crib where he stood weeping. As Mother had sharply pointed out this afternoon, the bruises weren't consistent with the normal bumps and bruises of childhood. Even he could see that. She'd also reminded him that Dana had come from an abusive home and that abused children often grew up to become abusers of the next generation. Reluctantly he'd promised her he'd ask Dana about the bruises. And he'd meant to, later this evening after dinner was over, and Josh was settled for the night. He'd meant to be gentle and understanding, and hoped she'd have an explanation other than the one his mother believed was the obvious one.

Matt stood in the middle of the room feeling helpless. He'd had to search for a rug cleaner, and he didn't know where to look for fresh pajamas for his son. Guilt reared its head. He hadn't spent much time with Dana and Josh lately. He'd been working long hours, trying to prove his worth to his father's company. All his life he'd been the smallest of the Bingham boys, the one who didn't compete in sports, and the one who was practically useless at a construction site. His father and brothers had sacrificed greatly so he could get the education he needed to take over handling the company's finances. Now, with the recent expansion, there was a tremendous amount that needed doing, and Matt was determined to show his family that he could not only fulfill, but exceed their expectations. He was aware that Dana didn't know many people in Salt Lake, and that she held his family at arm's length, but it had never occurred to him her loneliness might lead to something like this.

Slowly he squared his shoulders. No matter what, he would stand by Dana, but he wouldn't allow her or anyone else to hurt Josh again. He loved Josh with a fierce intensity he would have thought impossible before that moment when he'd first held his son in his arms. For two years that love had grown and expanded with each smile, each step, each gesture, and every shared moment. Before Josh's birth, he hadn't thought anyone else could come even close to mattering to him as much as Dana did. For the past two years, he had been almost smug in his belief that he had the most perfect wife and child in the world. But if Dana had done this, she needed help as badly as Josh, and it was his responsibility to see that she got it.

"I'll call Dr. Young." His words came out terse and abrupt. How was he going to deal with this? One thing at a time, he reminded himself. Josh needed medical care. That was his first priority, then he'd talk to Dana and convince her to get counseling. He'd spend more time with her and their son, even if his career suffered. His family came first.

The ride to the children's hospital, where Dr. Young said he would meet them, seemed interminable. He drove while Dana held Josh, wrapped snugly in the small quilt covered with rainbows and butterflies she'd made for him before his birth. It was his "blanky," the one he had to have in his crib at bed time, when he napped, or when something went wrong in his small world. Matt had always understood the quilt's attraction for his son. It was both light and colorful and spoke to a need he too harbored deep inside himself.

A picture of Dana rose in his mind as he drove. It was the first time he'd seen her. She'd walked down the aisle of the chapel where the student ward met in a blinding white two-piece outfit with huge splashes of red, yellow, and blue erupting across the brilliant white fabric like the wild brush strokes of an eccentric artist. Her auburn hair glinted fiery red as rays of light streamed through double glass doors near the front of the room and her own motion sent the flared skirt and filmy sleeves fluttering as though caught by a gentle breeze. When she began to speak, it was as though her radiance reached inside some dark spot in his heart and lit it with golden light.

Making an attempt to shake off memories of the past, he forced himself to concentrate on the traffic around him. They rode in silence, neither sharing their thoughts or fears. Once he glanced across the space between them and caught a glimpse of tenderness on Dana's face as she bent toward their son. In a way, he'd always seen Dana just the way his son saw his blanky—full of light and color, covering him with a special warmth meant just for him.

Pain settled more deeply, like a lead weight in his chest. He'd be a blind fool if he couldn't see how much Dana loved Josh. How could she hurt someone she loved with such intensity? Perhaps she hadn't. There had to be another explanation. His heart lifted; the woman he'd loved since he'd heard her bear her testimony at that Young Adult fireside almost four years ago couldn't possibly strike Josh. She'd told him before they married of the emotional abuse she'd suffered in her parents' home, and described the guilt and grief she'd suffered each time her father had beaten her brother. Dana abhorred any form of physical violence; she couldn't have done this.

He had tried to explain to his mother. "Dana's father never physically abused her or her sister. He mocked and ridiculed her, but he never struck her."

"I know you don't want to believe Dana would hit Josh," his mother acknowledged in her forthright way. "But you told me yourself her brother was always in trouble with his school or the law, and when he didn't obey his father's orders, his father beat him. Dana witnessed those beatings from a very young age. It's quite possible some part of her mind believes that is the way to deal with a disobedient boy. Josh is two. Two-year-olds generally try the patience of the most indulgent parents. I'm sure she doesn't want Josh to end up like her brother, so when he misbehaves, she likely punishes him the same way she saw her brother punished."

He felt like screaming. It sounded so logical he couldn't help wondering if his mother was right? Or should he trust his heart, which steadily protested Dana was innocent? He didn't know what to believe. He and Dana came from totally different backgrounds. He and his brothers had never questioned their parents' love for them. They'd hiked and camped and skied together. They hadn't had a lot of money, but there was always enough to fill the grill with hamburgers when their friends showed up after ball practice and to provide ice cream for the whole priest quorum and their dads after conference priesthood sessions. He'd been the third of four boys, all of which, with their mother's encouragement, had become Eagle scouts, then served missions for the Church. His younger brother, Hadley, was serving a mission right now. His family was close and did as many things together as possible. The Church had always been the center of their lives. His mother taught the Gospel Doctrine class and his father served on the high council of their stake. Respect and trust in his parents was as natural as breathing. He couldn't take his mother's concern lightly.

His thoughts turned to Dana's family. Her father was a prominent banker in San Francisco with little time or patience for his children, from whom he expected total obedience. He'd always scoffed at any form of religion. Dana's mother ran a small art gallery and entertained on a lavish scale. Wealthy and influential, they considered their social position of paramount importance. They'd had little time for their children, but had indulged them with expensive clothes, cars, and frequent vacations to exotic places. Marilyn, who was five years older than Dana's brother, was a high achiever who, while looking like a fashion model, seemed to do everything right. She graduated from high school and a prestigious college with honors, then promptly married a wealthy attorney with political aspirations.

Rick had been just the opposite. Too small to play football, he struggled with reading, chose friends his parents considered unsuitable, and skipped classes. At thirteen, he was arrested for breaking into a neighbor's house. After that he disappeared for days and sometimes weeks at a time.

Shortly after his eighteenth birthday he was found at the wheel of a stolen car with three teenage friends. A search of the vehicle produced a large amount of drugs and a gun used in the holdup of a convenience store, which had left a clerk severely wounded three days earlier. Rick had denied any knowledge of the gun or drugs, but as the only legally recognized adult in the group, and because he had a long juvenile record, he'd been convicted of drug possession, grand theft auto, and for possession of an unregistered firearm used in the commission of a crime. When he was sent to prison, his family had promptly disowned him.

Dana, a shy, quiet dreamer, had tried hard to please her busy parents and older siblings, but had always ended up feeling inadequate. Her older sister, Marilyn had made no secret of her dislike for her younger sister. Rick showed her more attention than any of the other members of the household, and she'd sneaked behind her father's back to patch his wounds when he got in scrapes and after their father punished him.

According to Dana she and her mother had grown closer during her early teen years when they'd discovered a common love for art objects and paintings. Her mother had discovered Dana's talent early and had made certain that her daughter had had the best possible instructors and supplies. They had frequently lunched together and browsed the shops and galleries, looking for nothing in particular. Dana's mother had even arranged for her to attend an art academy in Paris. When Dana returned to the states to attend college, she had come in contact with the Church. When her parents learned of her desire to be baptized, they told her she was no longer welcome in their home. Since she was of age, she chose baptism, with the result that she joined Rick in being completely cut off from her family.

"Josh's nose is bleeding again," Dana interrupted his thoughts. There was no inflection in her voice; she gave him the information, but revealed nothing of her own thoughts and feelings. Yet some instinct told him she was scared, and he found himself wondering whether she was scared for Josh or frightened for herself. His peripheral vision let him know she was trying to staunch the flow with a wad of tissues and that she wasn't being very successful. Fear such as he'd never known before sent his heart pounding. He found himself praying, *Please help me get Josh to the hospital in time.*

The freeway exit was coming up on his right. He put on his blinker and edged into the outside lane, then shot down the exit. Merging with traffic on the surface street, he moved ahead as quickly as he dared. Taking his eyes off the road for just a second, he realized Josh was unconscious and his own fear intensified. Two more blocks and he pulled into the circular emergency drive and shoved his hand down on the car horn. He'd barely stopped the car when two attendants in white coats began helping Dana and Josh out of the car. Dana didn't look back as she hurried toward the wide emergency room doors with her baby in her arms.

Someone told Matt to move his car to the emergency room parking lot before following Dana and Josh inside. He stood hesitantly for several seconds, feeling on some vague level the wind blowing through his hair while every impulse screamed for him to run after Dana and Josh. It took all the control he could muster to settle back behind the wheel.

He reached for the gearshift, then paused to watch the sliding doors close behind Josh and Dana. A stab of intense loneliness held him motionless for several minutes, then he gunned the engine. Pulling into the first parking spot he could find, he left the car at a run. As he entered the hospital, he spotted a bank of telephones and swerved toward them. It would just take a moment to let his parents know of the crisis and ask his father to bring some consecrated oil.

———•———

Warner Bingham scowled at the ringing telephone. He hated being interrupted when he was working at home, something he didn't do any more than necessary, but with Matt taking the afternoon off, there hadn't been time to get to these contracts all day. He'd wasted most of the day trying to untangle a bunch of misdirected orders. His son, Winn, who was his chief foreman, had ordered cement, which had been mistakenly delivered to his son Robert's construction site; and Bart Adams, his third foreman, had received wooden beams when he'd ordered steel. Warner just hoped Matt had spent some time this afternoon working on the Barringer bid at home. The added specifications would be difficult, but he didn't doubt his company could handle it. If they got a contract on that complex, they'd be well on their way, he thought with satisfaction.

The phone rang again and he reached for it. Barbara usually answered on one of the other extensions any time he closeted himself in his office, but he supposed she wouldn't this time. She'd been upset when she returned from Matt's this afternoon, and she'd cried when she told him about Josh. Renewed anger swept through him as he recalled Barbara's description of their grandson's injuries. What was Matt thinking of to let his wife get away with something like that?!

Barbara wouldn't answer the phone if she were still crying. She didn't often show deep emotion, and he didn't know how to deal with her unexpected tears now. If Josh's injuries were serious enough to cause her to weep, they must be pretty bad. He could count on one hand the number of times he'd seen his wife cry. He struggled to control his anger. This situation couldn't be allowed to continue. If Matt wouldn't deal with it, he would!

"Warner Bingham here," he answered brusquely.

"Dad, this is Matt." Good, he was glad the boy had decided to call. Matt would need to take a strong approach to this situation.

"Glad you called. Your mother said you wanted to talk to Dana before—"

"I haven't had a chance to talk to Dana about anything, Dad. Josh has a really bad nosebleed. I think he's unconscious. We're at the hospital—"

"We'll be right there," Warner interrupted.

"Will you bring some consecrated oil?"

"Of course, and son, I think we'd better call the police. This is serious."

"Not yet, Dad. I think I should talk to Dana first," Matt objected.

"Loyalty is a good quality, Matt, but your son's life may be in danger."

"I don't think Dana—"

Warner cut him off. "Matt, you need to be sure you have your priorities right. Your son's safety comes first. You married that girl against our advice after an extremely short courtship; you never even met any of her family. You've lived with her in an artificial college environment up until this year, and don't think we haven't noticed that you're disappointed in the way she fails to fit into your present life. You think you love her, but I doubt you even know her very well."

Matt's voice sounded tired. "Dad, you're the one who doesn't know Dana. The important thing now is to get Josh a blessing."

"All right, son. We'll be right there, but don't leave your wife alone with my grandson."

Matt hung up without saying good-by. Warner slammed the phone down and drummed his fingers against the heavy dark oak of his desk for several seconds before reaching for the phone once more. First the Barringer deal, now this!

———•———

Inside the hospital Dana was told to place Josh on a gurney. She laid him down gently and walked beside him holding his hand as he was wheeled down a hall and into a small examination room. The cessation of movement with its accompanying small jolt as the gurney's wheels were locked into place woke him, and he began to cry. When someone placed an ice pack near his face and began to examine his nose, he thrust out his arms, begging his mother to pick him up.

"Hush," she whispered. "Mama is here, and Dr. Young is coming to help you feel better." She knew he didn't understand, but she hoped what she said was true. She prayed Dr. Young could help her child, but she feared he could do nothing to relieve her own guilt. She was his mother; she should have protected him better. She should have been with him this afternoon. Her mind shied away from thinking about Matt. That he blamed her for Josh's injury cut too deeply to think about now. Right now Josh was all that mattered.

"Mrs. Bingham?" Dana looked up, startled to be addressed by the name she always considered belonged to her mother-in-law. A woman with short, dark hair and round, expressive eyes spoke to her. "Dr. Young is on his way. I'm Dr. Manderly. Dr. Young asked me to start a saline drip and begin some tests at once. If you would step out of the room, I'll begin."

"No, I can't leave him. I won't get in your way." Panic caused her to tighten her grip on Josh. He whimpered and she bent to soothe him.

"Ma-ma!" he cried. "Ma-ma!"

"All right, young man," the doctor said. "We'll let your mother undress you."

Gratefully Dana bent over Josh, taking great care not to bump any of the dark bruises as she freed his arms and legs from his one-piece suit. She cringed at the sight of his bruised skin.

"His diaper, too?" she asked.

The doctor nodded her head. Dana pulled back the tapes and automatically reached for a fresh diaper from her bag to cover the little boy as soon as the doctor finished her examination.

"Don't fasten it," the doctor cautioned. "Dr Young will want to see the bruise at the base of his spine when he gets here." Though nothing changed in the doctor's demeanor, Dana nevertheless felt a chill.

"Do you know how your son got these bruises?" the doctor asked.

"No. My husband discovered them when he picked him up from his nap. He showed me when I got home. Josh's nose was bleeding then, too."

"Has he had nosebleeds before?"

"No, his mouth bled a little a few days ago, but I'm pretty sure he's teething."

"Does he fall a lot?"

"Not a lot, but sometimes he does. He's only two." Dana thought the question strange. "At first I thought he'd fallen climbing from his crib, but my husband said he was standing in the crib when he went to get him. Our house doesn't have any stairs. He tripped over a toy about a week ago, but he wasn't hurt. He cried a few minutes then went right back to playing."

A nurse poked her head in the room. "Dr. Manderly, X-ray is ready,"she said. She was followed by an orderly.

"X-ray?" Dana felt confused. Weren't X-rays used to check for broken bones? There was no way Josh could have broken any bones when he tripped over his plastic truck in the middle of the living room carpet! She turned her bewildered gaze toward the doctor.

"Mrs. Bingham," Dr. Manderly spoke carefully as though explaining to a child, "we have to determine whether or not Josh has swallowed something or in some way sustained internal injuries that would account for his heavy bleeding. We will also take a blood sample to be tested. Wait right here, and we'll let you know as soon as we finish. Dr. Young should be here by that time, and he'll want to talk to you."

The orderly released the locks on the gurney's wheels and prepared to move the long, narrow rolling bed. She wanted to protest. Josh was just a little boy; he would be frightened to be left alone with strangers. She was his mother and she should be with him. She'd never left him with anyone except Matt before. She hadn't even gotten up the courage to send him to the children's class during Relief Society yet. But looking at his wan face, she acknowledged he needed help. Taking a deep swallow, she tried to smile at her son.

"Josh," she whispered. "Remember when Uncle Robert brought his camera over to take pictures of you? These people want to take pictures of you, too. Be a good boy, and don't cry, so they can take lots of nice pictures. They'll take good care of you and bring you back to Mommy in a few minutes." She bent to kiss his soft cheek.

She followed the gurney to the door, then stood back as the orderly pushed it down the hall. Josh's soft cries reached her ears and broke her heart. Wide doors at the end of the hall opened as if by magic and her son disappeared. She bit down hard on her clenched fist to keep from crying. She had to be brave. Whatever had happened to Josh, he would need her to be calm and reassuring when he returned.

"Mrs. Bingham?" Slowly she turned her head. A man stood a few feet away. She noticed his grim face first, then his uniform. "If you'd step back into the examination room, I'd like to ask you a few questions."

"Questions?" she repeated the word inanely. Why would a police officer want to ask her questions? Didn't he know her son was ill? She couldn't think about answering questions. All of her strength was required to walk and talk without falling apart. If she allowed any thoughts or concerns beyond Josh, she would shatter into tiny pieces. But a stray thought crept in, where was Matt? Had something happened to Matt? He should be here by now. She needed him. The hospital was a huge place; he must have gotten lost after he parked the car. She couldn't allow the policeman to tell her something bad had happened to Matt!

"If you would prefer to have an attorney present, that is your right."

She must be losing her mind. The officer wasn't making sense. She didn't need an attorney. She needed her husband. She needed her son safely back in her arms. Lifting her eyes, she searched the long corridor for Matt. He was closer than she expected, only a few feet away. She started to reach for him, then stopped. Something was terribly wrong. He looked stiff, frozen, and his eyes refused to meet hers.

"Matt?" She took a step toward him. The forbidding expression on his face stopped her.

"Matt . . . ?" she repeated.

He didn't answer. Realization dawned slowly. A great, jagged tear ripped painfully through her soul. Matt, the man she loved as though they shared one heartbeat, believed she had injured their child. In his eyes, she was capable of abusing her own baby!

She wanted to deny the unspoken accusation. No, she had to be wrong. That wasn't accusation she had seen in his eyes. Matt knew how she felt about physical punishment. He was tired; that was all. He'd been working too hard ever since he left school, and he was feeling a lot of stress because of the big project he was preparing to bid on.

The officer placed a hand on her arm. "I think we should talk alone for a few minutes, ma'am." She looked at him, then back at her husband. This time he didn't avoid her eyes. She recoiled in shock at what she saw. Revulsion, pity, and something she didn't understand. Could it be pain, or perhaps regret?

She felt as if he'd struck her. Slowly she became aware of the hand pulling her toward the empty room behind her. Fear caused her to shake off the hand, and before she stepped back into the room, she cast one last glance toward Matt, hoping she'd been mistaken and that he was coming to help her. She saw only the shattered look on his face and his mother's supporting arm around his shoulders. Over his head she caught the burning accusation in the other woman's eyes and understood. Matt had called his parents, and they had called the police to accuse her of injuring Josh.

Something warm and hopeful inside her—that small candle which had continued to burn even when her parents turned her away—shivered and faded. She wanted to die. Once more she had no one. No, that wasn't quite true. She still had Joshua. He loved her, and she loved him. No matter what happened, no matter what mistakes he would make in his life, she would never stop loving him. On mechanical legs she turned away and walked into the small room. She heard the closing of the door and heard its echo deep in her heart.

CHAPTER TWO

"Mrs. Bingham, please sit down." The officer indicated one of the two chairs in the small space. She sat. Actually she didn't have much choice. If she didn't sit down, she would probably fall down. Never before in her life had she felt so faint and distracted. An incessant buzzing in her ears added to her sense of unreality. As though from a great distance she heard the officer introduce himself as Sgt. Davidson. He said something else; she didn't know what.

"Mrs. Bingham," the officer started again.

"Please don't call me that," she choked out. "She's Mrs. Bingham. I'm just Dana." Suddenly it seemed tremendously important to establish a clear distinction between herself and Matt and all of Matt's family. They weren't her family. They didn't want her any more than her own family did.

"All right, Dana." The officer spoke slowly as if he understood her bewilderment. "Can you tell me what happened to your son today?"

"I told the doctor. Nothing happened to Josh. He didn't fall."

"How do you explain the nosebleed? The bruises?"

"I don't know. I just don't know. I should know," she started to cry. "I thought he had a cold or that he was cutting new teeth."

"Why do you think you should know?"

"I'm his mother. Mothers are supposed to know when their babies are ill. I promised God when I was a little girl that when I grew up I would take care of my children. I wouldn't go away and leave them when they had chicken pox or tummy aches. I shouldn't have gone, but I had promised, and I didn't know Josh was ill." Her words didn't make any sense; they spilled from her mouth between choking sobs she couldn't control. Somehow she had failed her child, little Josh whom she loved with an intensity that went beyond description. Her parents were right; she was a failure at everything she attempted. She'd been naive to think loving Josh would be enough.

"Mrs.—Dana, did you leave Josh alone?"

She lifted her head, feeling incredulous. "Of course I didn't leave him alone. Matt was there, and later his mother came over. Joshua was never alone."

"Why don't you tell me everything that happened today?" She sensed more than heard a change in her interrogator's voice. His face softened, transforming him from a stern policeman to the kind father she'd once imagined. Strange how she'd forgotten that fantasy. She'd been about eight or ten when the game began. She'd pretend she wasn't really a Dalby, that some evil person had kidnapped her and given her to the Dalbys to raise, but her real father never forgot her. He kept searching until one day he'd discovered where she'd been taken, and he'd come to get her.

"Dana . . . ?" Sgt. Davidson brought her attention back to his question. Slowly she struggled to recall the day's events. At more and more frequent intervals her eyes turned toward the door, searching for Josh's return. When she finished, the officer was silent for several minutes. Nervously she watched the door.

"Let's see if I've got this straight." The sergeant frowned. "The baby was quieter than usual all morning, but otherwise healthy. He ate breakfast, pushed most of his food onto the floor, which you say isn't particularly unusual. He played for a while, then fell asleep watching Barney. When he awoke, you fed him lunch, which he was eating in his highchair when his father arrived home. Your husband offered to clean him up so you could get ready for your meeting. You spent all afternoon at the church, and when you got home, Josh was sleeping, so you started dinner. You were preparing dinner when your husband called you. You rushed into the baby's room and saw blood everywhere. Your husband pointed out bruises on the boy's body, but you don't know what caused the bruises or why his nose suddenly started bleeding. Is that right?"

She nodded miserably and before the officer could say anything more, a commotion erupted in the hall. Above a cacophony of voices, Dana heard Josh call for her. Jumping to her feet, she raced toward the door and flung it open to find Josh crying and refusing to have anything to do with his grandparents, who were leaning over the gurney.

"Mama, ma-ma! 'Osh want ma-ma." He lay facedown on the gurney in almost a kneeling position with his little behind in the air and his hands beneath his face, covering his eyes and clutching at the sheet. Each time his grandmother reached for him his sobs grew louder, and he cringed further away.

"Josh, it's Daddy." Matt came forward and knelt beside him. Gently he patted the boy's back and his crying stopped. Dana stood paralyzed, watching. Slowly, carefully, Matt slid his arm under the small, shuddering body and pulled him against his shoulder. For a moment Josh snuggled against his father before spotting his mother standing in the doorway.

"Ma-ma!" He lunged toward her, and Dana reached to catch him. As he snuggled against her shoulder, her heart filled to overflowing with love for her son. No matter what Matt, his mother, or all the police officers in the city thought, she hadn't hurt Josh and Josh knew it. That was all that really mattered.

"You can't let her . . ." Dana shut her ears to her mother-in-law's loud protests. All the voices around her sounded like so much babble in her ears.

"Dana." One voice sounded kinder than the others and penetrated the shell she'd thrown around herself and her son. For a moment her heart tripped and she thought it was Matt speaking her name, but when she looked up she recognized Dr. Young.

"Take him back inside the examining room," he advised her. As he spoke he placed one hand on her back, urging her back in the direction from which she'd just come.

"I'm coming, too." This time she did recognize Matt's voice. His face looked ravaged and drawn, but determined, as he stepped toward them.

"I don't think so," said a firm voice. Dana had forgotten all about the police officer the moment she heard her son call for her. Now he stepped between Matt and herself. "Mr. Bingham, since your wife and the doctor will be needing the room behind us, I suggest we find another spot for our little visit."

"What?" Matt stared at the officer as though he'd lost his mind. "My son—"

"Your son is in good hands, but if you feel you need to call your lawyer before we talk, that will be fine. He can meet us here or at the station. It's your call." There was something implacable and cold in the gray-haired officer's eyes that made Dana shudder. She raised her eyes to her handsome young husband's face and saw the dawning horror there. She could identify with every emotion racing across his face, but she felt nothing. Ice was taking over her entire body, leaving only enough room for her son. Her final glimpse as she turned away was of an unmistakable plea for help in Matt's eyes. For a moment she wavered, then the coldness hardened her heart. Entering the small examination room, she closed the door firmly behind her, lest any of Matt's family follow her inside.

What seemed like hours later, Matt rose to his feet and stood awkwardly. Sgt. Davidson stood as well. What on earth was he supposed to do? Shake the man's hand? He would if he had to. He'd do anything to end this absurd cat-and-mouse game so he could go to Josh. Once he was sure Josh was all right, he'd have a few things to say to Dana!

He still couldn't believe he'd been so wrong about her. His parents had warned him that he didn't know her well enough to get married. They had advised him that because of her dysfunctional family background, she might be a poor choice to mother his children, but he'd fallen so deeply in love with her and had been so sure that she was all he would ever want, he'd married her anyway. And they had been happy, at first anyway, his heart reminded him. He didn't even know what had gone wrong. But something was definitely not right, he thought, bitterly remembering the cold, frozen look on his wife's face before she'd turned her back and left him to Sgt. Davidson.

While he was still going to school everything had seemed great, but after he graduated and moved his family to Salt Lake, their marriage had begun to deteriorate. Reeling with confusion and anger from his interview with the police officer, Matt tried to piece together the failure of his marriage. Right from the start, Dana had made no attempt to be friends with his mother or his brothers' wives. She spent her days painting sunsets and playing her clarinet beside mountain streams, all with Josh in tow. She had refused his mother's offers to babysit so he and Dana could have an occasional evening out, and to tell the truth, he was becoming more and more embarrassed by the way she dressed. He'd been enchanted once by her filmy, flowing gowns and untamed auburn hair. Flamboyant oversize shirts and tunics with leggings or jeans were fine on campus, but she was an adult now, a mother, and she ought to dress better. She should see a hairdresser and get something done with her unruly mop of hair. Why hadn't he seen this coming? How had the whimsy he'd once delighted in turned into something dangerous? After seeing Josh's injuries with his own eyes, why had he still found it impossible to believe she was capable of such violence? He'd been caught completely unprepared when she shifted the blame for Josh's injuries to him!

"Mr. Bingham." Something in the way the sergeant said his name raised his hackles. The officer had borrowed an office and kept him here more than an hour, asking the same stupid questions over and over, and he'd given him the same answers every time. It should be obvious Dana's accusations weren't true. The officer should have been concentrating on her, not him.

"Yes?" Matt carefully kept his face blank. He sensed that for some reason he couldn't fathom, the man would like nothing better than to arrest him or at least haul him down to the police station. He wouldn't give him an excuse. For just a moment he wished his brother Hadley was back from his mission and through with law school. One thing about his family; they stuck together.

"There's something you should know." The officer's eyes turned slate hard. "I asked your wife everything I asked you. She did her best to answer, in spite of the obvious shock she is suffering. She's scared and hurt, but not once did she even hint there was a possibility you might have injured Josh. I don't think that possibility has even occurred to her. Ordinarily I'm not called until after the doctor has had a chance to study all of the medical evidence, which makes me wonder why you pointed a finger at your wife before it has even been ascertained that any abuse actually occurred."

Matt didn't move for several seconds. An overwhelming sensation assailed him, a feeling much like the time his older brother Winn tackled him, knocking the wind from his lungs. He couldn't breathe, and the room dipped and swayed around him. He was barely conscious of the sergeant's departure. Was it true? Did Dana truly have nothing to do with the officer's decision to question him? A guilty sickness shook him to his soul. He felt confused, as if his whole world were collapsing, and he was helpless to put it back together. No, he wasn't helpless. He was alone in this room, and he would do what he should have done right at the start. Sinking to his knees beside the chair where he'd sat so long answering questions, feeling frightened for his son and resentful at the suspicion that had fallen upon him, he bowed his head and began to pray.

When he rose to his feet some time later, he felt shaken and chastised. Never before had he experienced such a deep sense of failure. He had failed his son—and what of Dana? Had he failed her, too? A sick certainty told him he had. He'd never known such a nauseating sense of guilt.

He left the office at a run. He had to find Josh and Dana. Dana shouldn't have been left alone to deal with doctors and the police. Authority figures frightened her, turned her speechless, and he had left her to deal with all that alone! He should have been with her to insist on the very best care for their son. He should have been there to hold his son and help him face the strangers who had invaded his world.

No familiar faces met him when he entered the ER. Frantically he searched the halls. Long corridors full of rapidly moving strangers met his gaze. Where were they? Where were Josh and Dana? Finally he approached the admitting desk.

"Excuse me." He cleared his throat and attempted to speak calmly. "Has Joshua Bingham been admitted?"

"Are you family?" the woman behind the desk asked.

"Yes, I'm his father."

The nurse raised her eyebrows and looked faintly superior before she answered, and he wondered how many people knew he'd been interrogated by the police because Sgt. Davidson thought he had physically abused his son. A slow burn crept up his neck.

"He's been taken to 4A, room 411. Dr. Young left instructions he's to have only one visitor at a time and gave the boy's mother permission to stay the night with him." The nurse spoke pertly and seemed to imply they didn't need him. Perhaps they didn't need him, but deep in his soul he knew he needed them.

"Thank you," he responded automatically. He searched for several minutes before finding the elevators. He pushed the "up" button and stood lost in thought as the elevator slowly moved upward. The nurse's words kept repeating themselves inside his head. *She said, "the boy's mother," not "your wife."* He couldn't help feeling there was some significance to her choice of words.

When the elevator stopped, he moved down the hall, searching for 411. After numerous wrong turns, he found it. The door was open and a dim light burned inside. Hesitantly he approached the door. He could barely make out the tiny form lying in a crib that resembled a cage on stilts. Two metal stands holding plastic bags stretched, via dangling tubes, to the tiny, still figure in the bed.

A small sound, the hint of a sigh, caught his attention and his eyes turned to the chair pulled up beside the crib. Dana lay there, curled in an uncomfortable ball. She too seemed to be asleep. A sliver of moonlight slanted through the closed blinds to light her face. She looked so sad and alone. His heart twisted. How could he have forgotten for even a minute how much he loved her. A quiet conviction stole into his heart; Dana hadn't struck Josh. She was only guilty of loving him so much she couldn't bear to let him out of her sight. How could he have thought otherwise?

"Matt?" A familiar voice spoke his name and a hand settled on his arm, drawing him back a few steps. "I hoped you'd get here before I left for the night."

"Dr. Young, how is he? Is he going to be all right?"

"I think so, son." The doctor who had treated his own childhood ills spoke with reluctance. "There are more tests we need to run over the next few days, but for now he's doing fine. I've explained it all to your wife, but she seems to be on the verge of succumbing to shock, and I'm not sure how much she understands. There's a room down the hall where we can talk."

Giving one last look over his shoulder at his wife and son, Matt stifled an ache to go to them and hold them both close. He wished he could turn the clock back. If only they could return to that tiny, cramped apartment near the Berkeley campus where they'd lived and loved for two and a half years before the real world had intruded. Funny how often he remembered that apartment with a hint of nostalgia. It was small and inconvenient, but Dana had painted the walls a pale sunny yellow and covered them with her bright, splashy paintings. He'd hooted with laughter when she painted the rickety kitchen cupboards pale green on the outside and brilliant orange on the inside. He always pictured the place in terms of light and laughter.

The room where Dr. Young took him was a smaller version of the waiting room he'd passed on his way to the elevator. Two comfortable gray sofas and a couple of tan chairs surrounded a square coffee table. A beverage dispenser stood against one wall, and a white telephone sat beside a box of tissues on a small table near the door.

"Sit down." Dr. Young indicated one of the gray sofas and Matt did as he was asked, though he perched on the edge and leaned forward anxiously.

"I'll get right to the point," the doctor began. "Your son is a very sick little boy. Preliminary tests show he is severely anemic. Dana gave her consent to begin a blood transfusion and that has been done. Tonight's tests indicate all three blood cell levels are very low, which means we will have to examine a small sample of bone marrow in the morning."

"Bone marrow! Does he have leukemia?" Matt's hands began to shake, and he felt as though his head were reeling.

"That's one of the possibilities we hope testing will eliminate. We won't know until we've run the tests."

"How painful are the tests?" He felt sick at the thought of anything hurting Josh.

"Novocaine-like drugs will be used to make the area numb," the doctor explained. "I can't promise the procedure will be painless, but it's probably not as painful as you imagine. A needle will be inserted into the large pelvic bone just below Josh's waist on either side of his spine. A small amount of marrow will be aspirated to be examined under a microscope."

"What about the bruises?"

The doctor frowned. "I'm not unaware that both you and Dana were questioned by the police tonight. I've assured everyone concerned, including your parents, that no abuse has occurred. Bruising, spontaneous bleeding, and fatigue are usually the first warning signs of serious blood disorders." His demeanor turned severe. "It's unfortunate the police were called in. Dana could have used your support tonight. In my opinion, she's very near the proverbial breaking point. Your family was upsetting her, so I sent them home."

Matt leaned back, stunned. Dana was innocent. If he'd listened to that quiet prompting which had insisted all along that Dana hadn't hurt Josh, she wouldn't have been alone tonight, and he wouldn't have been enduring Sgt. Davidson's questions when he should have been with Dana and Josh. He'd let his mother's fears become his own, and he'd denied his wife the support and comfort she'd had a right to expect from him. His son was critically ill, and instead of being beside him, he'd been closeted with a police sergeant who thought him a jerk. He was a jerk! He'd wanted to wait until Dr. Young saw Josh before involving the police, but he'd done nothing to stop his father from picking up the phone and making that call. He'd made a first-class mess of things!

Matt met the doctor's eyes fearfully. "How sick is Josh? He will get well, won't he?"

"It's too soon to answer that question with a great deal of accuracy at this point," the silver-haired doctor responded. "Blood disorders can be serious, involving blood and platelet transfusions, or even bone barrow transplants. There are drugs that can help in some cases, and once in a while we get lucky and find the cause, eliminate it, and the patient recovers completely."

Matt didn't know what to say; he couldn't collect his thoughts enough to even ask questions. His son was sick, possibly dying, and he didn't know what to do. He needed Dana. If they could just hold each other, perhaps everything would be all right.

"I'm going home." The doctor rose to his feet. "I suggest you do the same. There's nothing you can do here tonight."

"Dana . . . ?" he started to ask.

"It would take more than doctor's orders to pry her away from Josh tonight," the doctor chuckled. "Considering what a shy, little bit of a thing that girl is, she can be mighty stubborn when it comes to looking after that baby."

Matt walked down the hall beside Dr. Young. When they passed Josh's door, he paused and said softly, "You go ahead." The doctor hesitated, then wished him good night before walking on.

Matt stood in the doorway, watching, for a long time. At last he stepped inside the room. A terrible sadness filled him as he gazed at the tubes and monitors attached to his son's small body. He moved to stand beside Dana and watch her sleep. She'd had no one tonight. One telephone call and his parents and brothers had rushed to be with him. There had been no one for Dana. The one person she should have been able to count on had let her down. Never in his life had he felt such a miserable failure.

A blanket and pillow sat on a small table beside Josh's bed. He reached for the pillow and cautiously placed it beneath Dana's head. Next he pulled the blanket over her shoulders. Quietly he bent to kiss his son's cheek. Once more he gazed down at his sleeping wife and a lump swelled in his throat and tears slid wetly down his cheeks. Being careful not to wake her, he pressed his lips to her forehead.

His steps dragged as he left the room. He started toward the elevator, then retraced his steps to pause once more in the doorway to watch his wife and son sleep. After a few minutes he pulled himself away. Wearily he made his way back to the small consultation room, where he had just received the most painful blow he had ever received in his life. There he curled up on one of the gray sofas to stare sightlessly at a ceiling he couldn't see.

———·———

When they returned from the hospital, Warner went straight to bed but Barbara was too keyed up to sleep. She puttered around the kitchen, her thoughts in a turmoil. Her husband had been quiet all the way home. She wished he'd just say what was on his mind, but that wasn't Warner's way. After thirty-five years of marriage, she knew when her husband was upset about something. He preferred to mull a problem over in his mind and make it a matter of study and prayer before discussing it with her. For years his slow way of dealing with problems or differences had frustrated her, and she'd tried repeatedly to convince him that her way of dealing with problems by bringing them immediately out into the open was better.

That was what made this whole evening so difficult to understand. It wasn't like Warner to impulsively call the police, although at the time, she'd been glad he had. She shuddered, remembering the bruises she'd found on little Joshua. It was hard to believe that anything other than being hit could account for what she'd seen. Several times during their ride home she'd wanted to ask Warner if he blamed her for the conclusion she'd made, but he obviously wasn't ready to talk about it.

Whether her husband blamed her or not, she blamed herself. There was no way Warner would have acted as he had if she hadn't convinced him their grandchild was in grave danger from his mother. And she had no doubt whatsoever that Dana would blame her.

She'd worried about Matt's children's spiritual well-being from the moment she first met Dana. Her newest daughter-in-law was nothing like the strong, confident woman she'd always expected Matt would marry. Dana hadn't been raised in the Church, any church for that matter, and knew nothing of Primary. She had no well of spiritual knowledge from which to draw to help in teaching and training children in the gospel, no personal experience derived from being reared by loving parents. How could she teach her children what she knew so little about herself?

Both of Matt's older brothers had married well, and Barbara loved Sandra and Ann as much as she would if they had been born to her. Sandra was a little bossy, but she got things done, and she had a firm grasp of the gospel. Her father had been a bishop and was currently serving as a stake president, and she herself had served a mission. Ann's father had been Robert's mission president, though they hadn't met until Robert was released and both were enrolled at BYU. She was a little too "horse happy" to suit Barbara, but she never let her horses interfere with her church service, and Barbara felt confident that when the Lord saw fit to bless her with children, she'd be a wonderful mother. They'd talked about adoption lately, and Barbara wasn't completely comfortable with that. She wished they would give nature a little more time.

Matt had been popular and much sought after by girls in high school, perhaps not as much as his brothers, but still he'd dated some really nice girls. The girls he'd gone with were much like Sandra and Ann. Several had written to him while he served his mission, and he'd taken them out a few times after his return, but he hadn't shown a great deal of enthusiasm for any particular one.

She'd been skeptical when he wanted to transfer to UC Berkeley for his last two years of school, and appalled when after only a few months at the school, he'd announced his engagement to a girl he hardly knew. She and Warner had flown to California to meet Dana and for the wedding in the Oakland Temple. She'd felt that Matt had somehow been cheated when there was no reception, just a simple dinner planned by their campus ward.

Barbara looked around her kitchen. There was nothing left to clean or put away. She'd never been particularly fond of housework, but she hated dirt more than cleaning, so she cleaned. Wearily she sank onto a sturdy kitchen chair and rested her elbows on the table. She wished she could love Dana as whole-heartedly as she did Sandra and Ann, but the girl was impossible. She dressed like a hippy left over from the sixties and lived in some kind of dream world full of weird music and even more weird paintings. Without saying a word, she'd made it clear she didn't like her future mother-in-law the first day they'd met. The silly girl had cowered behind Matt and turned white the moment she'd offered to be her escort in the temple, and every time she'd asked Dana a question to encourage a conversation, so they could get to know each other a little better, the girl had managed to disappear.

Nevertheless, Barbara had been enchanted the first time she saw Josh and excited when the time came for Matt to move his family back to Salt Lake. She wanted to be part of her son's and grandson's lives. She'd missed Matt a great deal while he served his mission and during the years he'd been away at school. She'd felt closer to Matt than any of her other sons as he'd grown up and had been anxious to renew that closeness. She'd felt sure she could help him by filling in the gaps in Joshua's training and by using her own years of experience to help Dana be a good wife and mother.

She'd enjoyed finding them a pleasant, practical, small house in a good neighborhood. She'd had it repainted with a good quality off-white paint and selected a nice rich chocolate brown carpet with matching drapes for all of the rooms. Most of her own parents' furniture was still in storage and she'd gone through it, carefully selecting the sturdiest pieces to fill the little house. Remembering the garish paintings on the young couple's apartment walls, she'd picked up a couple of tasteful landscape prints at a discount store to complete the decor. Matt had mumbled his thanks, but Dana hadn't said a word. She'd stood in the door looking like she was about to cry. Her own disappointment still smarted.

Barbara shook her head, once more feeling foolish. She should have suspected that secondhand furniture and Wal-Mart art prints wouldn't be good enough for the ungrateful little snob. After all, Dana had grown up in a luxurious home where all her material wishes were instantly gratified.

Dana had looked down her aristocratic nose at Barbara's efforts to be helpful right from the start. She refused Barbara's offers to babysit, never contributed to any discussion, rejected her offer to enroll Josh in a play group, and instead took him to off-beat concerts in the park. She even turned up her nose at the backyard barbeques that were a family tradition. The girl ate fish and chicken, but she wouldn't touch beef—even though Barbara had spent hours marinating and simmering a perfect sauce for it.

Barbara sighed and leaned her head against her hands. She didn't know what to do. She loved Matt; there had been a special bond between herself and this third son from the moment he'd been born, and little Josh touched her heart in a way she couldn't explain. Dr.

Young said Josh was extremely ill and had hinted he might not be able to save the child. The thought of a world without Josh's cheerful grin was excruciating.

Her family had always approached difficulties with a united front and a deep reliance on God. Now facing one of the greatest challenges their family had ever known, they weren't united, and they hadn't prayed together. Matt was furious, and Josh was fighting for his life, isolated from those who loved him. Warner and Matt hadn't even been allowed to administer to him.

She'd made a mistake anyone might make, seeing a child covered with bruises. She still wasn't certain she could accept Dr. Young's explanation, but she and Warner were filled with regret for the action they'd taken. Yes, she accepted her share of the blame. Warner never would have acted without her instigation. She regretted the humiliation both Dana and Matt had endured in being questioned by the police, but that still didn't excuse Dana's refusal to let them see their grandson. She wished, too, that Warner would talk about it. She didn't like the uneasy feeling that a rift had opened between Warner and herself.

Dear Father, she found herself praying and felt an immediate sense of love and warmth. *My grandson, Joshua, needs your help. Please help him get well. I want with all my heart to help him. Please allow me to find a way to comfort and support him.* She paused as an overwhelming feeling stirred her mind telling her she should pray for Dana. For a moment she resisted the impulse. Deep inside she still blamed Dana for Josh's illness. Even though Dr. Young had said the boy's bruises were due to illness rather than abuse, she couldn't help suspecting Dana had exposed him to the illness through taking him to strange places, or that she might have passed on some genetic flaw from her dysfunctional family.

A strange coldness filled her heart, and she gasped with shock as she felt the warm spirit withdraw. *Please don't leave me,* she pleaded as before her eyes rose a picture of Dana's stricken face at the moment she turned back for one last look at Matt while Sgt. Davidson was ushering her into the examination room to question her. The enormity of what she'd done crushed upon her.

Forgive me, she choked out the words. *Please, forgive me.* No answering peace seeped into her soul. She continued to pray until at

last a quiet message she'd heard all her life, but never fully compre-
hended, filled her heart. God would forgive her. The promise was
sure, but it was Dana's forgiveness she must seek. That wasn't so sure,
but just as necessary.

CHAPTER THREE

Dana sat on the gray sofa in the small consultation room Matt had come to know so well, looking lost and empty, like an abandoned waif. Her features were pinched and drawn, and he suspected she'd lost weight she could ill afford to lose. Her jeans and the oversize, multi-colored sweatshirt she wore were clean, and she'd tied her bushy hair back with a leather thong. She wore no makeup, but then she seldom did. Feelings such as he'd experienced four years ago when he'd first met her swept over him. He'd first seen her as fragile and delicate as a lovely butterfly, needing nothing but that vibrant mane of hair and her shy sweet smile to set her apart as unique and beautiful beyond words.

She didn't speak or even look his way. He felt awkward and more than a little foolish. He didn't even know how to talk to his own wife. Very likely if he asked her a question, she would answer, but there would be no voluntary sharing of her thoughts and feelings. Once he'd been delighted by the almost instantaneous communication that flowed like a stream between them. But since leaving school he'd spent so much time and energy learning to shoulder his share of the burden for the family business, he had somehow let this unique bond with Dana slide into a secondary place. A touch of melancholy shadowed his heart, his shoulders drooped, and he sank lower in the sofa's cushions.

Dana sat six inches away, but there was no reaching for his hand, no snuggle against his side. If he reached across that short space and picked up her hand, he suspected she wouldn't pull away, but her hand would be lifeless in his. She lived only for their son.

But concern for Joshua wasn't the complete answer to her remoteness. That was his fault. He'd made a vow to forsake all others when he'd married her, yet the first time his trust had been challenged, he'd doubted her and placed his trust elsewhere. He'd been wrong, terribly wrong, and he feared that Dana would never forgive him. He couldn't blame her. He was having a difficult time letting go of his own anger toward his parents, which left him with no desire to see or speak to them any time soon. He'd never felt such anger toward his parents before, not even as a teenager. Dana must feel the same sense of betrayal each time she looked at him, only to a much greater extent.

"Dana. Matt." Dr. Young stepped into the room carrying a folder. He shook both their hands and inquired how they were holding up. He didn't seem surprised by their noncommittal answers. After a few minutes, he sat down across from them. Placing the folder on the table, he carefully steepled his fingers beneath his chin, brushing his fingers back and forth as though stroking a nonexistent beard. Finally he spoke. "The tests we've run this week rule out leukemia."

Before they could draw a collective sigh of relief, the doctor went on. "I have the report back now from the hematologist. His report is pretty much what I expected. Josh's bone marrow biopsy shows a great reduction in the number of cells being produced. The few precious stem cells in his bone marrow are not functioning properly."

"What does that mean?" Matt leaned forward to ask. "You've ordered blood transfusions for him, and he seems much better this morning. He was sitting up looking at his books when I was in his room a little while ago."

"Yes, he has responded well to transfusions, but blood transfusions only correct the anemia by supplying red cells. This alleviates some of the symptoms, but it is not a long-term solution. After continuous red cell transfusions, patients begin to accumulate toxic levels of iron in critical body organs. Eventually the level becomes intolerable and the patient dies. There is also a danger from excessive bleeding when insufficient platelets are produced. In Josh's case we may need to begin platelet transfusions right away to prevent a possible fatal hemorrhage."

"I don't understand. Aren't platelets part of blood?" Dana asked anxiously.

"They are, but the life span of a platelet is very short, at the most a few days, which makes several transfusions a week necessary. Platelets are also highly discriminating. Josh's body will quickly learn to recognize 'foreign' platelets and develop antibodies against them. When this happens, only 'matched' platelets will work."

"What are matched platelets?" Matt asked.

"Each person has tissue-type markers that are practically unique to that individual. However, close relatives, especially identical twins, may have markers that are nearly the same."

"Does that mean close relatives, like Dana and me, are the only ones who can donate blood for him? If so, I'll donate any time he needs my platelets," Matt impulsively volunteered.

"I will too, of course," Dana added. "Both of us have the same blood type as Josh."

"It's not that simple," Dr. Young explained. "Blood type is not the only measurement of compatibility. One small child, such as Josh, will need twenty matched donors to maintain him for one year. Even if we do find that many willing matched donors, it won't solve the problem. There are still white cells to consider. White cells transfused to another person only survive a few hours, making their transfusion on a routine basis technically impossible. Without normal white cells, Josh will be highly susceptible to bacteria and infections."

"What are you saying?" Matt surged to his feet and glared angrily at the doctor. "Is Josh going to die?"

Dana began to cry, and he regretted voicing the ugly word aloud. He quickly sat back down beside her and placed an arm around her trembling shoulders. For just a moment he felt her lean against him, then slowly, almost imperceptibly, she stiffened, drawing away. He loosened his hold and let her go.

"We'll do everything possible to keep Joshua alive," Dr. Young spoke, carefully choosing his words. "But it is going to require a great deal of cooperation from you and your families. Your son has a condition known as aplastic anemia, which means his bone marrow is not producing enough blood cells. As you may know, bone marrow is the spongy red tissue found in the center of bones. It usually produces all the various types of blood cells a body needs, but sometimes for unexplained reasons, this important function is disrupted. Our job will be to stimulate the stem cells in Josh's bone marrow to return to normal."

"How, doctor?" Matt asked.

"What can we do?" Dana spoke at the same time.

"There are drugs we can use which may help. They'll at least buy a little time. You both need to be tested to determine whether or not you are compatible platelet or bone marrow donors and you should approach your family members to see how many of them are willing to be tested. An identical twin or a sibling is the best match, but since Josh doesn't have that option, we need to look at other close family members. "

Matt felt confused. "I thought you said platelet transfusions wouldn't work,"

"I didn't say they wouldn't work, only that it is extremely difficult to find enough suitable donors," Dr. Young clarified. "Sometimes platelet transfusion provides the rest or boost the bone marrow needs to begin functioning again. In any case, they will give Josh a chance to regain his strength and prepare for the next step."

"Next step?" Dana raised startled eyes to the doctor's face.

"If a suitable, willing donor is found, Josh's best chance is a bone marrow transplant as soon as possible." Dr. Young's eyes never left her face as he gently explained. "A bone marrow transplant is a procedure where the patient's bone marrow is destroyed by radiation or chemotherapy and replaced with healthy cells from a donor. Finding a good donor match is sometimes difficult, and a search needs to begin immediately with family members. You should register Joshua with a registry as well. My office can help you with that."

"It's dangerous, isn't it?" Dana asked, her fear and dread showing clearly in each tense line of her posture.

"Most major medical and surgical procedures are dangerous," Dr. Young quietly acknowledged. "But it is his best option for a full recovery. The success rate for a bone marrow transplant from a perfect match is extremely good, and the sooner the procedure takes place, the higher the success rate. I'll have my nurse send you some pamphlets and computer printouts that may more fully answer your questions about aplastic anemia and the different types of transfusions. Any time you have questions, I'll try to explain the answers as well as I can. One more thing, you should be able to take Joshua home in another day or two, but it is essential that you avoid exposing him to any type of illness. It's best to isolate him from well-meaning family and friends and to restrict his activities. You'll need to help him avoid falls or accidents that might provoke bleeding."

"Why did this happen to Josh?" Dana asked hesitantly, and Matt wondered if she somehow thought he still blamed her.

Dr. Young shook his head slowly. "We really don't know. There have been cases traced to exposure to chemicals, radiation, drugs, a virus, or environmental toxins, but in most cases we never discover a direct cause."

After Dr. Young left, Dana and Matt continued to sit with downcast eyes. Matt wanted to put his arms around Dana and just hold her. He ached for the comfort only her closeness could give him. But instead of worrying about his own needs, he reminded himself, he should concentrate on Josh's needs. His son was in far more danger than he had imagined. He'd let Dana down; but he wouldn't let Josh down, he vowed. He rose abruptly to his feet. "I'm going to look in on Josh, then check with the lab to see how soon I can be tested."

"I'll go with you." Fatigue was evident in her voice, and Matt wished with all his heart, she really was "with" him.

———•———

When he finished the tests at the hospital, Matt tried unsuccessfully to convince Dana to go home and get some rest while he stayed with Josh. She wouldn't go. Faced with the choice of spending another night on the gray sofa or returning home to his empty bed, he'd opted to go to his office to work on the Barringer bid. Something about the new specs didn't feel right, and he wanted to go over the estimated costs to see if he might have missed anything. Bingham Construction wasn't exactly overextended, but their recent expansion, in addition to all of their new projects, had caused the company to push the financial line. They couldn't handle a costly mistake.

It was late and he was the only one in the building. Completely immersed in the project, Matt was oblivious to all else until something broke his concentration. Lifting his hands from the keyboard, he paused to listen. He waited several minutes, but whatever had disturbed his concentration didn't repeat itself. Rubbing his hand against the back of his neck, he chided himself for his own jumpiness. He was an adult, way too old to be afraid of the dark or to hear boogeymen simply because he was alone in a large building late at night. Technically he wasn't alone. Scott Lewis, the night watchman, and his dog were around someplace. He suspected his jittery nerves had more to do with worrying about his son and his marriage than the fact that he was working long after everyone else had left for the day.

Rising to his feet, he wandered toward the window. The view wasn't spectacular, but at the moment the view didn't interest him anyway. He wouldn't have noticed the lights moving along the freeway anymore than he did the lot full of heavy equipment that spread across the yard two stories below him.

He should return to the computer and do a little more number-crunching, he told himself. However, knowing what he should do, and doing it, were two different things. He was tired and his shoulders ached as though he carried a tremendous weight on them. It seemed to him the company was expanding too fast. This Barringer deal didn't thrill him the way it did his father and brothers. He saw too much potential for disaster, but his words of caution were met with hints that he was too green to appreciate how a job like this would secure the company's reputation. He sighed, acknowledging that his father and brothers were probably right. They had more experience than he did with the company, and he freely admitted that he had never been as adventurous as his brothers.

Right now he wished Bingham Construction, the Barringer bid, and the whole world would just go away and leave him alone. All he wanted was to go back to the hospital to be with Dana and Josh. Dana would likely prefer he stay away, but he couldn't. Unless he could be there with her and Josh, how would either of them begin to trust him again? And he was determined he would regain their trust. He had to believe Dana would give him a second chance to prove he could be the husband and father they needed. He couldn't face the alternative.

A flicker of movement caught his eye and he moved closer to the glass. He watched for several minutes, seeing nothing but the thick shadows of heavy equipment. It was probably Lewis's dog. The night watchman usually turned the big German shepherd loose to roam the yard at night. He might as well give up, go on home. He was so tired he was jumping at shadows.

———

Late the following morning Dana left Josh's room, and with shaking fingers pulled off the mask the nurses insisted she wear each time she visited her son. Josh wouldn't be going home today nor tomorrow either. His small bed was now surrounded by a plastic bubble, and she could only watch as he held up his arms and pleaded for her to hold him, causing her heart to ache. He had a cold, the kind of minor infection that should be no more than a mild case of the sniffles, but instead his temperature had risen dangerously during the night and each breath he took was dry and raspy. Someone, she didn't even remember who, had explained that because her baby's white cell count was so low, he had nothing with which to fight infection.

All night she'd remained as close as the doctor would permit to her tiny son. She had willed each labored breath he took and beseeched God to allow him to live. She only left his room now because the medical personnel insisted. Exhausted and drained, she moved slowly down the hall.

Lifting weary arms, she removed the hospital gown and shoe coverings a nurse had given her during the night and deposited them in a bin, a procedure that was now second nature to her. She hadn't left the hospital once in a week. Matt brought her a change of clothing each day and urged her to go home to get a decent night's rest, but she couldn't leave Joshua. More than ever, he was all she had.

Dr. Young had told her to go home, too, but she couldn't. Not only could she not leave Joshua, but she couldn't face the small dingy house her mother-in-law had picked out and furnished for them. Her father had badly damaged her sense of self-worth with his criticism and ridicule during her growing up years, but that nondescript, color-less house with its heavy furniture and dark drapes seemed to drain her soul of light and vitality. The happiness she'd shared with Matt and Josh had disappeared in its darkness. She'd wanted to repaint it, but Matt said his mother would be hurt if she did, so she hadn't done anything to it. She hadn't even replaced the bland, nondescript paint-ings that hung on the walls. With the cloud that hung between Matt and herself, and with Joshua fighting for his life, she couldn't face the dark loneliness of that house.

Matt should be here now, she thought as she wandered toward the waiting room. He'd gone home last night after their lab tests and had planned to go in to work early this morning so he could meet her at noon to take Josh home. She should have called him. He'd be upset when he learned Josh had faced a crisis and she hadn't notified him. Guiltily she acknowledged she would have been hurt had their roles been reversed. Still she was too tired to worry about it.

Her husband was just getting off the elevator as she made her way down the hall. At the sight of his quick smile of recognition, her heart lurched and she had to stifle an urge to run to him. For just a moment she allowed herself a small fantasy of leaning her head against his chest and feeling his strong arms settle around her, holding her tight, keeping at bay all the hurt and worry that weighted her down. Self-consciously, she lifted her shoulders and straightened her back. Some element of self-preservation kept her from yielding to her need for his comfort. She wished she didn't need him.

When she'd been a little girl she'd wanted her father to love her, but he hadn't no matter how hard she'd tried to please him. When Matt told her he loved her, she'd believed him because she needed so much to be loved and because she loved him. He was the hero she'd dreamed all her life would one day arrive to whisk her away from all the hate and anger of her childhood home. With him she would "live happily ever after." But she hadn't been able to hold his love any more than she had her father's. Somehow she had ruined everything.

"Josh had a setback during the night," she went right to the point when she reached Matt's side. "He's very ill and won't be able to go home today."

Matt's face paled, and he took a step toward Josh's room. She reached out to touch his arm. "You can't see him now. He's past the crisis and sleeping, but the doctor has ordered stricter isolation for him. He almost died." The last words were a whisper.

His lips tightened and he visibly swallowed. "You should have called me."

"I know." She didn't elaborate.

"He's my son, too. I should have known. I should have been here. Why didn't you call me?" His voice rose.

"I don't know," she whispered, but she couldn't meet his eyes.

Matt reacted as though she'd struck him. She hadn't meant to hurt him, and she wouldn't claim fatigue or fear as justification for not calling earlier or for breaking the news so abruptly. Her reasoning was more confused than that. Her father had never come when she'd been ill and cried for him, so she'd learned not to ask for him. But Matt wasn't her father; if she'd called, he would have come for Josh, but he wouldn't have come alone. His family would have come, too, and she couldn't bear that. They'd taken Matt from her; she wouldn't let them have Josh, too.

Matt struggled for a minute, then he grasped his wife's arm and propelled her toward the small waiting room where he'd slept almost every night of the past week. Only last night had he returned to their empty little house. Without Dana and Josh it had been bleak and cold, and he'd slept no better than he had the nights he'd sprawled on the hospital's gray sofa.

"How bad is he?" he demanded to know the moment they entered the room.

"He's asleep now," she whispered as though she was just beginning to see her failure to call from Matt's perspective. She trembled as she spoke and her eyes looked as dark and lusterless as Josh's. "He has a cold. It wouldn't even be serious if his white count were normal."

"But his white count isn't normal, and you should have called." He spoke through clenched teeth. He fought to control a spiraling anger. Since they'd brought Joshua to the hospital, Dana had behaved as though Josh were her child alone. Matt knew he hadn't been home as much as he should have been this past year, but he loved his child and spent all the time he could with him.

"There was nothing you could do. He's been sedated and given antibiotics. Dr. Young says he's passed the crisis point."

"This time!" Matt snapped. He attempted to calm himself. "Dana, don't you see he needs a blessing. If you'd called me, Dad and I . . ." The look on Dana's face told him he'd touched a trigger of some sort. He shook his head in anger and grief. It wouldn't help to yell at Dana, and he didn't wish to drive her further away. Slowly it dawned on him; he shouldn't have mentioned his father. In her mind Dana had reason to distrust his father. Since the night they'd brought Josh to the hospital, she'd made it quite clear she wanted nothing to do with his family, and he didn't fault her for being down on them. He just hoped she wouldn't expand her hurt and distrust to include the Church. Josh had done nothing wrong, and he had a right to the blessings of the priesthood.

"Maybe that's why I didn't call you." She surprised herself with her own words. A wave of pain swept through her and she knew it was true. She didn't want Matt's parents anywhere near her precious son—or her. They'd disapproved of her from the start and fed Matt's doubts, thus creating the nightmare that had occurred the night Josh had been brought to the hospital. They had subtly stolen Matt from her during the past year and had left her with an empty shell of a marriage. She'd passively allowed her own parents to dictate to her all of her life, and she'd suffered greatly the one time she'd stood up to them and proceeded with baptism. But she could never regret joining the Church! She'd been strong once, she would be again. No way would she trade one set of dictatorial parents for another!

"You don't want Josh to be administered to?" Matt asked incredulously.

"I've no objection to Josh receiving a priesthood blessing. You should know that," she responded angrily as resentment boiled to the surface. She said what once she would never have had the courage to say aloud. "If you really knew me, you wouldn't ask that. But you don't know me, do you? You don't have any idea what I want or how I feel. You think like your mother, that because you went on a mission and your family has held important church positions for several generations, your faith is greater than mine. You've never had to depend on the Savior as the only being who trusts and believes in you, and you have no idea what it is like to have only Him give you the unconditional love your soul hungers for. Josh has a right to every blessing the priesthood can give him, and you seem to think I love him so little, I would deny him that. But then, you think I'm the kind of woman who would hurt my own baby!"

Matt's face paled and his voice sounded stricken as he tried to explain. "Dana, I made a mistake, and I'm sorry. I regret with all my heart the ugly suspicions I subjected you to that night. Even at my worst, I don't think I really believed you had hurt Joshua."

"You were sure enough to call the police. You were so sure, in fact, that you considered punishing me more important than seeing that Josh got a blessing that night!" A well of bitterness burst bringing all the ugliness into the open.

"No," Matt attempted to defend himself. "I called Dad to ask him to bring some consecrated oil to the hospital. I tried to talk him out of "

"Obviously you didn't try very hard!" Dana let her pain run free. "But just for your information, Joshua didn't go without a blessing that night, or last night. Dr. Young and an orderly administered to him that first night, and last night there were two elders here visiting another child, and they responded to my request for a blessing. It isn't the blessing I object to. It's your father! Your parents control your life as completely as my father tried to control mine. I don't want to see your father or any of your family ever again! They're hateful and judgmental, and at the root of every problem we've had since we came to Utah!"

Matt slowly sank down on the sofa and placed his head in his hands. Watching him, Dana felt a twinge of guilt. It wasn't like her to throw a temper tantrum. She'd learned long ago not to verbally defend herself. She could blame it on worry and fatigue, but she knew there was more to it than that. She'd tried hard this past week to put

her hurt and shattered trust behind her, but all the months of sly
innuendoes from Matt's family, hinting that she wasn't caring for Josh
correctly, that she didn't know enough about the gospel to teach him,
that she didn't feed Matt properly, that her interests and style of dress
were somehow inferior, had eaten at her tender ego. She'd resented
Matt's gravitation toward his parent's counsel and his quick dismissal
of her opinions.

Her identity, along with her hopes and dreams, had slowly been
buried beneath Matt's career objectives and his family's constant barrage
of advice, and she had clung increasingly to her child. Josh became the
only person in the world who loved her just the way she was.

"Dana, please sit down," Matt sighed. She eyed him warily, but
did as he asked.

"You have legitimate cause to be angry with me—and with my
family," he acknowledged. "I've apologized for the stupid mistakes I
made that night. I want your forgiveness—I'll beg if need be—but I
don't think anything I say or do is going to reach you right now. I
pray that someday you will forgive me. I love you, but I don't think
you're ready to hear me say that either." He paused as if hoping that
in spite of what he had just said aloud, she'd say she loved him, too.
When she did not respond, he continued.

"Never have I doubted the sincerity of your testimony of the
gospel, and I hope that one day that testimony will enable you to
forgive me." He swallowed several times before plunging on. "I won't
force my family on you. At the moment, I'm terribly angry with
them, too, but they are my parents, and I love them. I let them know
they were to leave you strictly alone. Mother and Dad both regret
their part in what happened and would like to apologize to you." He
held up his hand when she appeared about to speak. "They've given
me their word they won't approach you until you're ready. They love
Josh, and you should know they've been here every day in the large
waiting room, waiting for any crumb of news about him."

Once more he paused and she found herself incapable of saying
anything. She didn't want to forgive her in-laws. Perhaps she only
needed an object for her fear and anger, and they conveniently
provided her with one, but her emotional hurt ran too deeply to let
go so easily.

"No matter how you feel—or how I feel—we have to put Josh first." Matt's voice became choked with emotion. "He needs donors, and the members of my family are the most likely candidates. We have to let them help Josh."

His words made sense. Somewhere in the recesses of her mind, she'd known since Dr. Young first explained about Josh's aplastic anemia, that it would come down to this. She couldn't save Josh alone. He needed his father's family. She had no choice but to ask for their help. Acknowledgment of need did nothing to alleviate her bitterness, however. Instead it only seemed to emphasize her inadequacies. For herself she would accept nothing, but for Josh she would compromise her pride.

As she slowly nodded her acquiescence, a stray shaft of cold, an early harbinger of winter, sent a shiver coursing down her spine, and she wondered if saving Josh's life would cost her more than she could pay.

"Are you Dana and Matt Bingham?" a voice from the hall interrupted them. When they acknowledged their identity, the young man dressed in hospital scrubs stepped inside the room. "Dr. Young sent me to find you."

"Josh!" They both jumped to their feet.

"Your kid? No, I didn't mean to frighten you. Dr. Young just wanted you to know he pulled a few strings, called in a couple of favors, and got your lab test results speeded up. They should be here before five tomorrow. He also said you should hurry with that list of possible donors."

Matt's eyes met hers and she realized he was asking her permission to contact his family. Her heart ached; if she said yes, would she be setting in motion the actions that could, in time, cost her the love and respect of her son? Would they take over her son until he saw his mother the way they did? But if she refused, Josh would die. No matter the cost to herself, she had to give him a chance at life. Slowly her lips formed the word, and over a roar like the wind in her ears, she whispered, "Yes."

CHAPTER FOUR

Matt strode across the parking lot, oblivious to both the rain and the puddles. Somehow it seemed a suitable backdrop to his mood. It did no good to kick himself for his faulty judgment or to try to excuse himself because he'd been afraid for Josh. He couldn't bear the possibility that he might lose his son, but seeing him weak and pale beneath that plastic bubble, with tubes and wires attached to his small body made the possibility all too real. And Dana? Was he losing her too? Perhaps he'd already lost her. The thought increased the ache in his heart. Though his anger was directed toward his parents, deep inside he knew he had only himself to blame.

He'd watched her struggle with the need to approach his family to ask for donors to help Josh. Even understanding her hurt and humiliation on the night they'd brought Josh to the hospital didn't quite explain her dislike for his family. He'd never told her of his parents' reservations about their marriage. Had she somehow guessed they hadn't wanted him to marry her, a recent convert from what his parents considered to be a dysfunctional family? Now he wondered if his own candidness in telling his mother of Dana's childhood and the brother who was serving time in prison had led to the aloofness between them. Shame swept over him as he realized he'd never once considered that Dana might not be the one at fault for the distance between his family and her.

His childhood had been warm and happy and he couldn't remember a time when he couldn't communicate freely with his parents. Some of his friends had had strong differences with their parents while growing up, but he'd considered himself pretty fortunate. He'd respected their advice and truly believed families were meant to be as close as his. Winn's and Robert's wives fit so smoothly into the family, it was hard to remember they hadn't always been there. But they'd both grown up in LDS homes, not much different from his own. Was that what made the difference? He'd once thought so, but now he wasn't so sure.

He'd assumed the distance between Dana and his family was her fault, but after the horrible suspicions his parents had voiced about Dana, and which he had far too easily accepted, his faith in his parents was greatly eroded. He wondered what else he had been blind to. In a way it was a scary feeling to lose that sense of security he'd always felt in trusting his parents' wisdom.

He reached his car and stepped inside. For all his hurry to enlist his family's aid in finding donors for Josh, he sat still, watching water sluice down the windows of the car and wishing he didn't have to ask for their help. If somehow he and Dana could work out their problems first, it would be so much easier. But time was a luxury they didn't have. Josh needed help now.

If there were some way to take Josh's suffering on himself, he would do it. A strange calm settled over him and a concept he'd only understood on an intellectual level touched his soul. His Savior understood. He'd taken upon Himself the suffering of so many because of His consuming love for them. He'd done for His younger brothers and sisters what he, Matt, would do for Josh if he were able. For the first time since this nightmare began, he felt loved and understood. The thought humbled him, and he wished Dana were with him so he could tell her of the insight that had shed light on his dark and weary heart.

His reluctance to face his family dissipated and he drove as rapidly as conditions allowed toward his childhood home. He knew the whole family would be gathered there. He'd stopped in the hospital lobby long enough to call his mother's secretary and request she pass on a message to Barbara Bingham. The woman had offered to put him through, but he hadn't wanted to speak to his mother directly. It would be hard enough to ask for her help when he stood face to face with her.

As he pulled to a stop in front of his parents' home, he spotted his father's truck parked next to his mother's SUV. Behind them were Winn and Sandra's custom van, Robert's F-150, and Robert's wife, Ann's, Fiero. Good, they were all here.

A voice on the radio caught his attention, ". . . seventy-four more shopping days until Christmas." He'd never concerned himself with Christmas in October before, but suddenly he wondered if Josh would survive until the holiday. Last Christmas Josh had kept Dana and him laughing as the toddler daily removed the decorations, which Dana had carefully crafted for their small tree, and hid them in his toy box. They'd taken delight in the way he clapped his hands in excitement every evening when they turned on the tree's tiny blinking lights. An ache touched his heart as he remembered how Josh had ignored his gifts on Christmas morning, but squealed with laughter as he played in the mound of wrapping paper. Suddenly Matt wanted to rush out to buy a train that whistled, dump trucks, a rocking horse, and the biggest ball he could find and wrap them in the brightest, shiniest paper in the whole world. If his son could never play the rough-and-tumble games other little boys played, how could he bear it? What if his son never had another Christmas?

Shaking off his gloomy thoughts, he took a deep breath, switched off the car, and opened the door. He squared his shoulders and marched up the walk. Josh would survive until Christmas. They would have many Christmases together. Matt wouldn't consider for one minute any other possibility.

Walking into the front room, he felt for just a moment a touch of an old annoyance. The room was as dark and gloomy as a funeral parlor. His mother had some kind of obsession with protecting carpets from fading. Surely with today's weather, she could open the stupid curtains without worrying about the sun fading her carpet. And what did it matter anyway if it did fade? It might be an improvement. The rest of the house was chaotic at times, but this one room was always immaculate. For the first time in his life he was struck by the phoniness of keeping one room constantly company-ready while just out of sight of guests, the remainder of the house was piled with the evidence of a family that put their activities ahead of house-keeping perfection.

Brushing aside the lingering annoyance, he greeted his family and moved to stand beside the fireplace. Everyone watched him expectantly, and he didn't know where to begin. After an awkward pause, his mother broke the ice for him.

"How is Josh this afternoon? Is he home?"

"He had a difficult night last night and won't be allowed to go home for quite a while," Matt responded carefully. He had no intention of revealing his own hurt that he had not been informed of his son's illness sooner.

"What happened?" "What's wrong with him?" Several voices spoke at once. His family's obvious concern for Josh warmed an icy spot in his heart. How could he cling to anger when there was no doubting his family's love for his dangerously sick child?

"Josh has aplastic anemia." He went on quickly to explain the little he knew about the disease. "Last night he started with cold symptoms and rapidly became seriously ill. His bone marrow isn't manufacturing enough white cells to ward off infection. He's on antibiotics, and his temperature is down this morning, but Dr. Young says he must be kept isolated."

"How soon will we be able to see him?" his mother asked and Matt sighed before answering. He really didn't want her to know that even if the medical staff would allow her to see her grandson, Dana didn't want her anywhere near Josh.

"Dr. Young says it's best if he has no visitors other than Dana and myself. He's in a plastic isolation bubble and we have to scrub and wear hospital gowns to enter his room." He swallowed back the lump that rose in his throat each time he pictured how small and helpless Josh had appeared when he'd gazed through the plastic at his sleeping child.

"Son, Josh needs a blessing." Matt's father stood. "Let me get my coat, and I'll go back to the hospital with you."

"Dad, they won't let you in."

"Of course, they will." Warner Bingham never paused in his march toward the closet where his coat was kept. "The hospitals around here always allow priesthood blessings to be administered to patients, no matter how ill the person is."

"No, Dad," Matt tried to explain. "Two elders already administered to him."

"You asked strangers?" Matt ignored the hurt in his father's voice. He had no right to be hurt. If he hadn't called . . . Matt swallowed back his own hurt, recognizing his reaction had been the same when Dana told him of the two elders who had placed their hands on his son's head and offered the blessing he would have preferred to give his son.

"Any faithful priesthood holder who blesses those in need is not really a stranger," he reminded gently.

"No, of course not, but at a time like this you should turn to family." Silence met Warner's pronouncement.

"It's Dana, isn't it?" Barbara voiced what he suspected the whole family was thinking. "She doesn't want us to see Josh."

"Well, Mother, can you really blame her?" Winn asked. "You and Dad practically had her arrested when she was already half out of her mind with worry. I can't blame her if she doesn't feel inclined to turn to family." Barbara's face turned red, and for once she appeared speechless.

"Winn, don't talk to your mother like that." Warner turned on his oldest son.

"Sorry," Winn apologized. "But just the same, I can certainly understand if Dana doesn't want to see any of us any time soon. When she could have used a little family support, we weren't there any more than her own family was." Matt winced at the truth in Winn's appraisal of the situation.

"I have to agree with Winn," his wife, Sandra spoke up. "The evidence looked bad, and I know you were thinking more about protecting Josh than punishing Dana, but it was premature to call the police before Dr. Young finished his examination. Now Dana's feelings are hurt and none of us are in a position to go to her and apologize." Matt had never noticed before how much Sandra resembled her mother-in-law. She was extremely adept at analyzing situations and bluntly taking charge. She even looked a great deal like Mother. Her hair was cut in a short no-nonsense style; she chose conservative, quality clothing with more concern for comfort than style, and she managed to juggle dozens of projects at once, including four-year-old twins and a first-grader. He'd always suspected two women as strong and outspoken as Mother and Sandra would clash someday, but he didn't want it to be over Dana.

"If only I had taken more time to get to know Dana better," Ann sighed.

"You've had your hands full. Between being Young Women president and having a full schedule of equestrian shows, you haven't had much time," her husband promptly defended her. Matt felt a prick of conscience at his brother, Robert's, quick defense of his wife. If only he'd been equally quick to defend Dana.

"Listen, all of you." Matt turned the family's attention back to himself. "You're right in believing that Dana is not anxious to see any of you, but it was not her decision to keep you away from Josh. You should know, too, that she is aware I'm here with you now. We discussed the situation, and she agreed we need your help. She didn't come with me because we felt one of us should stay with the baby in case he wakes up and is frightened. So that's why I'm here alone to ask if you'll help us." It was all true. He and Dana had discussed what had to be done, but he wasn't certain she would have come with him anyway. That was the real reason why he'd suggested she stay with Josh.

"Of course, we'll help," Matt's parents spoke in unison.

"If you need money—"

Barbara cut off Warner to say, "I'd be happy to watch Josh, so Dana can get some rest."

"We'll help, too, of course," Sandra spoke up. "You must be getting awfully tired of hospital food, I can . . ."

"No, that kind of help is appreciated," Matt interrupted. "But what we need—what Josh needs—is a great deal more than that. In order to live, he needs platelet donors, and as soon as possible he must have a bone marrow transplant. We've registered him with a donor registry, but his best chance of finding a suitable match is from family members."

"Oh, Matt, of course we'll help." His mother stepped to his side and grasped his arm. He knew her desire to help was genuine.

Warner too went to his third son and embraced him fiercely. "That baby is in far more serious condition than any of us thought, isn't he?"

Ann dabbed at her eyes, and Robert looked as though he might lose his own battle with tears. Winn and Sandra had identical stunned expressions on their faces. When they exchanged guilty glances, he knew they were thinking of their own healthy children.

"Thanks," Matt choked back his own tears.

"Surely, you didn't think we'd turn you down, did you?" Winn spoke quietly. The appalled expression on the faces around him confirmed his earlier feelings. Regardless of any unresolved differences, his family would stand behind him. It hadn't even occurred to him that they might not. He wished he could be as certain they would support Dana if she were the one asking for their help.

He shook his head slightly. "No, I knew I could count on you."

"Okay, what do we have to do?" Sandra, ever practical, symbolically rolled up her sleeves ready to go to work. "What about the girls? Are they too young to donate?"

"Dr. Young said we should have everyone tested. If the girls are a good match, whether or not they donate will be up to you and their pediatrician."

"What's involved in this platelet donor business?" Warner wanted to know. "Do we just give blood? I do that a couple of times a year, so that's no problem."

"Actually it's a different process. Platelets are collected from a donor through a process called hemapheresis," Matt attempted to explain his newly acquired knowledge as simply as possible. "It's a lengthy process that takes about three hours. Blood is drawn through a vein in the donor's arm and sent to a blood-separating machine, which keeps the platelets and sends the rest of the blood back to the donor. The platelets that have been separated are then given to the patient with aplastic anemia, in this case, Josh. Only a couple of days are needed for the donor's body to replace the missing platelets, but unfortunately Josh will need a transfusion every few days. That means we have to find as many donors as possible."

Silence met his explanation, but only for a minute, then everyone seemed to have questions. Finally Matt held up his hands. "I can't answer all of your questions. I brought some booklets on aplastic anemia and on donating platelets or bone marrow. I'll leave them here for all of you to look at. I do know we have to hurry with the testing."

"I'll call and make appointments for all of us," Sandra volunteered.

"Uncle George's family could probably help us, and Aunt Dorothy will be miffed if I don't ask her family to help. Let's see, where did I put our family reunion directory?" Barbara was already making plans.

"Are you all right?" Ann moved to his side. "And Dana, how is she holding up?" The question was asked softly, yet it seemed to carry over every other voice and once again silence fell over the room.

"It's hard," he answered simply over the ever-present lump in his throat, and he was struck by an awareness that Ann was the only one to ask about Dana. "But we'll be fine. It's Josh we have to focus on."

"Oh, Matt." Ann's eyes were soft with sympathy. "Dana doesn't believe it was just us who let her down. She blames you, too, doesn't she?"

Holding himself stiffly, he nodded his head. He didn't want to discuss the rift that had opened between him and his wife.

"It's my fault," Barbara claimed responsibility. "I saw those bruises all over poor little Josh and jumped to conclusions I had no right to make. If I'd kept my mouth shut, you wouldn't have made the assumption I did. If she'll only let me, I'd be happy to apologize."

"Mother, it does no good to try to assign blame," Matt said. "I'm Dana's husband and should have known better. More than any of you, I know how gentle her soul is and how much she loves our child. When she needed my support, I wasn't there. I have no one to blame but myself. Now if you'll excuse me, I need to get back to the hospital." He turned toward the door.

Warner reached out a hand to detain him. "Son, before you go, I think we should have a word of prayer." Matt nodded his head, unable to speak, and one by one they knelt in a circle.

Looking around at his family, Matt felt an aching loss. It was so natural for them to kneel together, but how many times had Dana been included in the family prayer circle? The few times she had been physically present, had she truly been included? He wished she were here now, her small hand clasped in his.

Warner cleared his throat several times before addressing Heavenly Father. *"We have been greatly blessed by the presence of little Joshua in our family and feel to thank thee for the love and joy he has brought into each of our lives. At this time he is gravely ill and needs not only our help, but thine. Please bless him that his little body will heal and that he will become strong and well. And we ask thee to protect him from pain and infection. Bless him that he will be able to grow and mature and fill his mission here on earth.*

"We also ask thee to bless Joshua's parents, Matthew and Dana, that they will be comforted by thy love and the love they have for each other. Our family has hurt Dana a great deal and we have failed her where we should have aided and supported her. We ask thy forgiveness and request thy help that we may atone for the wrong we have done her.

"Father, as we face the strain and worry of young Joshua's illness and seek to rectify our wrongs, please help us to be guided by thy will. Josh is in need of many donors; please be with all of his family that we may fill this need and that all of us who might be of service to him will be touched by thy spirit, that we may freely give." He closed the prayer in the name of the Savior and they all remained kneeling, their heads bowed for a few minutes, with only a soft sob and an occasional gruff clearing of a throat to break the silence.

When at last Matt rose to his feet, his father hugged him once more, followed by his brothers. At the door his mother drew him close before he could step outside. "What about Dana's family? Will they help?" she asked.

Her question shook him. He hadn't considered contacting the Dalbys, because just as he'd known his family would help, he knew hers wouldn't. "They've forbidden Dana to contact them for any reason. Through their attorney they let her know they don't even want to be informed if she should die."

"Oh!" Barbara looked stunned. Gradually the shock in her eyes turned to a militant flame Matt remembered well from a few unruly episodes in his own life as he grew up. "How could any parent . . . ? Oh, my! She must think we are as cold and indifferent as her parents!"

"No wonder she clings to Josh and is so protective of him!" Sandra exclaimed.

"She must be so lonely," Ann added.

"Well, this just won't do," Barbara went on. "Sandra, start making appointments. Ann, you look in my desk for those addresses. Winn, contact Bishop Barrows; there's no sense limiting this to family. Robert, you check with the Church Mission Department and see what is involved in getting Hadley tested. Warner, you better go back to the office and do as much of Matt's work as you can, so he can stay at the hospital as long as he needs to. Oh, and see how many of your employees might be willing to be tested. Matt, you'd better get back to the hospital. And see if you can get that poor, stubborn girl to eat something."

If he weren't so close to tears, his mother's words would have brought a grin to both his and his brothers' faces, along with a wise-cracking "Aye, aye, captain." They'd teased their mother for years about being a frustrated marine sergeant or a pirate ship captain. But not today. Today he seemed to be seeing his family through different eyes—Dana's eyes. When not seen through a lifetime of love and shared experiences, his family's organization and good intentions might easily be seen as controlling, dominating, even intimidating. No wonder Dana held back from them. If only he'd taken the time to help her see their good qualities, instead of expecting her to love them simply because he did.

Dana glanced at her watch. Fifteen more minutes. Time dragged as she waited to be allowed back into her son's room. She was only permitted ten minutes each hour with him. She paced the floor, eventually stopping in front of a large plate glass window. Far below she could see the parking lot with matchbox-size cars parked in tidy rows. Rain sheeted against the window, causing the shapes to twist and blur. A blue car wandered up and down the rows looking for a parking space, and she wondered if Matt had returned and if his parents were with him. Could she greet them, pretend nothing had happened? And if she couldn't, would they refuse to help Josh?

"Dana." She turned her head to see a familiar young nurse standing in the doorway. They'd spoken several times and the nurse had been sympathetic and understanding. "Josh is awake, and it would be all right for you to see him now."

"Thank you," she whispered and hurried to the room where she scrubbed her hands and collected a fresh gown and mask. When her fingers trembled, the nurse tied the strings for her, then walked beside her as she approached Josh's bedside.

"Ma-ma." Josh smiled faintly as she leaned toward the plastic engulfing his bed, and he weakly lifted his arms. If only she could clutch him to her and take him far from plastic bubbles, needles, restraints, and all the pain and fear that had invaded his life. She'd wanted Josh's childhood to be different from hers. She hadn't wanted him to ever cry for a mother who never came or to be lonely and afraid. What terrible mistake had she made to cause her child to suffer so?

"Mama is here." She attempted to smile and reached her hand toward the plastic.

"Dana, there are two circles cut in the bubble which work like small doors. Dr. Young said it would be all right for you to put your hands inside." The nurse pointed out the circular flaps. "That's how we feed and change him. Perhaps if you touch him, you'll both feel better, and in a couple of hours we'll let you give him a small amount to eat."

"Thank you." The backs of Dana's eyes smarted as she reached through the plastic and felt Josh's warm chest. Softly she brushed his cheek with her fingers and he turned his head to rub it against the back of her hand, reminding her of that blissful time when he'd nuzzled against her breasts, seeking life-sustaining nourishment. A tear splashed against the clear plastic. Josh sighed so softly, she barely heard the sound. He closed his eyes, and in moments he'd fallen asleep.

"He's very tired," the nurse spoke softly. "He's fighting a difficult battle, and he's been quite restless. For such a small child, he's really brave, but I think he'll sleep better now he's seen his mother."

Dana relished the nurse's acknowledgment of her relationship with Josh, but she knew she was being gently told her time was up. It was hard to withdraw her hand and break this small connection with her baby. Removing her hands from his warm body brought the ever-present tears to her eyes.

"You need to sleep, too," the nurse reminded her. "I promise I'll wake you if there's any change, or when it's time to feed him."

"I would appreciate that." She gave the young woman a watery smile, and slowly turned her steps back toward the small waiting room.

———•———

Warner parked in the spot that was always reserved for him and slowly climbed out of his vehicle, feeling weary and depressed. He made his way inside and paused, seeing the elevator close behind one of his foremen. He was going to have to speak with the man. He'd noticed for some time that Bart was spending too much time visiting with his wife, Josie, who was Matt's secretary, when he should have been at the job site. Bart had always been moody, but lately his temperament swings were really starting to upset Josie, and with Matt facing so much pressure from the Barringer bid and Josh's illness, she needed to be at top form.

With a sigh, Warner passed up the elevator for the stairs. At the top he paused to catch his breath and wondered just when he'd gotten so old and tired. Less than six months ago, he'd celebrated his fifty-eighth birthday and had congratulated himself on being as fit and energetic as he'd been two decades ago. Now a simple flight of stairs left him puffing and his knees wobbling.

He paused to catch his breath before approaching his secretary's desk, where he waited for her to hand him the usual stack of pink message slips.

"Is your grandson any better today?" Seeing the concern in Robyn's eyes, he was reminded of the loyalty of his staff. They were good people, and he intended to see that they all got bonuses once they got past the inevitable glitches of expansion. They had all worked long hours and taken little time off in more than a year. He pulled his thoughts back to the question.

"No, he's not well at all, which means Matt won't be here much for the next while," he admitted. "That's going to put a greater burden on all of us, but especially on his department."

"I'm so sorry," Robyn said. "Is there anything I can do to help?"

"Perhaps there is," Warner admitted. "The boy needs some kind of blood transfusions. You might see if any of the staff are willing to be tested for compatibility."

"I'll do that," Robyn promised.

Warner continued on to his office and nearly groaned as he eased into his large leather chair and automatically turned it to face the glass wall, which gave him a view of the mountain tops. As always he wondered how long it would take for the chair to assume the comfortable contours his old one had developed with the passage of time. Above the freeway that horizontally bisected his view, Warner could see the dome of the capitol building, the spires of the temple, and the multiplying high-rises of the city. He loved the view and took a special kind of pleasure in picking out buildings constructed by his company. The window was the best part of his office.

He turned back to look at the sleek furniture Ann had chosen for him and found himself longing for the old oak rolltop Barbara had found at a yard sale for his first office. He didn't need such a fancy office, but Winn and Robert had insisted it was his due. He hadn't been able to convince either of them that he'd been happiest when his office consisted of a battered brown briefcase, a hard hat, and a rusted yellow pickup truck.

No, he wasn't being completely honest with himself. He enjoyed many of the perks that had come his way as his business had grown. He'd struggled for many years to start his own business and the position of respect he now almost took for granted from his peers did matter. Perhaps more than it should.

He'd never quite gotten over the hurt he'd felt when his former partner had deserted him, just when he'd believed they were ready to expand the company. Even worse, his partner had taken half of the company's assets. It was about that time that Barbara had left the company as well, and he'd never been quite sure whether it was because she lacked confidence in his ability to lead the company, or if Hal had had something to do with her leaving. Hal had accused

Warner of lacking the drive and ambition to be really successful, and the years following the dissolution of the partnership had extracted a heavy financial toll. Consequently Warner derived a secret satisfaction in knowing his company was now just as successful as the company Hal had formed, maybe more so.

Over the years he'd heard rumors of several suits filed against his former partner's company for using substandard materials and shoddy workmanship. All in all, he was glad his association with Hal Downey had ended. Warner valued the reputation he'd built and didn't want his company's name associated with questionable work or business tactics.

Warner was older, a little heavier, and certainly much better dressed than the young man who had first envisioned owning his own company, but he didn't think his values had changed. His family and the Church still came first, although his actions lately made him wonder if he may have lost sight of his priorities for a time. His son's face haunted him, and he held himself responsible for inflicting so much pain on him. Not only was Matt's child seriously ill, but his marriage was obviously in deep trouble.

The expansion needn't have been pushed through so rapidly, he berated himself, realizing that he'd given no thought to the pressure he was putting on Matt's marriage. He had simply thrust his son straight from college into the demands of completing the construction and moving into their new building, acquiring additional equipment, and undertaking many larger, more complicated contracts than the firm was accustomed to handling.

He sensed that a good share of Matt's marital problems went beyond the night he'd called the police. He and Barbara had entertained doubts about Matt's marriage from the beginning. They'd never been able to see what Matt saw in the childlike bride he'd chosen. Their family was outspoken, assertive, and self-confident. Matt's wife was shy and reticent, never voicing any opinions, or having much to say. She had clung to Josh as though she feared Matt's parents were going to take him away from her. Warner knew that Dana had grown up with a great deal of wealth, but to be perfectly honest, she looked to him like those hippies who used to hang out at airports passing out flowers.

Barbara had tried to help the girl, but that hadn't worked out too well. Near as he could tell, Dana had been avoiding Barbara long before this fiasco. He'd seen Barbara's frustration as she tried to help her daughter-in-law fit in better, and he'd been annoyed by the girl's silent resistence. Now he wondered if Dana had been just plain overwhelmed. He was well aware of his wife's strong personality. He enjoyed Barbara's quick mind and air of authority, but some people were intimidated by those qualities, especially in a woman. Personally, he'd never felt comfortable around small women or artsy types, and he preferred both men and women who said straight out what they meant.

Hindsight told him that he and Barbara both should have taken more time to get to know Dana rather than being so quick to assume she needed changing. Guiltily he realized he scarcely knew the girl at all; most of what he knew about her had come from Barbara. He should have also seen the danger in keeping Matt late at the office for such an extended period of time. Hadn't he been taught all his life that such absences were dangerous to marriages?

It would be easy to excuse himself. Expanding the business was for his sons' sake. They would never have to go through the financial insecurity he and Barbara had endured until recently. Their wives wouldn't have to work the way Barbara did. First, she had helped him start his business, and then when Winn had left on his mission, followed less than a year later by Robert, she'd gotten her realtor's license and supported them both. He wanted his sons to have the best opportunities. And the best eternal companions. Funny how those goals now sounded more like excuses.

Though he and his wife viewed Matt and Dana's marriage as one of being "unequally yoked," once they'd realized they couldn't change Matt's mind, they'd determined to support the marriage. But had they really done so? Had there been some negative force behind his keeping Matt away from his home so much that his marriage had been weakened? Why had he, a man who rarely acted impulsively, been so determined to push the expansion forward at so much greater speed than necessary? And why had he been so quick to believe the worst about Dana? Not only to believe, but to act upon that hasty assumption? He shook his head, not understanding his own uncharacteristic actions.

So far, Joshua was his only grandson, and it bothered him that Dana hovered over the boy whenever he was around in an obvious attempt to protect her child from his grandfather. His heart ached with the love he wanted to shower on this lovable little boy. He'd loved each of his sons, and he adored his granddaughters, but something about Josh touched his heart as no other child ever had. Perhaps he was being fanciful, something else he rarely indulged in, but he often felt a link with Josh that went soul to soul. He wanted to be there to protect and reassure the child through this terrible illness. Instead he was forbidden access to his grandchild. It was inconceivable that he would never be a real grandfather to Josh.

Please, he prayed softly. *Give me a chance to show Joshua how much I love him. Soften Dana's heart that she'll forgive my mistakes and allow me to spend time with Joshua. Please grant him a healthy body and mind. Father, please tell me what to do to help him.*

Long after he finished praying, he continued to sit with head bowed, hands clasped. At last an ember of warmth filled his heart, growing and expanding until he knew. *To love the child, he first had to love the child's mother.* How on earth was he to go about doing that? Love had always seemed to him to be one of those things that just happened, not something a person could make happen. A person couldn't just turn love off and on.

Or did he really believe that? Hadn't he been trying for years to win back his wife's love? There had been no doubt in his mind that Barbara loved him during those early years, but he'd made some costly mistakes that had brought them to the edge of financial ruin, and she'd lost faith in his ability to support them or lead his company. While he'd struggled to re-establish his company, she'd acquired her own successful business and had become the major support of their family. For a long time he'd believed he wouldn't regain her trust until he proved himself capable of managing a major firm.

Now he questioned whether he knew anything at all about what had gone wrong in his own marriage. Barbara wasn't mercenary. He'd realized a long time ago that it didn't matter nearly as much to her as it did to him that she made more money than he did, but the skills that went into leadership were important. She admired the ability to be firm and decisive, and he'd struggled to develop those attributes.

One day he'd show her she'd been wrong about him. He wasn't weak or lazy. He was truly capable of fulfilling those dreams they'd shared in the early years of their marriage.

CHAPTER FIVE

Dana knew her husband had entered the room, but she kept her eyes closed, hoping he would think she was asleep. She had slept for a short time on the gray couch in the room just down the hall from Josh's room, but not long or well. Her mind would not leave the small room where Josh, her precious baby, lay. She couldn't erase from her thoughts the pleading in his eyes as he struggled to move arms that wouldn't move because they were strapped to the sides of his bed, a gesture made necessary by his repeated attempts to remove the needles from his arms.

"Dana." She felt the cushion beneath her sink as Matt sat beside her. She hadn't fooled him; he knew she was awake. She wasn't sure why she'd even bothered to steal a few more minutes of privacy. She'd never been able to be still enough or good enough so no one would notice her.

"Dana, a nurse stopped me in the hall. She said Joshua is awake and that she had promised you she'd wake you so you could feed him. I offered to do it."

For a moment she thought he meant he'd offered to feed Joshua, and she felt a surge of resentment. Then she understood he meant he'd only offered to wake her, and she felt shame that she had assumed he was usurping a task she coveted for herself. She struggled to a sitting position, only to find herself so close to Matt that his chest brushed her shoulder, sending a flutter of awareness through her. Quickly clamping down on the sudden urge to lean against her husband, she jumped to her feet and felt a moment's dizziness from the sudden movement.

"Are you all right?" Matt reached out a hand to steady her.

"Yes, I'm fine." She withdrew from his touch, forcing herself to turn away from him. This wasn't the time to think about Matt. She couldn't bear to think about him or her shattered dreams. Later, when Joshua was well again, then she'd have to think about Matt, about their marriage, but not now. Now she must concentrate on Joshua. Only Joshua mattered. Still, a lingering sense that she should apologize to Matt haunted her as she turned to flee down the hall.

———•———

Matt cursed his clumsiness. The sound of her hurrying footsteps sounded more like she was running *from* him than that she was running to Josh. He shouldn't have touched her. He knew she was scared and vulnerable, and that each time he touched her, or spoke to her, she relived that awful moment in the emergency room corridor when her eyes had pleaded with him for help, and he'd turned away. A feeling of self-loathing came over him. That moment haunted him, too. He couldn't forgive his own actions that night; how could he expect her to dismiss them from her mind?

After a few moments, he followed her down the hall. Only one person at a time was allowed in Joshua's room, but he couldn't resist hovering near the door to the room, searching for just a glimpse of his son. One part of his mind told him he had as much right as Dana to be with Josh, even to feed him if he chose to, but another part warned him not to push the issue.

Remembering his mother's admonition to make certain Dana ate, he turned away to make his way to the cafeteria. He selected a crab salad and a couple of rolls for her. She never drank anything but milk or fruit juice, so he selected both a carton of milk and a small bottle of orange juice.

When he arrived back on the fourth floor he found Dana curled in one corner of the gray sofa. He watched her for several minutes before she became aware of him. A sense of shock ran through him as he noticed how thin and worn she'd become. She wasn't very big to begin with, but the past week had taken a terrible toll on her. Her vibrant hair had lost its luster and her jeans hung in unbecoming folds from her slender hips. Something told him that one week of worry and sporadic meals didn't account for all of the changes in his wife.

A longing he'd experienced several times recently assailed him. He wished they were back in their apartment close to the college campus. Those two years had been the happiest of his life, even better than the two years he'd spent on his mission. In that apartment he'd felt strong and confident. His actions weren't measured against his brothers' achievements, there had been no quotas, and best of all, Dana thought him some kind of hero.

He loved his brothers, but they were a tough act to follow. He'd never been as handy with tools as his older brothers were, and Hadley could think faster on his feet than anyone had a right to. Consequently while they helped Dad, he'd mowed the lawn and run errands for his mother. His brothers had all been football heroes in high school, while he'd barely made the track team; Robert's football scholarship paid most of his college expenses. Even as missionaries, his brothers had advanced rapidly to leadership positions and baptized dozens of people, while he'd spent most of his mission with an aging computer in the mission home, serving as a finance clerk. He'd only baptized two people and one of those was a girl the sister missionaries had taught.

Dana had made him forget his inadequacies. Around her everything was light and new, even his testimony had felt brighter, and Josh had brought an added glow to his life. Where had his sparkling, laughing bride gone?

A blinding flash of clarity left him feeling like a fool. One instance of doubt and betrayal hadn't done this to Dana. Not even Joshua's devastating illness was alone responsible. He'd forgotten that his family and friends, the people in their ward, the whole city were strangers to Dana, and that Dana was never comfortable with strangers. For the past year he'd focused on his job, feeling satisfaction in knowing he did it well and that it made a tremendous difference to his father and brothers. He'd basked in their approval, and taken joy in being reunited with his family. He'd reveled in sharing their lives and activities, and in measuring up to their expectations.

For the past year he had been more son than husband. On some level he'd known Dana wasn't happy and had felt vaguely annoyed with her. It was easier to dismiss her dissatisfaction than admit his own selfish preoccupation.

Focusing on his job, he'd concerned himself with proving his ability to his father and brothers. He found the work challenging and satisfying, and if he ever felt guilt over the long hours he worked, he assured himself he was doing it for Dana and Josh, and they should appreciate how hard he was working for them.

Dana never complained. Sandra might march down to the office or even to a construction site and demand that Winn put family home evening or a school performance for his daughters ahead of completing a job on schedule, but Dana never would. She'd learned at a young age to avoid conflict and to never make demands. She'd made it easy for him to neglect his responsibilities at home.

He became aware she was watching him and felt a momentary awkwardness. "Here." He thrust the food he'd brought toward her. "I thought you might be hungry."

"I'm not." She stated it as a simple fact.

"No, I don't suppose you are. I haven't been hungry lately either, but Dr. Young told me when I went to the lab for testing that we both needed to eat and keep our strength up because even if we test positive, we can't donate blood, platelets, or bone marrow to Josh if we're run down or ill. If either of us becomes ill, we'll be banned from his room as well."

"Oh!" She looked stricken and he regretted sounding so threatening, but he'd only told her the truth, and it looked as though she might need to be shocked into caring about herself. She took the cardboard tray he handed her and set it on a low table beside her. Busying herself with opening the milk carton and nibbling at a roll, she ignored him without appearing to blatantly do so, but he knew what she was doing. Dana had a tendency to play ostrich, to bury her head in the sand. By pretending a conflict didn't exist, she seemed to think it would go away.

"It won't work, you know." He settled himself on the sofa across from her. "You can't pretend I didn't hurt you or that you're not angry with me. I've apologized, and I'll be happy to apologize again if it will help." He waited, but she didn't respond, so he went on. "We have to talk about it sometime."

"I can't. Not now," she whispered in a stricken voice and he sighed.

"All right, I won't pressure you, but I want you to know I love you." How he ached to hear her respond with the same three little words, but she remained silent.

"Dana, we've got a rough time ahead of us. Do you think we could at least declare a truce? For Josh's sake?" This time she nodded her head.

"I won't ever doubt you again," Matt promised. "And I'm asking for your word that you won't shut me out from anything to do with Josh's care or condition. If you don't want my family around, I'll keep them away, but both you and Josh will have to have some contact with them if any of them are suitable donors. They've all agreed to be tested and are anxious to do anything they can to help."

"I'm afraid," she spoke so softly he almost didn't hear her.

"Afraid I won't keep my word?" he queried almost as softly and held his breath, fearing her answer.

"N-no. I'm afraid of losing Josh."

"Oh, honey." He moved across the narrow space between them and reached for her hands. "We have to have faith that if we do all we can, Josh will get well." She lifted her head until their eyes met and he saw the sorrow there. His heart constricted and he wondered if she sensed something he didn't. "I can't bear to even consider the possibility that he might not make it," he admitted slowly.

"There's more than one way to lose someone you love." She spoke softly and the pain in her eyes told him she spoke from firsthand experience. Guiltily he wondered if she meant their own estrangement. Or did she mean her brother? Surely she couldn't think she could lose Josh to anything but death. Another layer of sorrow spread across his heart as the truth sank in. That was exactly what she feared. Where he saw his family's love and concern as a kind of solace, she saw their involvement as a threat to take over her child.

"I've told myself over and over that if this is his time, I have to accept that, but I don't believe it is." She removed one hand from his and brushed it across her eyes. "Somehow I think I'm being tested. If I can just be strong enough he'll be all right. But I thought that when Rick was taken away. I thought if I prayed hard enough, and believed enough, he would come back. Matt, I just can't lose Josh, too. I'm not strong enough."

Without conscious thought, Matt put his arms around Dana and held her while she cried, knowing that not all of the tears were hers. "Listen to me," he whispered in her ear. "Rick's conviction and his refusal to allow you to visit him are not your fault. He's an adult and he made the choices that separated you. Whether Josh recovers or not has nothing to do with your faith or how much you love him either. Faith and love can't be discounted, but you can't take all of the responsibility upon yourself. I love him, too, and whether or not you want to believe it, my family loves him and prays for him."

He wasn't sure where the words came from, but they seemed to tumble from his mouth. "Even our combined faith and love may not be enough to save him. I've known all my life that there are times when tremendous faith creates a miracle, but when a miracle doesn't occur I don't think we can blame it on a lack of faith. If we make certain everything is done medically to save him, and we believe with all our hearts in God's healing power, and we still lose him, then somehow we'll just have to dig deep inside ourselves to find the faith to accept God's will."

"I don't know if I can do that," Dana whispered through her tears.

"I think I've always known that each person's faith must be tried, but I pray that losing our child is a test we won't have to face." He buried his face in her hair, and he held her until his arms ached and his back turned stiff. Sleep finally claimed her exhausted body, but still he couldn't let her go. Never, for all eternity, did he want to let her, or their son, go.

"Mr. Bingham," a quiet voice spoke from the doorway. "There's a call for you at the nurses' station."

Matt glanced toward the nurse, then back at Dana. He didn't want to leave her, even for a few minutes, but the call might be important. It could be Dr. Young with the results on his and Dana's tests. Slowly he eased her head onto one of the cushions and shifted her slight weight until she lay on the sofa. Overcoming his reluctance to separate completely from her, he forced himself to stand. Looking back at her, he wondered if she might become cold. He wouldn't be gone long, and he could ask for a blanket at the desk. Instead he slipped off his jacket and laid it across her slender shoulders.

When he reached the nurses' station, he took the phone someone handed him and quickly identified himself to the caller. His father's voice came over the line.

"There's been a break-in here," Warner announced without any preamble. "Can you leave there long enough to come down and check over your office? That seems to be where most of the damage occurred."

"I'll be right there," he promised. He hung up the phone and his mind was immediately flooded with questions. When had the break-in occurred? How much damage? Why his office? He could be there in twenty minutes . . . but he hesitated. Dana might awaken and need him. He hadn't seen Josh at all this morning, and hadn't he just vowed that from now on he'd put his wife and son first? His preoccupation with his job was partly responsible for the estrangement between him and Dana, yet here he was, already rushing off to see about the family business.

A break-in wasn't exactly business as usual. Dana would understand an emergency, and he really did have obligations and responsibilities to his family, too. He had to go.

When he reached the door to the waiting room, he saw Dana was still asleep. He sensed she hadn't slept much for a long time, and he felt reluctant to wake her, even to tell her he had to leave. Reluctantly he backed away, hurrying back to the nurses' station.

"Could I leave a note here for my wife?" he asked the nurse behind the desk. "She's asleep, and there's an emergency at work. I need to let her know where I'll be, but I don't want to wake her."

"Yes, of course," the nurse responded. "I was just going to let your wife know she could see Josh again for a few minutes."

Matt paused. Dana needed to rest, and he wanted desperately to visit Josh. The break-in had already happened, and getting there quickly wouldn't change a thing. He made a decision.

"Dana is so exhausted, I'd like to let her sleep a little longer. May I be the one to spend a few minutes with Josh?"

Forty minutes later Matt punched the elevator button for the third floor of Bingham Construction. The ride was brief, and he made no apologies when the doors opened, and he stepped into the midst of the crowd gathered in front of the receptionist's desk. If they didn't understand, that was too bad. He certainly didn't regret the few minutes he'd spent at his son's bedside. Josh's smile of welcome had gone far to mend his shattered spirit, and when the nurse told him his time was up, Josh had wanted him to stay.

"Pway, Dada. 'Osh pway, Dada," he'd whispered, even as his exhausted little body drifted toward sleep.

"Daddy will be back soon, and we'll play," he promised with tears in his eyes, and a prayer in his heart that Josh would soon be able to play.

———•———

"The police have already dusted for prints." His father wasted no time getting to the point the moment he arrived. Matt was glad there was no comment on the amount of time it had taken for him to arrive after he'd said he'd be right there. If his father had said one word, Matt wasn't sure he would have been able to hold his temper in check.

"We need you to go through both your paper files and computer files to see if anything is missing," his father informed him.

"How did someone get in?" Matt asked as he hurried down the hall beside his father and brother Robert.

"We're not sure," Robert answered before Warner could speak. "Winn came in early to pick up some equipment he needs at the Forsby site. Scott met him at the back gate. He was anxious to leave because his dog was sick, and he wanted to get him to a vet. He wasn't aware that anyone had entered the building. After Winn went upstairs and discovered the break-in, he checked around and found a small amount of meat we suspect was poisoned near the west fence."

"Didn't Scott hear anything?" Matt paused, remembering the shadow of movement he'd attributed to imagination around midnight the night before.

Warner shook his head as he responded. "Apparently not. The break-in probably occurred while he was inside the building. He leaves the dog alone in the yard when he comes inside. The burglar probably sedated the dog, then waited until Scott was back outside to sneak inside the building. "

"The lock on your outer office is scratched." Robert pointed out the damage as they entered the accounting office. "We might not have even noticed, if I hadn't come in early and surprised him before he could get out. I think he was in a hurry and got careless when he heard the elevator coming up."

"I was here until almost three . . ." He started to explain about the shadow he might have seen, but he stopped when he saw the disaster his office had become. Files lay everywhere. His wastepaper basket had been overturned, and computer disks and papers littered the room as though someone had made a hasty search. Drawers hung open, their contents spilling out. A residue of fingerprint dust covered every surface. He found himself unable to speak for several seconds.

"We figure the intruder broke into your office while Scott searched for the dog and worried over the dog's apparent illness," Warner explained. "If you didn't leave until three, and Winn got here before five, he might not have found what he was looking for."

Matt looked around with a sense of helplessness until he spotted his staff huddled together in the outer office. He could see their sympathy and concern. He suspected they also dreaded the increase in their workload that would be required to replace missing or damaged records. A surge of resentment shot through him. He didn't want to spend more time here; he wanted to be here less. Dana and Josh needed him with them.

"Bob Evans helped me do a quick survey of the files to see if we could determine whether or not anything had been taken," his father explained. Bob was one of Matt's assistants who, after having managed payroll and accounts payable for Bingham Construction for close to twenty years, was looking forward to retirement in a couple of months. Warner continued, "We didn't find anything missing, but he said we shouldn't disturb things until you have a chance to go through everything."

"I'll start immediately," he responded even as he wondered where to begin.

"If you need any help, I'll send Robyn down," his father offered.

"No, I think we can handle it." Matt deliberately included his staff, knowing that the mess would ultimately involve them all, but that initially only he could sort through the debris. With an odd awareness, he realized the significance of the thought. It didn't only refer to the mess his office had become. His marriage, too, was a shambles, and no matter how much he would like to think his marital problems would be resolved if his parents would apologize to Dana and try harder to accept her, he knew it wasn't going to be that easy. He had to take action himself.

Each computer disc had to be dusted and returned to its proper slot in his media file. Josie, Matt's secretary, was enlisted to help shake dust from the papers, smooth and mend them where necessary, and then return them to their files.

"I can't find the file folder for this one, Matt." Josie held up a stack of papers. "It's the Barringer file, and it seems to be intact."

"Make a new one," he told her. She set the papers on his desk while she looked for the file folders.

"What about this stuff?" she asked a few minutes later, indicating the odds and ends of papers, post-its, and torn scraps she'd piled on his desk beside the Barringer file.

"It looks like the contents of my waste paper basket and the stuff on my desk got dumped together. I'd better keep all of it until I can go through it. Most of it's phone numbers and quotes I've scribbled on envelopes and note pads while I was on the phone. If we have to reconstruct any files, we may need them." He looked around tiredly. Nothing seemed to be missing and his office was beginning to look better, but the real work was just beginning.

He looked up to see a young clerk standing at the door. She glanced at him apologetically, then turned to his secretary. "Josie, your husband is on the line. He says he *has* to talk to you immediately."

Josie sighed and returned to her desk. As Matt watched her leave, he felt a heightened awareness of the woman's unhappiness. His own marital problems had increased his sensitivity for others with similar problems, he supposed, and he'd suspected Josie and Bart had been having problems for quite some time. It was none of his business, he acknowledged. He certainly didn't envy Josie living with anyone as moody and opinionated as Bart, but it was her business, not his.

Matt switched on his computer and heaved a sigh of relief when it hummed to life. Slowly he began a meticulous scan of his desktop files. They were the most likely to have been pulled up in the short amount of time the burglar could have been in the building. The directories appeared intact, so the next step was to review the active files for projects currently underway. He began with the Atkinson project out in Draper that Josie's husband, Bart, was supervising. It was a small office complex, and everything seemed to be moving as it should. He then moved to the new school in North Salt Lake that Winn's crew was constructing. Everything appeared as it should be there, too. Robert's crew had been plagued lately by a number of petty thefts and a couple of minor injuries at the warehouse site along California Avenue, but they were still on schedule and hadn't exceeded budget in any way.

"Matt!" Bob Evans' voice held a note of excitement as he spoke from the doorway. "I think you should see this." The older man held a paper in his hand.

Matt swivelled his chair around to accept the paper from his assistant. It was a plain piece of 8 1/2 by 11 bond paper with two columns of numbers. About a third of the way down the page was a two-inch square blank spot.

"It was in the trash basket beside the copier," Bob explained.

Matt's hopes dropped. He knew what it was; he'd tossed it there himself late last night. Bob had prepared the proposal for the bid committee yesterday, but Matt didn't want to take the originals with him to the hospital, where he'd hoped to look over the pages while sitting with Dana. So he'd made a copy, then noticed, while stuffing the papers into his briefcase, that he had missed a small section of three or four consecutive pages. He had already turned off his computer and didn't want to take the extra time to turn his computer back on, so he went to the file on his desk to pull the needed pages and copy them. Seconds later he discovered that he'd left a post-it on one of the original pages, which had blocked out a tiny square on one of the copied pages. Disgusted at himself for not noticing, Matt had thrown the useless page in the trash and pulled off the post-it, making a new copy and replacing the post-it back on the original. The last thing he'd done before leaving the office was to set the originals back in the wire basket on his desk with his backup disc.

Gradually Matt became aware Bob was still watching him expectantly. Before he could explain about the paper, his assistant asked, "Can you tell which proposal this page came from?"

Since the older man frequently assisted Matt in preparing bids, he was familiar with the way Matt worked, and had therefore recognized immediately the significance of the single page. Even though the font was clearly the same as his own printer produced, this was a copy, so it had to have come from Matt's proposal file. Bob never used the copier to duplicate the pages from his printer because he used a color printer.

Glancing down at the paper again, Matt said, "It's from the Barringer proposal." He set the page on the desk next to the file that Josie had set there earlier as he explained how the paper came to be in the trash. "I'm afraid it won't . . ." He stopped mid-sentence to look from the single page to the thick stack of paper, and then back again. Rolling his chair back, he grabbed for his briefcase and fumbled for the papers he'd stuffed inside. Spreading his own red-penciled copy across his desk, then the stack from his wire basket, he invited Bob to take a closer look.

"These two sets of papers look the same," Bob concluded as he thumbed through the papers on Matt's desk.

"But they shouldn't," Matt muttered as he grimly shook his head. Neither set of papers was the one he'd left on his desk during the night. The papers he had left on his desk the night before had come from Bob's printer and had the same look as the sheet found in the trash. Something was wrong. He just didn't know what yet.

He handed the two stacks of paper to Bob, who wordlessly carried them out of the room, and headed for his corner of the outer office. Matt turned back to the computer to pull up the Barringer file.

Some time later Matt looked up when his father spoke his name. "The clerks have all gone, and I'll be leaving, too, unless there's something else you'd like me to do. It looks like your people did a good job of cleaning everything up." The older man stood in the doorway. Matt glanced toward him absently, then looked back at the monitor.

"Did you find anything?" Warner asked.

"Yes, Bob found a page from a routine supply list from the Barringer project that had been discarded in the waste basket next to the copier. He recognized it, because I had flagged it when Paul Barringer requested the addition of a couple of skylights, and Bob knew that a page from a proposal didn't belong in the outer office."

"You think someone broke in here to copy our proposal so they can underbid us?" Warner bristled at the idea.

"No." Once again, he explained how the paper had come to be in the trash. "Come look at this," he called his father closer. Together they leaned toward the computer. "At first I thought the computer files hadn't been tampered with. Everything looked the way I'd left it. Then I noticed the paper from the trash had come from a different printer than the papers sitting on my desk."

"How can you tell?" Warner wasn't a computer enthusiast; he considered them merely a necessary evil.

"Because Bob Evans' printer is an inkjet color printer," Matt laughed. "He chose it so he can use lots of red ink. Mine's a black and white laser printer because I'm more interested in speed than graphics. The type fonts are different, which is quite noticeable when pages from the two different printers are mixed together. When I finish a section of a proposal, I give my disk to Bob to proofread and to verify my figures. When he finishes, he hands back my disk and a paper printout from his printer. The copy we submit is always from Bob's printer because it looks a little more polished. I left the original Bob printed here on my desk. The copy we found in my office today was printed on my printer."

"Why didn't the thief just take the copy and go?" Warner asked.

Matt looked at his father. "I think he wanted me to find a doctored version of the original and think it was the one I had already approved. His plan might have worked, if Bob hadn't found the page I threw away last night. The intruder made some changes in my computer file and copied the changes to the backup disc. Then, not noticing that the document on my desk came from a different printer, he reprinted the amended proposal on my printer and left it on my desk, taking the originals with him. When the font on the page from the trash didn't match the copy on my desk, I knew that wasn't the proposal I'd left there."

Warner stared at the screen, clearly baffled. "Why would someone go to all that trouble just to get a peek at our bid? If he wants to underbid us on the project, all he needs is the total."

"Oh, he doesn't plan to underbid us," Matt answered in a grim, tight voice.

"Then what's this all about?" his father demanded.

"We've taken on too many projects, we have expansion debts, and we're just two days away from bidding the biggest project the company has ever handled," Matt said steadily. "If our bid is too low, and we can't deliver for the amount specified, we're out of business. Bankrupt."

Warner's mouth opened and closed soundlessly several times before he managed to ask, "Someone shaved the figures, so we'd bid too low?"

Matt nodded.

Warner's eyes narrowed. "Can you reconstruct the bid we originally intended?"

"I can," he affirmed. "But are you sure we should go ahead with the bid? Sabotage might be the next step."

Warner was silent a moment. "It's too late to make any decision tonight," he said carefully. "Winn and Robert should be in on our decision, too. Go on home and get some rest. We'll meet here at six in the morning."

Startled Matt glanced toward the window. Night had fallen and a faint spatter of rain dotted the glass. He'd been away from the hospital for hours. A picture of Josh as he'd last seen him rose in his mind along with a heavy dose of guilt. Once again he'd left Dana and Josh alone.

CHAPTER SIX

Matt stopped to check the small waiting room before going on to Josh's room. A young couple sat on one of the gray sofas, holding hands and looking scared. There was no sign of Dana. He'd found her there last night, asleep, when he'd finally been able to get back to the hospital. He'd watched her sleeping for several minutes, then had gone to Josh's room. A nurse had allowed him to stand a few feet from his son's bed to watch him through the plastic shield draped around his bed. He'd gone home feeling frustrated, much the way he felt now.

His father was expecting him at the office this morning, but he wasn't leaving the hospital until he talked to Dana and saw Josh. He turned to move swiftly down the hall, but two steps past the public phones he spun around. Dana stood with her back to him, a telephone pressed to her ear. She turned, recognizing him, as he took a step toward her. A jumble of emotions he couldn't identify crossed her face as she slowly replaced the receiver without taking her eyes from him.

"I tried to call you," she whispered. "I didn't know—"

"Is Josh all right?" He tried to refrain from shouting as he cut her off, remembering how angry he'd been at her failure to call him the last time Josh faced a crisis and the distance she'd immediately placed between them.

"Yes, but he's very weak," Dana said, the strain of the past few days evident in her voice. "He has some patches of little red dots on his skin the doctor called petechiae. That means there's bleeding under his skin. Dr. Young increased the antibiotics in his IV and started another blood transfusion. He said it's critical for Josh to have a bone marrow transplant right away."

Swallowing hard, Matt asked, "Can one of us donate? Did Dr. Young get the results on our tests?"

"Yes, I tried to call you last night, but the switchboard was turned off, and you weren't home." He felt, more than heard, a note of accusation in her voice. "Dr. Young said your blood isn't a close enough match for you to be a platelet donor."

Matt felt a stinging disappointment that he couldn't do this for Josh. "What about you?"

She shook her head. "My compatibility is closer. I could donate platelets, but I'm not close enough for a really good bone marrow transplant. He doesn't want me to donate platelets at this point anyway; he doesn't want to risk Josh building up antibodies that might interfere with the bone marrow transplant in case another family member is compatible."

"Most of the family were in yesterday for testing," Matt told her. "More of them are scheduled for today."

"What if we don't find a match?" She began to cry softly. He stepped toward her, intent on placing his arms around her, then hesitated, feeling awkward. By now he knew she would endure his touch, but not welcome it.

"We will," he tried to promise, but wasn't sure he could make such a promise. The alternative was more than he could face.

"Dr. Young is going to give him something called cytokines. He said that sometimes alternative therapies work by suppressing the immune system and can occasionally stimulate the stem cells to begin functioning on their own. But we shouldn't count on therapy as a cure, he said. Just as a means of buying time to locate a donor." She wiped her tears and glanced behind him. "He's probably awake. He'll need to be fed and changed."

"I'd like to see him," Matt said.

"Do you . . . want to feed him?" He sensed she had difficulty making the offer.

"No, much as I'd like to, I need to be at the office today. Someone broke in and tampered with some important files. I promised to be there early this morning to help straighten them out. I just want to see Josh for a few minutes before I go."

"All right." She sounded disappointed and he wondered if she wanted him to stay.

"I'll call Dad and tell him I can't make it, if you want me to stay with you," he offered.

"No, I'm all right." But her eyes were bleak and she looked small and fragile. He felt torn between his desire to comfort and be with her, and his responsibility to the company. The whole family's financial security was dependent on the business. Even if he stayed at the hospital, there was nothing he could do but sit and wait. If he went to the office, he could at least begin untangling the mess their intruder had left behind.

He was thirty minutes late when he walked into his father's office. Warner looked pointedly at his watch, but again he didn't say anything about his tardiness.

"How long will it take to get back up to speed on the Barringer bid?" Winn asked immediately.

"Two or three days," Matt answered. "That is, if there aren't any more surprises hidden in my files—and I'm not needed at the hospital."

"Any change in Josh's condition?" Robert asked. Warner frowned, listening intently, as Matt explained.

"Dr. Young thinks Josh needs a bone marrow transplant right away. The doctor's starting chemical therapy to buy some time and prepare Josh for the transplant if a donor can be found."

"Dad and I have appointments later this morning to be tested," Winn informed him. "The women and Robert were tested yesterday."

"I appreciate that." Matt made every effort not to reveal how much his family's prompt response to his request for donors meant to him. His father and brothers weren't the kind of men who expressed sentimental emotions easily, and if he said too much, he was likely to embarrass them, or worse yet, burst into tears.

"Bids are supposed to be in by five tomorrow afternoon," Warner spoke up, changing the subject to Matt's relief. "Can you be ready?"

"I can try, but after the break-in, I'd prefer a little more time to check my numbers and set up a stronger security system on the files," Matt said frankly. "I also think we should take another look at the Barringer project, as I've mentioned before. Getting the project will squeeze our resources tighter than I think we should risk. Even our original estimates were low and allowed for little leeway if we were to encounter any trouble. We'll also have to consolidate all three crews into one large unit, which will limit our flexibility and take us out of the running for the kind of projects that have built our company." Matt was aware that his father and brothers were more comfortable with risk taking, whether physical or financial, than he would ever be, but he wanted them to know about his uneasiness with the project.

Robert was the first to speak up. "What kind of security system do you have in mind, and why haven't you already taken care of it? I thought we all had passwords to get into our computer files."

"Our system is outdated, and none of us have web access, so I thought passwords were sufficient," Matt explained. "The new system we have on order will have modems and be networked so we can pull up the files we all need; we won't have to copy discs for each other. It'll be more efficient but it will also require greater blocking and security. Under our current system a hacker can't get into our files unless he's physically present, so there hasn't been a need for more than passwords until now."

Warner didn't understand computers but he knew about passwords. "So that means someone has your password," he said, scowling.

"I'm afraid so, but I have no idea how he got it, or if he somehow found a way to bypass it. That's why I need time to set up a new password, then put a second password on individual files," Matt explained.

"Who have you given your password to?" Winn asked.

Matt nodded his head towards his father. "Dad has it. So does Bob. At times either of them may need access to files I'm working on. Both of our secretaries also have access. They enter both of your daily logs, as well as Bart's every morning, so Dad and I have current work-in-progress statistics on a daily basis."

"Well, none of them are our burglar," Warner asserted. "Robyn's been with the company for twenty years and I trust her completely. Josie's been with us almost as long. In fact," he paused, as if remembering, "she and Bart met here, right after I hired Bart as assistant foreman, back when you boys were still in grade school."

"The burglar probably doesn't even know you've already caught on to what he did," Winn said, looking at Matt. "We can hire an extra security guard for a few days until the bid is submitted, so what's to stop our going ahead?"

"It seems to me we've had more than our fair share of mixed-up orders and minor accidents lately," Matt pointed out. "We need to take a look at those foul-ups. They might be related to the break-in."

"No way," Winn scoffed. "Those things just happen from time to time. They certainly call for paying more attention to details, but they're not deliberate."

"Few projects have the potential for profit the Barringer job offers," Robert spoke thoughtfully. "Still, if the risk is too high, maybe we should drop out. We've got enough work to meet payroll and our present loans."

"Barringer will establish our credibility in the major project market," Warner reminded his sons.

"Besides our expenses just went up." Winn's voice carried a hint of impatience. "We've already ordered excavation equipment with price tags that almost equal the national debt, and Hadley will be home and ready to enroll in an ivy league school this fall. Ann has her heart set on a state-of-the-art equestrian school, and Josh's expenses will easily outstrip our insurance."

"I'm afraid Winn is right," Warner sighed. "We need that contract."

"Ann's stable can wait, and we could cancel the equipment order," Matt muttered. "There are other projects out there that would meet our needs with far less risk."

Robert nodded his head as though in agreement, but didn't say anything.

Neither Winn nor Warner were willing to cut back, Matt could tell. They both thrived on challenges, and this project would certainly be a challenge. A seven-hundred-and-fifty-room hotel complete with restaurants, shops, parking, convention space, and all of the amenities, covering a full city block, was definitely big time. Almost a year had gone into bid preparation. It was insane to try to check and verify the reconstruction of that bid in just two days. One costly error could plunge a resource-poor company into bankruptcy. Besides, Matt didn't particularly like working with Paul Barringer. He had a hunch the man's arrogance and tendency to make changes would end up costing their company plenty.

At times he wondered how the business had stayed afloat as long as it had. Growth had happened too fast, and the company's finances showed a reckless disregard for building any kind of reserve for dealing with emergencies or slow-downs. Over the past six years of booming economy, profits had been invested almost exclusively in expansion. He'd tried to talk to his dad about his concerns, but Warner had brushed them off, saying the secret to his success had always been the ability to see an opportunity and grab it.

Once Matt had brought up the subject to his mother, since she had handled the books during the company's early years. She'd reminded him that his father had been running the company for more than thirty years and knew better than any of them what he could handle. But Matt wasn't so sure.

Feeling the eyes of his father and brothers upon him, Matt conceded defeat. "I'd better get started," he said.

"Use any of the staff you need," his father told them. "I'll have Robyn hold your calls and get a memo out, letting everyone know your project has priority for the next couple of days."

Back in his office, Matt slouched in his chair, glaring at his computer screen and wondering when his wife and son would get to be a priority. His father's final words sank in, and he sat bolt upright.

"Josie!" he turned to yell toward the outer office. Startled, she leaped to her feet and ran toward his open door.

"Yes," she puffed as she slid to a stop.

"Take my credit card and go pick up a couple of those little cell phones." He handed the plastic to her.

"Phones? What kind? What . . . ?"

"I don't care what kind. Just get them activated—one for me and one for my wife." He turned back to the computer. If he was going to be stuck in the office for the next two days, he intended to make certain Dana could reach him any time night or day. Cell phones were nowhere near as good as being there, but they were better than being out of touch.

———

Warner paced the floor after his sons left the room. Finally he halted before the vast window to look out over the industrial park and the top of the city on the other side of the freeway. He wondered if Matt was aggressive enough for the job. This wasn't the first time he'd showed hesitation in moving forward with bold decisiveness. He was his mother's son, brilliant with numbers and organization. But he was his father's son, too. He was far too conservative, afraid to take chances.

Barbara had always been impatient with Warner's slow way of making decisions, and he'd tried to change. In the beginning she had kept the company's books, and he'd considered her an indispensable part of the business. She'd had a strong voice in urging him to grab opportunities or to steer clear of projects she considered unprofitable. When he and his partner, Hal Downey, had combined their small businesses to form a larger company, Barbara had at first backed Hal's more aggressive style, and Warner had sometimes felt left out as they joked and teased in a way she had never laughed with him. Then one day he had walked into the office to find his wife and his partner arguing furiously over something to do with one of their current projects, something he hadn't quite understood. After that, the two had argued frequently; Barbara suddenly began opposing projects Hal considered essential, and she protested the rapid expansion of the company. There had been a fierce battle over taking out a larger loan for one project. Even though he hadn't fully understood his wife's concerns, he too had been nervous about getting too deeply in debt and had sided with her.

A fearless risk taker, Hal had derided Warner for listening to his wife's pessimistic advice. Their differences over taking chances, and Barbara's reluctance to encumber the company with more debt when the fledgling company had been given an opportunity to build a big sports complex, had played a large role in the breakup of the partnership. Hal had told him that Barbara really wanted to go ahead; she was simply opposing the project because she didn't think her husband had the ability to succeed in a project that size. Even then he hadn't changed his mind. That was when Hal took his half and left the company.

After they'd split the business, Warner thought Barbara would be more comfortable, but instead she seemed to lose interest in the company, and a gap had developed between them, convincing him Hal had been right. He was a disappointment to her, and she doubted his ability to succeed on his own. Once, out of the blue, she'd suggested that Hal had cheated them, and Warner had defended Hal, insisting she was mistaken. Even though finances were a lot tighter than he'd expected after Hal left, and they'd skimmed pretty close to the edge a few times, Warner had been shocked when Barbara told him she couldn't take it anymore.

"You don't need me," she'd said. "Bob Evans can write checks and bill clients. He can even figure your taxes."

"But he doesn't understand strategy or long-term planning," he'd protested. "I thought we were a team, that together we'd build an empire. When the boys are a little older, they'll be partners too, and there will be no stopping us."

She'd had a strange, sad look on her face as she sat uncharacteristically silent watching him. Finally she'd said, "I guess I'm not an empire builder. I've already accepted a position with Dunbridge Realty. I told Mr. Dunbridge I would start in two weeks."

The business had done all right without her, Warner told himself. He even suspected he'd been able to move forward a lot faster because he felt he had something to prove to her. Still, he missed her by his side, and he knew full well some of the headaches and near-disasters the company had faced could have been avoided, if he'd had the benefit of her financial expertise.

She'd been right about Hal, too. In time Warner had learned that his partner had been hiding assets purchased at company expense for almost the entire length of their association, assets that enabled him to start a new company and grow at a dizzying pace. He'd never told Barbara of his discovery, and every time he passed the large building and yards Hal now owned, or the huge home perched like an eagle's nest above the capitol, he had to remind himself not to be envious or angry. He'd chosen not to pursue legal recovery, primarily because letting others know how gullible he'd been was more than his pride could bear. But he had spent long hours with Bob Evans, trying to get a better grasp on the company's finances.

Sometimes he still resented the way Barbara had jumped ship when he'd been struggling to save the company, and he was pretty certain that the only reason old Dunbridge had managed to retire in such comfortable style was because of the way Barbara had managed his money. Her income had paid for Winn's and Robert's missions and schooling, too, he admitted with some reluctance. Knowing she paid most of the bills and made a lot more money than he did had been humbling. But those years were just a temporary setback. Watching Hal Downey's company grow faster than his own, and his old partner becoming a wealthy man, bothered him at times, but everything was fine now. His income matched Barbara's and with the Barringer project in his company's pocket, he'd finally surpass Hal's success. He just had to make sure Matt didn't start dragging his feet.

A twinge of conscience caused him to wince. Matt was under a lot of pressure. It was only natural that he'd prefer to be at the hospital right now rather than here reconstructing that bid. But since there was nothing he could do, even if he were at the hospital except sit and worry, it was probably best for him to keep busy. Hard work was the best possible antidote for worry.

"Mr. Bingham." Robyn's voice interrupted his thoughts. "You said to remind you of your appointment at the lab."

He started guiltily. The appointment to be tested had slipped his mind. Something else had slipped his mind, too. He remembered just last week he'd needed something from Matt's files while Matt had been at the hospital and had sent Robyn to get the information. She knew the password, but she couldn't have had anything to do with the break-in. She'd been his secretary for twenty years. She was the only secretary he'd ever had. She was practically family. This break-in business was making him jumpy, he thought, and if it was causing him to doubt loyal employees, then the damage went much deeper than the possible loss of a contract.

"I'm leaving right now," he spoke abruptly before grabbing his car keys off the desk and heading for the elevator. As he passed Matt's office and saw him hunched over his computer, his mood lightened. Matt would be okay. He was worried about Josh. That was all.

Dana huddled in one corner of the gray sofa. Every few minutes she checked her watch to see how soon she could return to Josh's room. Her head ached, and her mind felt fuzzy. Intellectually she knew she needed a meal and a good night's rest, but she couldn't risk being unavailable if Josh needed her. Perhaps if Matt were here . . . no, he couldn't sit around waiting for those few precious minutes one of them might be with Josh. He had to work. His family needed him. The company needed him. Bitterness crept into her thoughts as she questioned where Matt placed her needs and Josh's on his list of priorities. Her father had always placed business first. She'd been naive to think Matt would be any different.

"Sister Bingham?" a voice asked hesitantly from the doorway. She looked up to see a young woman with boyishly short, white-blond hair that poked out at odd angles. She wore jeans with a dirty smudge on one knee and an over-sized purple t-shirt. In her hand was a single, long-stemmed pink rose. "Are you Dana Bingham?" she asked.

"Yes," Dana acknowledged, wondering who the very pregnant, jeans-clad teenager might be.

"Good! I'm Mandy Brockhurst." The girl held out her hand as she hurried across the room. "You don't know me; I just moved into the ward two weeks ago. Sister Taylor called me this morning to ask me to be a visiting teacher. When she told me about your little boy, I decided to come right over to meet you and see what I can do to help." She beamed at Dana, then quickly sobered. "She said you moved here recently from California and you're kind of shy. I'm not a bit shy, and I only came from Manti, but isn't it just awful not knowing anybody?"

"My husband's family lives close . . ." Dana didn't want the girl's pity. She didn't want her to see how terribly alone she was. Besides she was used to being alone. She'd learned a long time ago not to count on other people.

"Relatives are okay . . . even in-laws sometimes," Mandy giggled before going on. "Mine are the greatest, but I mean friends. I just know we're going to be friends." She plopped down on the sofa beside Dana. "Here!" she thrust the rose into her hand. "I was pruning the roses when Sister Taylor called, and I looked at that flower and I thought, it's the last rose of the season. It should have been gone long before now, but since it isn't, there must be a reason. Right then I knew it was because it was for you! I picked it, and I didn't even take time to change my clothes, as you can see. I looked up the bus schedule and came right over here!"

Dana blinked. Mandy certainly wasn't shy. She'd never met anyone quite like this girl before. She didn't encourage strangers speaking to her as a rule, but something about Mandy Brockhurst intrigued her.

"What happened to Sister Thompson and Sister Roberts?" It occurred to her that the two elderly ladies who called on her every month hadn't been to see her for a while. They were sweet old ladies, but it was always a struggle to talk to them. Sister Roberts was hard of hearing and Sister Thompson always seemed to be in a hurry.

"Oh, Sister Taylor said one of your visiting teachers moved into a senior care facility and the other one was assigned to someone else and given a new route. I haven't met my partner yet; she's away on a trip with her husband. I've never been a visiting teacher before, so you'll have to tell me if I don't do it right."

"I'm sure you'll do fine." Dana almost felt like smiling.

"My mother has had the same visiting teachers my whole life, and they're really super. They sometimes bring her little things, and they always say really polite things about Mom's garden even though it sometimes gets out of control, and she gives them armfuls of zucchini and tomatoes. They fixed dinner for our whole family after

Mom brought each of my brothers home from the hospital and that's a lot of dinner 'cause there's eleven of us. Twelve, now I'm married. They just showed up to help me clean house the day after my littlest brother, Benjy, was born, and we had lots of fun. They brought us dinner, too, when one of my little brothers broke his leg, and one of them drove Mom to Petey's school to get him when he came down with chickenpox and she couldn't get the truck started. And they always talk and talk with Mom, just like my girlfriends and I used to do. They giggle too. I'm so glad I get to be your visiting teacher, because I know we're going to be friends. Do you feel that way, too?"

This time Dana smiled. "I think I'd like to be your friend," she admitted shyly.

"Now, tell me all about your little boy. I bet he's just darling. Does he look like you? I hope my baby looks like my husband." She patted her swollen abdomen. "He's really good looking. It will be just terrible if my baby has eyes like mine. And my hair! Brent, he's one of my brothers, says only some weird kind of dog has eyes like mine, one brown and one blue."

"Your eyes aren't weird at all," Dana attempted to reassure the girl. "They're unusual, but they suit you. I think you're very pretty."

"Oh, Dana!" Mandy threw her arms around Dana. "I just knew our friendship was meant to be. Like inspiration or something!"

When she pulled back, she tried to look severe as she reminded Dana, "You haven't told me about your little boy yet."

"His name is Joshua, and he looks like his daddy, except for his hair. It's lighter than mine, but has reddish streaks. And it's really curly, like mine," Dana replied obediently.

Mandy clapped her hands. "I can't wait to see him. All of my brothers have blond hair like mine and were as bald as a bunch of old grandpas when they were born. They're not going to shave your little boy's hair off, or anything like that, are they? When my brother Cory fell out of a tree and had to have stitches on his head, the doctor shaved part of his hair off. David and Max said that looked funny, so they shaved the rest off."

"No, I don't think they'll shave his hair off. There's nothing wrong with his head." She explained what she knew about her son's illness.

"Your doctor can test me. David, too. David's my husband," she tacked on to her offer.

"That's really nice of you, but I don't think you can be a donor while you're pregnant. If we haven't found a good match before your baby is born, maybe you can afterwards."

Mandy nodded cheerfully. "Okay."

A nurse came to the door to let Dana know she could visit Josh again, and she was surprised by how quickly the time had passed. She paused only long enough to thank Mandy for coming before hurrying down the hall.

"I'll be back," Mandy called after her, and Dana found she hoped the young woman really would return. Her chatter had made the time go faster, and it certainly felt good to feel someone cared.

Of course, Matt cared. About Josh anyway. She was no longer sure how much he cared about her. He stopped to see their son every day, but he kept himself slightly aloof from her. A wave of sadness swept over her. She'd vowed never to have a marriage like her parents. To her it had always seemed they lived separate lives. They each went their own way until some important social occasion, when they would both dress up, wear expensive jewelry, and phony smiles. They didn't fight. Instead they were formally polite to each other. If her mother had ever disagreed with her father over anything, that disagreement had been long in the past before Dana was born.

As long as Dana could remember, her father had made all of the decisions in their family. If her mother had disagreed, she hid it well behind a facade of bored indifference. If her own marriage was going to be like that, she'd rather leave.

———◦———

It was late when Matt turned his car into the hospital parking lot. For once he had his choice of parking spots. Picking up the box lying beside him on the car seat, he tucked it under his arm while he locked the car. When he reached the fourth floor, the night nurse was just leaving Josh's room.

"How is he?" He asked softly.

"Restless," the nurse answered with a smile. "Perhaps a short visit with Daddy is what he needs."

Matt's heart lifted, and he turned to follow the nurse to the closet where gowns and masks were kept. He removed his jacket, and handed it with the small box, to the nurse.

"They'll be at the desk," she told him. "Just go on into your son's room when you're ready."

Matt hesitated in the doorway for a couple of seconds before approaching Josh's bed. The nurse's words echoed in his head and he wondered if he'd ever be ready to see his son looking so pale and help-less hidden behind a balloon of clear plastic. Finally he took the steps that brought him to the baby's side, and he thought his heart would burst when Josh's eyes lit up. The little boy pulled himself to a sitting position and grinned happily.

Matt was relieved to see the restraints had been removed, and Josh was able to move around a little. The drug therapy Dr. Young started that morning seemed to be working.

"Pway, Daddy," Josh spoke in almost normal tones. Matt wasn't certain whether Josh wanted him to pray or play. It had been a long time, too long, since he'd done either with his son.

Matt doubled up one fist and moved it slowly over the plastic bubble, making engine noises as his hand moved.

"R-r-r-r! Truck!" Josh giggled. He doubled up his small fist and repeated the action.

"N-n-n-n." Matt spread his thumb and pinkie wide and mimicked the drone of an airplane. This time he swept his hand rapidly over the plastic.

"Zoom!" Josh laughed in delight.

In only minutes Josh tired and lay his head back on the bed. Matt let his fingers become a horse that clip-clopped slowly across the barrier separating them. Josh's eyes closed, and soon he was asleep. Matt clasped his hands together as he stood looking at the sleeping child. He'd played; now he prayed.

Reluctantly he left Josh's room to make his way to the small room where Dana lay curled in one corner of the gray sofa. Her thick curls obscured most of her face. Disappointment struck him. He'd known she was likely to be asleep since she wasn't in Josh's room when he arrived. Still he'd harbored a hope he could talk to her, be with her for a few minutes. He wanted to tell her he missed her. It seemed like forever since they'd really been together, and he had no one to blame but himself.

Watching her chest rise and fall, he wondered if she would ever forgive him for his doubts and neglect. But why should she? He couldn't forgive himself. Even now when he needed to be with her and their son, he was spending all day and half the night at the office.

Stepping closer he set the small box he carried on the magazine-strewn table in front of Dana. He could see her face now. She looked exhausted. Somehow, she had to be persuaded to return home to get a full night's rest and to eat decent meals. He noticed a flower, a rose, clutched in her hand. It had been pink, but now the petals were turning brown and it looked limp and wilted. For some reason that made him feel sad.

He wouldn't waken her. As much as he longed to touch her and to spend a few minutes talking with her, he could see she needed rest more. Removing a pen from his pocket, he wrote a brief note.

Dana, I bought us cell phones today. There's a little booklet with yours that explains its features and how to use them. The first speed dial number is already programmed to my cell phone, or dial 244-8996. I'll keep my phone on all of the time, but you'll have to step outside of the hospital to call me since cell phone use isn't permitted inside the hospital. Please call me often.

He hesitated before he added, *I love you, Matt.* She might not want to think about their relationship, but he wanted her to know that though he'd been stupid, he truly did love her.

CHAPTER SEVEN

Tapping a pencil impatiently against the edge of her desk, Barbara listened to the nurse repeat the lab results. She couldn't believe it. Not one family member was a match! There were several with the same blood type, but the other factors weren't even close. She thanked the nurse and hung up. How could she tell Matt? Twenty-seven family members had been tested and were eager to help, but not one of them was a close enough match for a bone marrow transplant. A few could do initial platelet donations, but as Josh's antibodies built up resistance, they would quickly be eliminated as suitable donors.

Her thoughts turned to Josh. He was an adorable child who looked just like his father, except for that curly reddish-brown hair. He got that from his mother, at least the curls. Dana's hair was really more red than brown. She hadn't seen Josh since the day he'd been taken to the hospital, and though she'd never seen him as much as she'd liked, she missed him terribly. She loved her sons with all her heart, but there was something between a grandparent and grandchild that was impossible to explain. Her throat felt thick and her eyes burned. She absolutely refused to consider the possibility she might lose this precious child.

Rising jerkily to her feet, she paced the narrow confines of her office. She should call a few clients. The Anderson house she'd listed yesterday was just what the Fosters were looking for; she should call, make an appointment. There was a lovely home on Brentwood with a hand-lettered "for sale by owner" sign on the lawn. She should inquire to see if the owner could be persuaded to list with the Dunbridge agency.

She returned to her seat and reached for the telephone, only to set the receiver gently back on the cradle. Today she didn't care about houses or clients. She wanted to help her grandson; she wanted to see him.

She'd promised Matt she would stay away from the hospital until Dana was ready to see her. That would probably be never. She sighed heavily and wished there were some way to improve her relationship with Dana, but she'd never been good at relationships with other women. The interests of most of the women she knew seemed small and petty, holding little real purpose or value, and she knew her own interests in business and academics tended to intimidate them. It had been a lovely surprise to learn that Ann and Sandra were not only well-educated, but each was also a competent businesswoman in her own way. She felt closer to them than she'd ever felt before to another woman, but she had no idea how to connect with her newest daughter-in-law.

Perhaps if her own mother had lived, she'd understand her own gender better. Growing up, holding her own in a family of rough and tumble boys under the care of a father who devoted every minute away from the job to the Church, hadn't left her with much motivation for pursuing the usual feminine pursuits. To this day she kept hidden the "sampler" she'd had to sew back in Primary.

She'd never in her life been comfortable around women who were small and fragile and blatantly feminine. Somehow they made her feel like a clumsy elephant and a failure as a woman. She didn't own one article of clothing that sported so much as a scrap of lace; she'd avoided homemaking meetings for years, since she couldn't contemplate a much worse fate than to be stuck with a paint brush or glue gun in her hand, and just the thought of sticking some concoction of twisted vines and paper flowers on her walls made her shudder. Growing up, her best friends had been males. She'd never had much to say to other women, finding few were interested in stock options or prime rates, and she had no interest in fashion, hair, crafts, or aerobics groups. She didn't understand Dana at all, nor understand what had drawn her son to the girl. She wished with all her heart Matt had found a sensible wife more like his brothers' wives.

She shouldn't really be surprised at Matt's choice. She'd figured out while in her early teens that males tended to choose beauty over brains and had uncharitably concluded that was because most men could see better than they could think. For that matter, she'd never been really certain why Warner had asked her to marry him. They'd been good friends since high school, but she was nothing like the beautiful, stylish women he'd dated in college. Since he couldn't possibly have married her for her looks, she'd happily concluded he'd married her because he loved her, until an overheard telephone conversation had robbed her of that theory.

She'd always suspected she was a disappointment to her husband, but that call had confirmed her worst fears. Warner was a big, handsome man who fit in easily anywhere. Even now he had little gray in his hair, just small streaks in his sideburns that gave him a distinguished air. In contrast, her hair was heavily streaked with gray, and her large frame carried considerably more pounds than it had thirty-five years ago when they'd married. She wasn't fat, but neither did she have the model thin shape of the women with whom successful men like Warner were usually seen. Worse, she hated the social events she was expected to attend as Warner Bingham's wife. More than once she'd wondered if her husband weren't so committed to the Church, and set such high moral standards for himself, might he leave her behind and find a trophy wife who would be more of an asset than she could ever be in his determined pursuit of the professional heights.

She tapped the pencil against the desk a bit more sharply. In all the years they'd been married, she'd never doubted Warner's commitment to her and the boys, and she'd assumed he was as happy with their marriage as she was until Warner and Hal had broken up their partnership ten years ago. She sighed. She usually avoided thinking about that unhappy time, but Hal's hurtful words still lingered in the back of her mind no matter how hard she tried to dismiss them.

In her mind she paused once more outside the office Hal and her husband shared. With one hand raised, ready to knock, and the other hand holding a stack of invoices for materials she couldn't remember ordering, she heard a voice raised in anger. The door had been ajar and she could see Hal with the telephone held to his ear. He was shouting into the instrument.

"Forget Warner! That fat cow he's married to controls the purse strings. She won't let him spend a nickel without her okay, and there's no way she'll let him in on this . . . Yes, he knows it's the deal of a lifetime . . . Sure it was his idea to begin with, but she won't let him actually do anything . . . No, that's why the payments have to be in cash. She'd consider it beneath her moral ethics and make his life a nightmare . . . It's not that simple. He told me marrying her was the biggest mistake of his life, and that he can hardly bear to look at her now, but at the time he thought her father's connections in the construction business would offset the personal disadvantages, and he needed the old man's financial backing. Now his religion keeps him from divorcing her. He has to sneak around behind her back to get anything done. . . No, he's not a happy man, but he's stuck! She's stifled the life out of this company and out of him. . . I'm getting out of here! If he wants to let her hold him back, fine, but she's not going to keep me from reaching the top."

She'd gone back to her desk and worked like a robot the remainder of the day. She'd never told Warner of the overheard conversation, but in the days that followed and as the men dissolved their partnership, she'd tried to block out the hurt Hal's words had inflicted on her. In many ways discovering Warner's professional ethics didn't match up to her lofty image of her husband's integrity hurt more than the personal insults. Why hadn't she guessed that Warner was aware of Hal's dealings? He was too astute to have not seen, and therefore agreed to, what was going on. It was her fault the partnership broke up, and it was her fault the business wasn't as successful as Warner wanted it to be.

She faced a quandary that taxed her own ethical standards. If she reported Hal, Warner's role would come to light, and he would lose everything, possibly even go to prison. She'd agonized over what she should do, and in the end, had done nothing. She couldn't be a part of a business that didn't meet her ethical standards, so she determined to leave. Mostly she couldn't continue working with Warner, knowing she was a disappointment to him both personally and professionally, and that he'd never truly loved her the way her romantic fantasies had led her to believe.

Sadly she discovered she could sever their business association, but their marriage was another matter. She loved him and still believed in his innate goodness. Blindly she'd trusted he would rectify his unsavory business practices without Hal's influence surrounding him, and this, she believed had proven to be the case.

As Warner had struggled to keep the small part of the company he'd been able to retain, she'd searched out a small business she could lavish her attention and business acumen on. Time had proved she'd made the right choice. Her earnings over the years had compensated for the loss she'd caused her husband's company, and given him the breathing room necessary to expand his company and fulfill his dreams. She didn't doubt that Warner was far more successful now without either Hal or herself, than he would have been if either had stayed. Only occasionally, did she admit she missed the excitement she'd once felt when she thought they shared a common dream. She was okay with the business aspect of their lives; the part she'd never come to terms with was Hal's less than flattering description of her and her conviction that her husband was as disappointed in her as a wife as he had been by her as a business partner.

Enough of this thinking. She did Warner a disservice when she doubted his commitment to her and to their family. She'd never been a beautiful woman, and she hadn't improved with age, but there wasn't much she could do about that. Besides, she was the one who bowed out of their professional partnership, the one who couldn't match his vision, who questioned his ethics, and who couldn't withstand the uncertainty each time he gambled on a bigger project. His business had flourished over the years, and though she sometimes felt Bob Evans played a larger role in that success than Warner suspected, she was happy running the business she'd gradually taken over from old Mr. Dunbridge. She liked being her own boss and enjoyed the challenge inherent in buying and selling property, and if the pleasure and excitement she'd once cherished in their marriage had waned, she had to accept that. Few marriages remained the romantic love match she once imagined she and Warner shared.

It was time for action. In spite of her promise to Matt, she couldn't just sit here and do nothing. Could the lab have made a mistake? Who else could she badger or cajole into being tested? It wasn't in her nature to sit by and do nothing while her grandchild needed help.

She picked up the phone once more and began calling every relative she could think of. When she finished, she still wasn't satisfied. There had to be more she could do. Her family resources were exhausted. The only possibilities left were Dana's family. Like it or not, Dana would have to ask for their help. Not even the most indifferent parents could refuse to save their grandson's life! Matt would be angry, but there was no other recourse. She'd arrange a family council, and this time Dana would have to be there.

Her hand suddenly froze as a picture of Dana rose in her mind. Dana was tiny and feminine with naturally curly hair. She wore lace and gauzy fabrics. Her house was spotless, and her child clean and adorable in little play suits she designed and sewed herself. Flowers grew in her house and garden, and she was familiar with composers and artists whose names were impossible to pronounce. In short, Dana was everything Barbara was not.

The comparison made Barbara squirm. Had she rejected her son's wife because of her own insecurities? The idea was appalling and untrue. She wasn't insecure. She was an intelligent, self-confident, and highly successful business woman. But a thirty-five-year-old picture of Warner sitting on a low wall close beside a young girl in a flowered dress, her curls blowing in the spring breeze sweeping across the college campus, came painfully to mind. The girl had begun to cry, and Warner had held her, never suspecting his fiancée had witnessed the scene. Two weeks later she and Warner had married, and Barbara had never asked who the girl was, or why she'd been crying. She'd locked the memory away, believing she didn't want to know. Now she wasn't so sure. Her forthright nature insisted she examine the dislike she'd held for Dana from the moment she first met her. She didn't like the self-portrait that formed in her mind.

Matt ran the numbers through his computer once more. He'd found at least a dozen changes in his earlier calculations so far. None were glaringly obvious. The two totals were nearly identical. Only one digit differed, but that one digit made a tremendous difference. He probably wouldn't have even noticed the changes if he hadn't gone searching for them.

"How's it going, son?" He looked up to see his father standing in the doorway.

"Look at this," Matt pointed to an area on the screen. Warner leaned closer.

"That's shaving it a little close, but I guess we could do it," Warner continued to stare doubtfully at the screen.

Matt tapped a few keys and Warner took a few minutes to review the new projections before him. "I don't know," Warner muttered before Matt took him to the next area. In minutes Warner was shaking his head. "I want that contract. I want it badly. Undertaking a project like the Barringer Complex has been my dream since I was younger than you. I'm willing to shave costs as close as possible to get that opportunity, but those figures don't give us *any* leeway. You know I won't cut quality, but there has to be some profit margin. If nothing goes wrong, we can just make it with those figures, but the first increase in materials, stretch of bad weather, or mechanical problem will kill us."

"That's my point," Matt spoke evenly. "We could go bankrupt if we submit a bid that low. Someone changed my projections, which were already as low as we can safely go and still guarantee delivery. All of the changes I've found are actually possible, but all of them together are too constrictive."

"I don't understand." Warner shook his head.

Matt's face was grim. "Someone wants to make certain our bid is the lowest."

"You mean whoever broke in here thinks he's helping us?" Warner asked incredulously.

"No, I wouldn't go that far," Matt corrected. "I suspect someone wants to sabotage either our company or the project. If our bid is too low, and we face delays that increase our costs, or work has to be redone, we could lose everything."

"And if it's Barringer they're after, and he had to replace us with another construction company, the process could drag out so long, he'd lose heavily or be forced to pay tremendous penalties," Warner added.

"Right. So what are we going to do?" Matt leaned forward in his chair.

"Seems to me we need to get that corrected bid turned in." Warner's tone was definite.

"That's all?" Matt stared at his father incredulously. For some reason, getting this contract held a disproportionate sense of importance to his father. "Have you considered the Barringer bid might not be the only bid our intruder tampered with?"

Warner looked startled. "You think our other bids were changed, too? That they're all too low?"

"I don't know," Matt admitted. "I haven't had time to check the others. But I don't think anyone would go to all this trouble to fix one bid, where if we're lucky, we could conceivably come in this low. If someone really wants to stop the project, they could either sabotage the job site to make certain we get the delays and extra costs, which would then force us over the estimated costs, or they could arrange for us to underbid on all our contracts to stretch our resources too thin."

Rubbing his chin thoughtfully, Warner remained silent for several minutes then he asked, "How soon can you check the other bids?"

"I have Bob looking at bottom line totals now," Matt responded.

"All right, finish up here, then go on over to the hospital and get Dana. Your mom called, that's why I stopped in here. She seems to think we need a family council."

"I don't think Dana will leave the hospital," Matt responded reluctantly.

"She'll come if you convince her it's for Josh's benefit," Warner spoke confidently. "Bring the Barringer papers and whatever Bob finds. After your mother gives us the lab results and we set up some kind of schedule for helping Josh, we can brainstorm about this problem."

Matt watched his father leave and smothered an edge of resent-ment. It was easy for Dad to say "go get Dana." But Matt knew it wouldn't be that easy. First, Dana didn't want to leave Josh's side, and second, she wanted as little to do with his family as possible. He had no idea how he was going to persuade her to meet with his family. Or if he should even try. On the other hand, if there was any possibility his mother had found enough platelet donors, he and Dana had better be there.

When Matt reached the hospital he was surprised to see that Dana wasn't alone. A young woman, who looked like she ought to be in a maternity ward, sat close beside her. Her arm was around Dana, the white telephone receiver in one hand. She said something, and Dana smiled, the first smile Matt had seen on his wife's face since this ordeal began.

"Is this a private party, or can anyone join in?" Matt slid onto the sofa beside Dana and held his breath. She didn't shift away, but her smile disappeared.

"You won't have to call him now," the young woman pronounced in a positive voice, setting the receiver back on its cradle.

"Is Josh worse?" Dread filled Matt's heart.

"No, he's just the same." He thought she was going to say more, but after a moment's hesitation, she introduced Mandy Brockhurst to him.

"Hi, Mandy." He held out his hand. Mandy took it and gave it a firm shake.

"Oh! If I'd known you would get here this soon, I would have brought enough dinner for you, too. I could have. David, he's my husband, says I always cook way too much. That's because I have so many brothers, and brothers eat a lot, so I learned to always fix plenty. It's just chicken and noodles, but it turned out pretty well. I'm glad Dana liked it, and I don't mean to be critical, but she's much too thin." She had a pleased look on her face as she glanced toward an almost empty plate sitting on the coffee table.

"It was very good. Thank you." Dana smiled faintly at Mandy. Matt felt a wistful tug of jealousy. It had been a long time since Dana had looked on him with a fraction of the warmth he sensed between the two young women.

"I suppose I'd better go now that your husband is here," Mandy spoke to Dana. "I'll be back tomorrow."

"Should you be making this trip every day?" There was concern in Dana's voice.

"Oh, I'm fine," Mandy laughed and patted the obvious mound that had obliterated her waistline. "Junior isn't due for two more weeks, and he'll likely be late. All of Mama's babies came late, and she said I should keep busy because ladies who sit around and get waited on don't have strong muscles, so their deliveries are worse. Besides it's kind of an adventure. Can you believe I had never ridden on a bus until this week? I was kind of scared, but shoo, it was as easy as mud."

Matt watched in fascination as a corner of Dana's lip twitched. The girl was entertaining, and his wife obviously liked her. He wasn't certain why Dana had befriended the girl, but he was glad she had. He had just recently become aware of how painfully lonely his wife was in his hometown.

Mandy struggled into a pair of sandals sitting on the floor in front of her, then reached for Dana's empty plate. "What would you like me to fix tomorrow?" she asked Dana.

"Mandy, you don't have to fix dinner for me every night." Dana reached out and took the young girl's hand. "Not even the best visiting teacher in the whole world has to go that far. Besides, I worry about you riding the bus home alone after dark."

"You worry about me?" Mandy appeared touched. "You don't need to worry about me. I can take care of myself just fine. Besides no one is going to bother a woman with a tummy that gets to the bus stop half a block before the rest of me gets there."

Dana smiled at her friend's joking words, but from the quick frown that made two small creases between her eyes, Matt knew she thought her friend terribly naive. Matt did too.

"And fixing dinner is no trouble," Mandy went on. "I like doing it. David is working the evening shift now. He won't be off until eleven, and I like to keep busy. Besides, I like you and your little boy, and I really want to help. I don't know many people yet, and you're the only friend I've got in this whole town. Anyway in our neighborhood, everyone is awfully old and kind of boring, except you. I've already knit so many booties, Junior will need twenty feet in order to wear them all before he's a year old, so I don't have anything else to do. But if you'd rather I didn't come, I won't. Daddy says I talk so much, I make people tired."

"Oh, Mandy." Dana reached out to hug her friend. "You can come as much as you want. I love having you here."

An idea began to click in Matt's mind.

"Mandy, if you don't have any other plans, perhaps you wouldn't mind staying here for a couple of hours while I take Dana somewhere. You could talk to Josh if he wakes up, and if there's any kind of problem, you could call us on Dana's cell phone. Then when we get back, I can give you a ride home, so you won't have to take the bus after dark."

"I don't want to leave—" Dana began.

"It's just for a short while, and it concerns Josh," Matt coaxed.

"That's a great idea," Mandy beamed. "I'd love to be here for Josh."

Matt held out his hand. With obvious reluctance, Dana accepted it.

CHAPTER EIGHT

She shouldn't have come. Oh, they were all being as polite as can be, but there was an awkward strain. Matt's brothers spoke too loudly, Sandra was too hearty, and Ann dripped sympathy. Matt's mother oozed nervous energy and avoided meeting her eyes, which was a pretty good indication she wasn't going to like what was about to happen. For that matter, Matt was avoiding eye contact, too. She wondered if he was in on it, too, whatever *it* was. She wished they would get on with it, so she could get back to the hospital.

Barbara glanced toward Warner's office for the umpteenth time. Dana couldn't quite decide whether her mother-in-law was nervous or irritated. Nervous wasn't likely, but she'd certainly seemed annoyed when Warner got a call right after she and Matt arrived. He'd disappeared inside his office and hadn't emerged yet. Dana peeked at her watch. It had been almost an hour since she'd left Josh, and she wanted to get back to the hospital.

Matt leaned over to whisper in her ear. "There's no need to be nervous. Mom just wants to tell us the results of everyone's lab tests."

"But I already know." Her voice rose slightly with a hint of indignation. "Dr. Young stopped to tell me just before Mandy arrived at the hospital. No one matches. I'm the closest, but not close enough for a good transplant. I can donate platelets without a problem, but with my bone marrow, Josh would only have about a ten to twenty percent chance of long-term survival." Tears stole down her cheeks. "I should be at the hospital. Please take me back."

Blindly Matt reached for her, and passively she let him hold her. Several minutes passed before he became conscious of the room's silence. Everyone was watching them with varying degrees of pity on their faces. Did they already know? Was he the last to be informed of the failure to find a donor for Josh? Grief and fear were replaced by anger. Why hadn't he been informed? Why was he always the last to know what was happening to his own family?

A picture of Dana and Mandy at the hospital rose in his mind and he remembered Mandy had mentioned something about Dana trying to call him. All right, he conceded, Dana might have tried to call him. But why hadn't she said something on the drive over here? But no, that wasn't fair either. He hadn't given her a chance. He'd talked the whole time, telling her about the Barringer bid problems, trying to distract her from her obvious reluctance to come with him. Besides he'd made the mistake of blaming Dana before.

His anger shifted to his job. This wasn't the time to be tied to his work. The Barringer project was a risk he didn't want to take. He didn't want to be tied to the demanding project. He wanted to be with his son. His dad ought to cut him some slack, let him be at the hospital with Dana and Josh where he belonged.

Warner stepped into the room and Matt found it difficult not to express his anger. Perhaps it was the tight lines around his father's mouth or the tired slump of his shoulders that held him back. Why couldn't the stubborn man see that the Barringer bid was costing them all more than they could afford?

"Now that your father is here, there are a few things we need to discuss," Barbara began.

"We need to get back to the hospital," Matt cut in, his grip on Dana tightening. "We're already aware none of the family can provide a match for Josh. You shouldn't have dragged us over here when we belong with our son." He stood, pulling Dana up beside him.

A stunned silence met his words, followed by a barrage of words.
"None of us?"

"There must be some mistake."

"What about the donor registry?"

"What are you going to do now?"

"We can repeat the tests."

"I don't know what we're going to do," Matt snapped, "except be there with him. Here!" He thrust an envelope toward his father. "You'll just have to settle this Barringer thing without me." He moved toward the door.

"Wait, Matt." His mother stepped forward, placing her hand on his forearm. Angrily he shook it off.

She ignored his behavior. "I wasn't aware you knew about the lab tests, and I thought it would be easier if you learned of it surrounded by your family. We want to support—"

Matt's voice was curt. "How could you think I would enjoy being the last to know?"

"Matt, your mother meant well," Warner spoke sternly.

"I should have learned from Dr. Young, and I would have along with Dana, if I'd been at the hospital with Josh. But no, *you* decided I should do two months' work in two days because getting that Barringer contract is the most important thing in the world!"

"Take it easy." Winn was on his feet now, too. "You're under a lot of pressure, but losing your temper isn't going to help."

"You're right." Matt turned to his older brother. "Nothing is going to help. My son is dying, and there's absolutely nothing I can do about it."

"I thought the drugs were helping," Ann whispered.

"They're keeping him alive. But they won't cure him." Dana raised her head to reveal twin streaks of moisture on her cheeks. She spoke equally softly. "They're only meant to build up his strength and prepare him for the transplant." Her voice broke, and she leaned her face against Matt's shoulder. Voices of his family broke around him like waves crashing against the shore. He didn't know how much more he could take, and he felt certain Dana had had enough. It was time to get out of here.

"Listen to me!" Barbara's voice raised sharply to be heard over the noise in the room.

"No, Mother, not this time." He headed for the door, pulling Dana along beside him.

"You can't give up." His mother's voice followed them.

"I'm not giving up—just facing reality," he spoke through clenched teeth.

"Reality is that everyone in this family has been tested and is willing to do whatever is needed to save Josh. Many of our blood types match, and I've made appointments for us to donate blood tomorrow morning. But what about Dana's family?" Barbara's voice held a note of accusation.

Matt felt Dana stumble beside him. Her muscles locked and she would have fallen if he hadn't had a firm grip on her. There was no way to make his family understand how badly Stephen Dalby had hurt his daughter, nor how badly his threats frightened her.

"They won't help Josh," he stated flatly. "And I won't allow you to blame Dana because her father—"

"Matt!" Warner roared. "That's enough. No one is blaming Dana, and losing your temper isn't helping anyone."

"How do you know they won't help, if you don't ask?" Barbara persisted. "Josh is their grandchild, and no matter how bad Dana's relationship is with her parents, I can't see any grandparent refusing to help their own grandchild."

"The Dalbys can and will refuse," Matt growled. He tightened his grip on his wife's arm. He had to get her out of here. In spite of his physical urging, she didn't move. She stood as though glued to the floor.

"I-I'll ask them," she whispered. Then she was practically running. He let the door slam behind him as they hurried toward their car.

———

He seemed possessed by some kind of urgency as they sped toward the hospital. Dana kept her head bowed, and he wasn't certain whether or not she was crying. He felt like he should apologize for his family. He probably should apologize for losing his temper, too. While he was at this apology business, he supposed he owed his family an apology, too.

"Dana?" She mumbled something, or at least he thought she said a word or two, so he went on, "If I'd known Mother was going to bring up your family, I wouldn't have taken you there."

"She's right, though." He watched her twist her hands. "If I'm a closer match than you or any of your family, then doesn't it make sense that someone in my family might be the perfect match Josh needs?" The resigned finality in her voice told him she didn't expect him to answer, neither did she expect her parents to agree to be tested.

He thought about what she said and found himself agreeing, but instead of cheering him, his anger grew more acute. That cold fish attorney who spoke to Dana and him just before they got married left no doubt in Matt's mind that Dana's parents considered her dead. They probably would like nothing better than to refuse to save her child. Approaching them could even bring some form of retaliation.

When they reached the hospital, Dana hurried to Josh's room while Matt kept his word to drive Mandy home. Dana's young friend chattered freely the twenty minutes it took him to see her safely home. Once more he wondered how Mandy had managed to get past Dana's defenses. He would never have guessed anyone so talkative could manage to befriend his wife, but he was glad she had. He had a hunch he owed her a great deal, just for being there at a time when Dana was terribly scared and alone, a time when he should have been there.

When Mandy climbed out of his car, he watched her slow progression up the sidewalk. She walked with the same lurching waddle Dana had before Josh was born, keeping one hand splayed against her side in an attempt to soothe a persistent backache. He'd teased Dana about being a penguin and assured her he found penguins adorable. His nostalgia for a time when he and Dana had laughed and dreamed together led him to thoughts of having another child. They hadn't meant to wait this long, but the time had never seemed right since he left school and joined the family business. Now he wondered if he and Dana would ever have another child. With a start he realized he wanted one.

His mood darkened as the thought occurred to him that his desire for another child might be connected to the possibility of losing Josh. He wondered if a hidden corner of his mind had given up. Was he seeking a replacement for Josh? No, his heart rebelled. If they were unable to save Josh, there was no way another child would ever take his firstborn's place. What he really wanted was to see Dana swollen with his child once more and for her to be happy and excited, full of dreams again. He wanted Josh to have a brother and to be able to do all the things with him that he'd done as a boy with his brothers. Or perhaps Josh would like a little sister to tease and protect. He'd always wanted a little sister and never gotten one. He hoped Josh would be luckier.

He watched Mandy fumble in her purse, but before she found her apparently elusive key, the door opened, and a young man swept her into his arms, then inside the house. He heard their combined laughter and felt a twinge of envy.

He guessed that Mandy's baby would be born soon, then she wouldn't have as much time to distract and sooth Dana. Anyway that was his job, one he intended to start doing. The new Barringer bid was complete, and as far as he was concerned his father could do whatever he liked with it. He was going to spend his time with Dana and Joshua, and if Dad didn't like it, Matt would find another job.

He spent the night at the hospital with Dana, taking turns visiting their son's room at two hour intervals. He got little sleep and wondered if Dana slept at all. Added to her concern for Joshua was her fear of contacting her parents. He sensed her trepidation and wished she would talk to him, but knew she wouldn't. He had a long way to go to regain her trust.

He finally broached the subject a little before seven. "Dana, you don't need to approach your parents personally. I could have the attorney who represents the company call."

He could see she wanted to accept his offer but wasn't surprised when she shook her head. "I think that would only make Daddy angrier. I-I have to do it myself."

"What about a letter?"

Her eyes filled with tears. "Letters take too long, even registered letters, and I wouldn't know for days whether or not he got it."

"You could call your mother at the gallery. From what you've told me, she's more likely to help than your father is." He persisted in searching for a way to lessen Dana's dread of contacting her parents.

Once more Dana shook her head. "Mother won't speak to me without Daddy's permission."

Matt ground his teeth in frustration. He found Dana's family incomprehensible. He couldn't fathom how any woman in today's world could be so completely under her husband's thumb as Linda Dalby seemed to be. He couldn't even remotely imagine his own mother accepting that kind of dictatorial control. From all Dana had told him about her mother, he suspected the woman was bright and competent. So why did she put up with it?

"I think I better call now," Dana spoke in a strained whisper. "Daddy will be almost through with breakfast. He'll be angry if I wait to call him at the bank."

Standing, he walked beside her to the pay phone. Someone was using it, so they took the elevator down to the lobby. As the elevator slowly descended, Dana bit her lip and her shoulders shook. Instinctively he reached for her, and when she didn't resist, he held her to his side. He was thankful she trusted him enough to allow him to support her in what he knew was a difficult action. When they reached the lobby, they stepped outside to a wide patio. He released her and watched as her trembling fingers tapped in the number on the small phone. She shouldn't have to do this. He ached to take the phone from her hand and tell the man, who had hurt her so deeply and made her afraid, what he thought of him. For his son's sake he had to stand aside, with clenched hands, watching his wife's face twist in an agony of hope as she listened to the hollow ringing in her ear. Dana's eyes widened and she swallowed convulsively. He watched helplessly as her hands tightened against the instrument she held gripped in her hand.

"Dad?" Dana's voice shook. It had been four years since she'd heard her father's voice.

"Who is this?" He sounded angry and her fear escalated.

"Daddy, this is Dana." She spoke rapidly, trying to get in all the words as quickly as possible. "Our baby, Joshua, is really sick. We need help . . ." A loud click sounded in her ear breaking the connection.

"Please, Daddy," she begged, though she knew he could no longer hear her. Pain twisted in her stomach and she thought she might be sick. A deep wrenching sob broke free, and her whole body shook as she struggled to press the off key. She'd thought she could handle it. Over and over she'd told herself not to count on his help, but even though she knew he wanted nothing to do with her, some little part of her hadn't believed he would refuse Joshua.

Arms came around her and Matt held her against his chest. Wordlessly he held her while she cried. There was nothing delicate and lady-like in the way huge gasping sobs tore from her throat. The hurt went deep and was laced with fear. Her family was Josh's last hope.

"Matt? Dana? Is Joshua worse?" A voice broke through her misery. Slowly Matt released her and turned to face his mother. He shook his head and Dana knew he, too, was having difficulty controlling his emotions. She could feel waves of anger rolling off him. He turned some of that anger toward his mother.

"Dana called her father. He hung up on her." His voice sounded belligerent, then his shoulders slumped, and Dana felt a wave of compassion for him. At least she was feeling something for her husband, she marveled in a stunned attempt to avoid thinking about her father. He's exhausted, she thought with a kind of numb awareness. How long could he go on working long days and spending every moment away from the office at the hospital?

"Just like that? He wouldn't even discuss it?" Barbara Bingham's mouth tightened to a grim line and she glanced indignantly at her daughter-in-law. Dana's heart sank. One more thing Matt's mother could fault her for. She shrugged her shoulders, thinking she was too tired to care any more whether her mother-in-law approved of her or not. If her own parents cared nothing for her, how could she expect her husband's parents to find anything in her worth caring about? The only solution was for her to stop caring. Nothing mattered anymore except finding a bone marrow donor for Josh. Obviously family was out; they'd just have to pray for a nonrelated donor.

"We'd better hold a family council and decide our next step," Barbara spoke decisively. "Most of the family is still in the lab donating blood. I'll call there and find a room where we can meet." Giving Matt's arm a pat, she turned to walk away. Dana didn't protest. It no longer mattered whether Matt's family hung around the hospital or not.

Dana watched Barbara cross the patio, her heels tapping a rapid, no-nonsense tempo all the way to the double doors. Her tailored suit and perfectly coiffed hair added to her authoritative air. Dana sighed. She was being immature to resent her in-laws. Unlike her parents, they at least cared about Joshua, even if they didn't like her. When Matt told his parents that Josh had been diagnosed with aplastic anemia, they had immediately volunteered to be tested for compatibility and to become blood, platelet, or bone marrow donors. They had rallied his brothers, aunts, uncles, and cousins to the cause. Calling the police hadn't been so bad, she reasoned. They'd only done it to protect Josh. They meant well.

"Dana, we better go upstairs." Matt placed an arm around her shoulders. "I don't know what a family council will accomplish. Every relative Mother could find has been tested and none of them are a close enough match for a bone marrow transplant. We've already registered with the bone marrow registry, but if we're not up there in a few minutes, Dad will send one of my brothers after us."

"Sometimes I wish they'd all just go away and allow us to be alone with our son," she said wistfully, but nevertheless turned obediently toward the door.

"They're just trying to help," Matt said quietly.

"I know," Dana admitted. She tried to be fair. She just wished they didn't leave her feeling so inadequate.

Exiting the elevator a few minutes later, they walked slowly down the hall. At the door to their son's room, they paused to peer inside where a clear plastic barrier prevented them from going further. Josh lay curled on his side with a small, clenched fist just touching his cheek. His dark eyelashes contrasted against his pale cheeks. Only a month ago his cheeks had been as fat as a little chipmunk's, pink and healthy. Now their exuberant little boy was wan and listless; dark shadows made his eyes look like sunken holes, and he didn't run or giggle any more. A needle was taped to his thin arm and fluid dripped from a plastic bag into his tired little body. How she wished she could snatch him from his barred bed and hold him close. If only she could flee with him to some place where he would be safe.

Matt's fingers squeezed hers, and she knew he was experiencing the same desire.

When they reached the small waiting room where the Bingham family waited, Dana dropped to a seat, and after a moment's hesitation Matt sank down beside her. She didn't look at the others gathered there. She didn't want to see them look past her to Matt with pity in their eyes. She didn't want to see the accusations. She closed her ears to their polite arguments, to their evaluations, to their plan.

She could only think of Josh. He was so little, and he needed to be held and told she loved him. The short visits she was allowed each day, wearing a sterile gown and mask were too brief. *Please Father,* she prayed, *don't take Joshua. He's too little to suffer so much. Please make him well.*

She felt oblivious to everyone around her. Voices traveled in the air above her, but she didn't hear them. She was too tired. The pain went too deep.

"I won't take no for an answer. I'll go to California and talk to him myself." Her mother-in-law's voice cut through the haze surrounding her. Surely she didn't mean that the way it sounded. It almost sounded like Barbara Bingham planned to confront Stephen Dalby. The picture that came to her mind was too absurd. If she weren't so tired she would laugh. For a moment she almost felt sorry for her father, but not quite. Somehow the idea of her father having to face her mother-in-law was extremely comforting. Her head slumped against Matt's chest. The voices that had been a faint buzz disappeared behind a dense fog.

"That poor girl is asleep," Barbara pointed out unnecessarily to Matt. "Take her home, and make sure she gets some rest. You need some rest as well. Sandra can stay right here until the girls get out of school, then Ann can take over. Warner can take a turn, too. By that time you should both be rested enough to come back."

"But no more spending the night," a voice spoke from the doorway. Matt looked up to see Dr. Young. Looking straight at Matt, the doctor added, "Two platelet donors besides Dana have been found. Josh is responding well to the chemical treatment and with three donors available, he is in no immediate danger. Dana is the one at risk right now. Make certain she eats and sleeps, or she'll be unable to help when the time comes. I don't want her to become a patient, too."

Matt's sisters-in-law nodded their agreement, and Matt realized he was hopelessly outnumbered. Carefully sliding his hands beneath Dana's slight form, he lifted her into his arms. Dr. Young held the door and Robert hurried to press the down button. He glanced regretfully toward Josh's closed door, then stepped onto the elevator. Dana would likely be furious when she awoke to find herself in their bed, miles from Josh.

CHAPTER NINE

Up ahead a van pulled out of a parking spot and Warner edged closer to make certain someone didn't beat him to the only empty space in the entire short-term parking garage. Giving the departing vehicle barely room to back and turn, he darted into the space and braked hard.

"You could have let me off at the entrance. It really isn't necessary to park and go in with me," Barbara reminded him.

"I'll carry your bags and make certain your ticket is waiting," Warner spoke tersely as he wrenched open the trunk and reached for his wife's suitcase, while she shouldered a matching flight bag.

"I know how anxious you are to get to the office, and I really can handle this," she spoke purposefully as she started toward the sliding doors leading to the airport. He matched his steps to her long stride and said nothing. Most of the time he appreciated Barbara's independence and capable way of dealing with obstacles, but there were times she made him feel next to useless. A man should carry his wife's bags and no matter how busy he might be, he could take time to see her off on a trip, especially when he had no idea how long she might be gone. Admittedly time was at a premium, but making certain Barbara caught her plane wouldn't exactly cause his business to fold!

To tell the truth he didn't feel good about this trip. He'd tried to talk Barbara out of traveling to California, going so far as offering to go with her when he couldn't dissuade her, but she'd insisted she could handle it, and with Matt away from the office, he really did need to be there. Barbara could hold her own with most men, but the thought of her going to see Stephen Dalby made him uncomfortable. Matt was certainly convinced his mother was wasting her time, maybe worse.

After checking Barbara's bag, they made their way along the concourse, arriving at the gate just as her flight was called. Turning, she gave him a quick kiss on the mouth, then speaking matter-of-factly, she said, "I'll call from the hotel tonight to let you know what progress I've made."

He felt a moment's amusement. It was so like Barbara to assume there would be progress. "It might not be so easy. Matt seems to think the man is some kind of two-headed monster."

"He may be, but he's about to meet a determined grandmother." There was a hint of a smile, as though she looked forward to a challenge. "It may take a little while to track down Dana's parents." She patted her bag, and her eyes revealed her stern determination. "Matt gave me their home address. He said it's surrounded by a wall and has security gates, so I can't just walk up and ring the bell. I'll try their businesses first, but if that doesn't work, I'll find a way to get inside."

He didn't doubt she'd succeed. Barbara always accomplished whatever she set out to do. Her abundant self-confidence wasn't misplaced, he knew. He couldn't think of a single instance when she hadn't accomplished what she set out to do. Watching her walk away, never looking back, he couldn't shake the feeling that this time might be different. She disappeared inside the accordion pleats of the jet bridge, leaving him behind to make his way back to the parking garage alone.

Heavy traffic between the airport and his office made the return trip slow and he found himself becoming increasingly frustrated. Barbara would likely reach San Francisco before he reached his office. He, for one, would be glad when all of the road construction was finished, the Barringer project was in hand, and little Joshua was back home. He was getting mighty tired of so much upheaval in his life.

He'd barely reached his desk when Robyn signaled he had a visitor. "Paul Barringer to see you, Mr. Bingham."

Before he could respond, his office door opened and Paul Barringer stepped inside, followed quickly by another man. Warner scarcely glanced at the second man, and Barringer made no attempt to introduce the burly young man with him. Warner's attention was focused on the tall, thin man extending a hand toward him. Quickly he stood and reached for the proffered hand. Introductions were not necessary between Warner and Paul. The two men had met briefly at various social functions and twice at planning and zoning hearings, and Warner had known Paul's father for many years.

Paul Barringer was young for the amount of influence he wielded, not only in the city and state, but internationally. He was not quite forty and had already served as president of the huge conglomerate of businesses and financial interests his grandfather had started and his father had expanded. His bearing suggested he knew very well the importance his name carried.

The younger man's grip was firm and he exuded an air of confidence, but for just a moment Warner longed for the old days when he'd dealt with this man's father. Something about Paul Barringer, Jr., rubbed him the wrong way. The older man had been blunt—some would say domineering—but his word and a handshake were better than a contract. His death two years ago had shaken the business world, but Warner was one of the few who knew that had he lived, he would have retired, turning the business over to his son, anyway. The older Barringer had confided to Warner just weeks before his heart attack that he'd had "a little discussion" with the "brethern" and that he was expecting a mission call. Warner didn't doubt the man had gotten his "mission call," only it hadn't been to any of the missions he might have expected.

Warner waved the two men toward the sofa at one end of his office, and settled into the matching armchair Ann had insisted was necessary for a proper conversation corner.

"Warner, I'm pleased you submitted a bid," Barringer began. "I'd heard a rumor that you might. I'd also heard it would be much lower." He lifted his eyebrows as though his last statement were a question.

"I'd like to know where that rumor started," Warner responded unhurriedly. No way would he allow anyone to see how much Barringer's words disturbed him. *The person or persons involved in tampering with the bid would have expected the submitted bid to be lower.* If Barringer got a lower bid from one of Bingham's competitors than the total Matt had painstakingly inked as a bottom line to their bid, the corporate giant should do more than a little checking to see where the bidder expected to cut costs.

"My board just opened the bids this morning, so I'm not familiar with the details," Barringer went on smoothly. "I only peeked at the final figures, but it appeared to me they were all quite close and higher than anticipated."

"Close bids are to be expected." Warner leaned back as though the conversation were idle chit chat. "It will be an expensive project, and we all have the same material and labor costs to work with. Quality has a price tag. My understanding is that's what you're looking for, both in workmanship and material."

"Quality is synonymous with your name," the younger man inserted smoothly. "You built my mother's home twenty years ago, and you were a friend of my father's, so I will, of course, recommend you to the board of directors. Not all of our directors are family, and we do have shareholders we must answer to, so their opinion counts, but ultimately the choice is mine. You do understand that the firm that builds the complex which includes the Barringer corporate head-quarters and an internationally rated five-star hotel will achieve worldwide name recognition?"

Warner nodded his head, wondering where this was leading.

"I wouldn't be adverse to looking at a second submission if you were so inclined," Barringer answered Warner's unspoken question. "I've made the same offer to two or three others, including your former partner. Two weeks should be enough time." He smiled know-ingly and rose to his feet.

A chill slid down Warner's back. Could Barringer himself have something to do with the changed numbers in the original bid? A corporation such as the one this arrogant young man headed could easily hire or find someone among its numerous employees who could break into a computer system to customize a bid to meet their own agenda. Paul's father would never have done such a thing, but did the son share his father's iron-clad ethics?

Though Warner remained calm and affable on the outside, he seethed inwardly. The Barringer Group wasn't a government entity; it didn't need to ask for bids, and it wasn't required to accept the lowest bid. Paul could have come to him and openly discussed costs and fees. He could have gone to any of the other applicants. So why was he playing this cat-and-mouse game? Was it some kind of power trip, or was there a more sinister purpose?

After Paul Barringer and his still unnamed companion left his office, Warner sat very still, thinking. The younger Barringer had enjoyed throwing his weight around; he knew the extent of the power he wielded and was one of those men who took satisfaction in making other men acutely aware of his wealth and power. Would Warner's company be better off if he passed up this project? A wave of loneliness swept over him, and he longed for Barbara's blunt appraisal. Unfortunately, she was a long way away. Besides, she'd washed her hands of his business a long time ago. Finally he pressed the call button on his phone to ask Robyn to locate his sons and send them to his office as soon as they could feasibly leave their present projects.

———•———

Matt returned from the nurse's station where he'd been summoned to the phone. He folded his arms across his chest and leaned back, closing his eyes. Dana observed him quietly for several minutes. She noted the dark shadows down the sides of his face and across his chin. It had been too many hours since his last shave. The gauntness of his face spoke of meals missed, and the coldness she'd felt in her heart since he'd accused her of beating their son lessened. Silently she acknowledged that his suffering was as deep and real as her own. Though his eyes were closed, she knew he wasn't asleep.

"Your father wants you back at the office?" Dana asked softly.

"Yes," he answered monosyllabically.

Dana sighed, but said nothing more.

"I'm not going." Matt's voice held a petulant edge, but she under-stood. She too had long ago reached that point where duty and responsibility, along with the expectations of others, mattered little. Along with the need for food and sleep, her own hurts and disap-pointments seemed trivial. Her world had narrowed to the room down the hall, where her baby struggled for his life. There was a kind of solace in knowing Matt inhabited that narrow little world as well.

He'd made too many wrong choices. The company faced a crisis, yes, but his being there wasn't critical. He'd done all he could do. His father and brothers had managed for years without him; they could continue to do so.

Dana didn't say anything further, so he didn't know whether she agreed with his decision, or if she wished he'd go. He sensed she wasn't ready to discuss their marriage or even commit to trying to fix any of the things that had gone wrong, but she didn't seem to resent him anymore. She no longer flinched when he touched her, and he took that as a good sign. He was too tired, and too worried about Josh, to think about rebuilding his marriage right now. Besides, he suspected Dana was incapable of focusing on anything beyond their son, and as long as she didn't actively resent his presence, then he was willing to settle for simply being beside her for now.

It would soon be his turn to visit Joshua. He found himself checking his watch every few minutes. Each small noise from the hall set his heart pounding in anticipation. Yet as much as he looked forward to those precious minutes with Josh, leaving Dana behind, knowing he was depriving her of being with her baby, filled him with guilt.

This visit was fixated in his mind as being of special importance. He intended to do something he should have done right at the begin-ning of this nightmare. He was going to give his son a father's blessing. His eyes went to Dana and he wondered if he should tell her. His heart told him he should. If he truly wished to make amends, and regain her trust, he had to be completely honest with her.

"Dana," he began hesitantly. When she looked up he went on, "When I see Joshua this time, I want to give him a blessing. It's not the same as administering to him. It will be just me." His voice trailed off.

She was silent so long he thought she might be angry, but at last when she turned to face him, he saw the gleam of moisture in her eyes. He wondered if he should back off from blessing Josh tonight.

"I-I'm glad," she whispered in a husky voice.

"You're sure?" He had to clear his throat to get the words out. She sat with her head bowed and her fingers pressed against her lips. When she spoke, he could barely understand her words.

"The first time I gathered my courage to attend Relief Society, the teacher talked about something she called a father's blessing. She talked about Abraham and Lehi, but what really impressed me was when she talked about modern fathers who bless their children when they start school, go away to camp, or just because the son or daughter asks for help with a problem. As others in the room told stories of times their fathers or husbands had blessed their children, I started to cry. If only I'd had a father who loved me enough to offer me a blessing. I-I'm thankful Joshua has a father who-who wants . . . can . . ." Her words disappeared and he reached across the space dividing them. She settled against his side, and his arm wrapped around her in a motion so familiar and so deeply missed, he ached with a sense of homecoming.

"Dana, I'm so sorry you didn't have a father like that," he whispered. "If I could change the past and give you the security and blessings you had a right to expect from your father, I would."

"Mr. Bingham?" A voice reached him from the doorway. "Your son is awake and you can visit with him now."

Dana pulled away from him. "Go give Josh that father's blessing," she whispered.

"You're all right?" he whispered as he slowly stood up.

"Yes." She smiled, and his heart rocketed. "Go to Joshua."

Feeling that he and Dana were united for the first time in much too long, he left the room, lightened by a sense of hope and purpose. When his hospital gown was in place, he stepped into his son's room.

His steps faltered as he once more took in the reality of little Josh's illness. The machines and tubes, the plastic bubble, and Josh's pale face undercut his confidence, and he wondered what kind of blessing he could give this child he loved so much. With all the mistakes he'd made, was he worthy to give his critically ill child a blessing?

Reaching through the plastic, he hesitantly touched his son's face and was rewarded with a tiny smile loaded with trust and love. Feeling a wrenching pain in his own heart, he smiled back. With that small exchange, his faith returned. Though there had been times he'd joined with another priesthood holder to anoint and bless someone who was ill, and he had prayed by himself and with others, he'd never stood alone before God to ask a blessing quite like this.

During his growing up years his father had occasionally called him into his office and laid his hands on his head, but he didn't remember the words his father had said nor been aware of any special impact on his life from those prayers. But as his hands gently stroked the dear face of his son, he recalled the sense of love he'd imagined creeping from his father's fingers down through his body like water trickling through the soil to nourish his roots. Sudden strength moved like a wave through his entire body, humbling him with its power and majesty. Slowly at first, then gathering strength and faith he began.

A shimmering curtain of moisture blocked Warner's vision as Matt walked from the room, going right past him without seeing him. He'd come to insist that Matt return to the office with him, but he found he couldn't speak. With a crisis he didn't fully understand looming over his business, he particularly wanted to hear this son's reaction to Paul Barringer's visit. Though he found Matt's fiscal conservatism frustrating at times, he also recognized Matt's business acumen. Like his mother, Matt had a grasp of numbers and an under-standing of his competitors that he and his other sons lacked. Matt had expressed doubts several days ago that he was only now begin-ning to suspect had their basis in reality. As badly as he needed Matt's business expertise, it would have to wait. The few minutes Matt would be allowed to spend with Josh superceded all else.

He watched Dana blink back tears and knew he was invading his daughter-in-law's privacy. He hadn't meant to eavesdrop, and he didn't know why he hadn't immediately announced his presence when he realized Matt and Dana hadn't noticed his arrival. Now standing alone, Dana appeared a lost and lonely glass waif who might shatter if he spoke.

With one part of his mind, he was conscious of Matt's disappearing footsteps, with the other, he saw only Dana. Perhaps for the first time in his association with his son's wife, he really saw her. Beyond her baggy clothing and thick tangle of hair, he saw a scared little girl who brought a pain to his heart. For just a moment he saw another little girl. Larissa had lived next door and been his best friend. She had followed him everywhere, and at first he'd reveled in the child's hero worship. He'd tied Larissa's shoes over and over, held her hand when they crossed streets, pushed her swing for her, and made certain she got home safely from kindergarten. The summer he turned nine and she was six, her parents' fighting escalated, and frightened, she'd clung to him until his friends teased him about having a girlfriend. Her constant presence had then become an embarrassing nuisance.

He'd taken drastic measures to evade her after that, ignoring the hurt and loneliness on her thin little face. Then suddenly he woke up one day to discover she and her mother had moved away, and he wasn't anybody's hero anymore. Like a ghost, her sad little face had haunted him for years.

Funny, how he'd never quite gotten over missing Larissa and feeling guilty for the way he'd turned his back on her when she'd needed a friend. Perhaps if he'd had a daughter . . . There had been a girl back in college who had briefly reminded him of his childhood playmate . . .

"Dana," he spoke gently, not wishing to startle her. Slowly she raised her head and he winced internally at the wariness in her eyes and noted an aura of tenseness, a tightening of her shoulders, lending her the appearance of a doe set to flee. "I know you don't want me here. I only came because there's a matter I need to discuss with Matt."

"He's with Joshua." She explained Matt's absence with a minimum of words, but there was no rudeness.

"I know. I'd like to wait." She shrugged her shoulders indicating she couldn't stop him from waiting, or perhaps she didn't care what he did.

"Has there been any change?" he asked softly.

"No. Tomorrow morning he'll receive his first platelet transfusion. If Josh improves even slightly, he'll get the second one toward the end of the week."

Encouraged by her answer, he ventured another question. "Will you be the donor?"

Dana shook her head. "With just three donors, Dr. Young wants to stretch the period between transfusions as far as possible, and he said I should be last."

"Why is that?"

"He's still hoping a family donor will be found, and he doesn't want Josh building up antibodies against my blood, which could affect the success of a related bone marrow transfusion." Her shoulders drooped and the defeated tone of her voice told him she didn't hold out much hope that anyone related to her would step forward to save Joshua.

Feeling awkward he continued to stand near the doorway. He couldn't sit if she continued to stand, and she certainly wasn't giving any indication she'd welcome further conversation. It occurred to him that he'd never been alone with his daughter-in-law before. Always Barbara or Matt had been around. Accustomed to being surrounded by people who were assertive, outspoken, even forceful, he'd dismissed Dana as being of little consequence. He'd never bothered to get to know her. Matt said she was shy and beautiful with a keen mind and a love for art; Barbara described her as immature and secretive. He'd never gotten beyond annoyance that she kept him from his grandson.

Her words spoken to Matt a few minutes ago rang in his ears and filled him with shame. Long ago he'd let down a little girl who needed a big brother. Now his mistake was far more serious; he'd let down a young woman who needed a father and who had as much right to a father's blessing from him as Josh did from Matt. Josh would welcome Matt's touch and be comforted by his father's words, but Dana . . . ? Years ago, with each of Barbara's pregnancies, he'd secretly hoped for a daughter, but he'd been content with sons. His patriarchal blessing said he would have sons and daughters. Funny, he hadn't thought of that phrase for years. Had the Lord meant his daughters would be his sons' wives? Dana's own father had thrown away his relationship with his daughter. Had he just as carelessly lost the right to be a father to Dana? His thoughts troubled him.

Dana wouldn't welcome a blessing from a man who had never progressed beyond being her husband's father, a man who was a virtual stranger to her. A window opened in his mind and he remembered a fervent prayer of long ago when he'd asked his Heavenly Father to give him a chance to make up his wrong to Larissa. That girl back at college, the one who reminded him of Larissa, had been headed for trouble. He'd tried to be a big brother to her, but she'd made it clear she wasn't looking for a brother, and since he wasn't looking for anything more, he'd ended their friendship. Now he knew. He could never personally make up to Larissa his callous indifference, but he could be forgiven if he accepted the challenge of becoming Dana's father. It shouldn't be too hard; he really had always wanted a daughter.

He wasn't sure where to start. He'd never had a daughter or a sister; he wasn't certain he was even much of a husband. He enjoyed his granddaughters. He was practically in awe of them, but Dana wasn't a child. He couldn't treat her the same way he did them. He was on friendly terms with his other two daughters-in-law. He enjoyed Ann's sense of humor, and knew he could count on Sandra's quick mind and determination to get a job done. They both were daughters of exceptionally fine men, and he'd never thought about either of them as being literally a "daughter." They were his sons' wives and good friends in their own right. Certainly he considered them family, but they already had fathers.

Or was he looking at this whole fatherhood thing wrong? To begin with his love for his sons was an extension of the love he shared with Barbara, a tangible product of that love. But now his relationship with his sons was a mixture of memories built during their dependent years, his pride in their abilities, and the friendship he enjoyed with them as strong, competent fellow adults. Perhaps that's where he should start, by being first a friend, then see where that might lead.

"You know, Dana, I came here to talk to Matt, but now I wonder if it might be better to talk to someone who hasn't been involved, who might not already have an opinion." When she didn't say anything but merely looked at him, waiting, he forged ahead. "Something curious happened at work this afternoon that might have something to do with the break-in we had earlier. I'd like to tell you about it. The Barringer Corporation is planning a massive project encompassing an entire city block . . ."

CHAPTER TEN

Stepping from the cab, Barbara added a generous tip to the fare before turning to face the multi-storied gray edifice. For just a moment she wondered how earthquake-proof the building was. After all this was San Francisco. The thought was fleeting and her mind immediately returned to the business at hand.

Armed with a medical report and a picture of Joshua no grandparent could possibly resist, she wasted no time checking her appearance in the gleaming tinted windows. She'd learned long ago that no amount of fussing would make her pretty, but an expensive, well-tailored suit and a precise haircut lent her a power image. Concern for her personal appearance was always left behind the moment she left her dressing room mirror.

Though prepared to appeal to Stephen Dalby's heart, if he had one, she suspected a calm, rational argument from an articulate equal would carry more weight. But just in case it became necessary, she wouldn't hesitate to use a subtle bit of blackmail. She was prepared for that, too.

Refusing to allow marble floors and ceilings that disappeared into dazzling heights to intimidate her, she stepped smartly toward a pale young man seated at a massive desk in regal boredom.

"Could you direct me to Stephen Dalby's office?" It was no accident the request was more command than question. Minutes later she was on the plexiglass elevator, headed for the bank president's private suite on the fourth floor.

Bluffing her way past the young man on the first floor and stepping past the security guard monitoring access to the elevators was simple compared to getting past Dalby's secretary, a formidable woman whose hardness spoke of "past forty" while her clothes created a faux-twenty-something look. Her black suit just missed severe by being a mite too tight and by revealing a decolletage that would have benefitted greatly from the simple addition of a shell. Her blond hair was lacquered to perfection as were her gleaming dagger-like fingernails. Obviously she didn't do a lot of typing or filing.

"Do you have an appointment?" the woman asked in a voice that made it clear she knew Barbara didn't, and that there was nothing in Barbara's appearance that either impressed or intimidated her toward fulfilling Barbara's request to see her boss.

"I don't believe an appointment is necessary to deliver a message to my son's father-in-law." Barbara let a note of disdain creep into her voice. She was long past being cowed by the dragons guarding the portals of the rich and powerful.

"Hardly." The secretary's voice dripped sarcasm. "I know Preston's mother well."

"Preston?" Barbara arched an eyebrow. "Oh, you mean that Vincent boy Marilyn married." Barbara knew very well the "Vincent boy" was nearly forty and had recently announced his candidacy for the legislature. She also knew her response was a petty, impulsive reaction to the haughty secretary's insinuation that Stephen Dalby only had one daughter. She had been critical of Dana since the day she first met her, but somehow hearing her dismissed as of no consequence by the secretary struck a discordant note in Barbara's heart, immediately bringing out a fierce protectiveness for her daughter-in-law. "Of course not. My son married the pretty, younger daughter, Dana," she responded smoothly.

Feeling a moment's satisfaction as the other woman failed to conceal either her surprise or a quick glance at a large framed painting behind her desk, Barbara let her eyes follow the secretary's. It was her turn to be surprised. The mural-like painting was bright with a great deal of white space. It had an ethereal quality, showing an endless array of formless, but vivid dancers swirling about in a vast ballroom. It spoke of noise and laughter, with an almost chaotic harshness that left the viewer exhausted. Barbara's eyes gradually focused on one small figure that didn't seem to belong in the ballroom, but stood with her back to the gay confusion, every line of her body suggesting she was drawn to something outside a massive, arched window. It was the view outside the window seen through large panes of glass that brought an unconscious gasp to Barbara's lips.

Through the ballroom window, the figure gazed at a raging river with a faint path along its far rocky shore. The path was hidden in places by the cascading water and mist of the river. A few struggling hikers clung to a rope strung along the path paralleling the river. Barbara's eyes were drawn to one particular figure, a seeming twin of the one watching through the ballroom window, who strained to maintain her grip on the rope while waves crashed across her feet, turning the path slippery. Rocks blocked the path and the mist nearly blinded her while it sinuously beckoned toward the river. But instead of cowering in terror, the woman radiated joy and purpose as she looked steadfastly ahead toward the last pane of the ballroom window.

Barbara knew what she would find in that last scene. Her eyes followed the direction of the struggling figure's hopeful gaze. She wasn't disappointed. Once more there was vivid color, but this color revealed a kind of muted joy. Love and caring radiated from happy people greeting one another. Children played beneath a great sheltering tree, couples strolled hand-in-hand, and a woman, again the same woman, her apron filled with fruit, sat looking back at the dancer with infinite sadness.

"The Dream by Dana Dalby" was engraved on a small brass plate beneath the painting, and Dana's signature appeared in tiny, neat slanted letters across one bottom corner of the large canvas. Surely if Stephen Dalby kept one of his daughter's paintings, especially this one, he must have some feeling for Dana. Her hopes rose.

She sensed the painting was exceptionally good, though she was no connoisseur of fine art. More importantly, it told her something significant about her daughter-in-law. Dana understood Lehi's joy and sorrow far better than Barbara had assumed. Like Nephi, who felt compelled to understand his father's dream, and who had been subject to rejection by his brothers for choosing the gospel path, Dana had chosen the Lord's way over the wealth and glitter that was her birthright. The artist who painted the picture before her didn't possess a shallow testimony.

"Dana?" The secretary repeated with a nervous glance toward a closed door. Her brassy gloss seemed to soften. "Is she all right? I thought . . . We were told . . . Didn't she join the Mormons and enter some religious commune someplace?"

Barbara shook her head. "Until last January, she and my son lived in Berkeley while he finished school. Since then, they've been in Salt Lake City. They have a beautiful little boy." Making an abrupt decision, she decided there was no harm, and it might actually help her cause to tell the secretary a little of Dana's life. "She's fine, but their son is critically ill. I stopped by here to let Mr. Dalby know his grandson's condition."

"He won't give you any money." The hardness crept back into the secretary's voice.

"Money isn't needed," Barbara snapped back. "Any bills not covered by insurance will be paid by our family."

"I'm sorry," the other woman apologized, but the wariness didn't leave her eyes. "Mr. Dalby doesn't have an opening until toward the end of next week."

"Next week could be too late," Barbara responded in a burst of anger. "Joshua could die before then." She didn't know what the secretary's response might have been if her attention hadn't been captured by the door the woman had glanced toward several times opening, allowing Barbara a glimpse of two well-dressed men with bulging brief cases just leaving Dalby's office. They paused in the doorway for several seconds with their attention focused on someone still in the room. When they moved, Barbara darted past them to find herself in a large office filled with gleaming, black furniture.

The single occupant of the room sat behind a large desk. He didn't lift his head or acknowledge her presence in any way. Silver wings highlighted his dark hair and a narrow mustache topped a hard, tight mouth. Something about the man sent a cold chill down her spine.

Ignoring the secretary's shout of dismay, Barbara proceeded directly to the wide desk where she slapped a small portrait of Joshua onto the shining surface. The man didn't reach for it, nor turn his attention toward her.

"This is your grandson!" Barbara spoke without preamble, hoping to shock the man into an awareness of her presence. "He's going to die of aplastic anemia unless he receives a bone marrow transplant right away."

"Get out." Dalby raised his head and said the words with little inflection, but his lip curled in an unmistakable sneer. His eyes were hard and cold.

"I tried to stop her." The secretary's voice, filled with anger, and perhaps fear, came from behind her as Barbara stared in astonishment at the man who didn't deign to even glance at the picture lying on his desk.

Determinedly, she forged ahead. "His name is Joshua Fielding Bingham and he will be two years old the end of next month. He's big for his age, and his hair isn't as red as Dana's." Dalby's features hardened and he made no attempt to hide his contempt at the mention of Dana's name.

"You can leave, or I can have you thrown out." His attempt at indifference failed to conceal the malevolence in his eyes. Barbara's own eyes narrowed.

"Perhaps you didn't hear me," she spoke slowly and distinctly. "I am Barbara Bingham, owner of Dunbridge Realty and the wife of Warner Bingham of Bingham Construction. You and I have a grandson in common who is critically ill. A bone marrow donor is needed, and since a match cannot be found in my family, the search must be widened to include your side of the family."

"Must? I think not. When Dana chose to become a Mormon, she ceased to be my daughter. Ms. Frances, please call Security." He turned his back to reach casually for a sheaf of papers lying on a low cabinet.

"You would deny your own grandchild?" Barbara asked incredulously. Stephen Dalby perused the papers in his hand, pretending not to hear her words, and she felt an unfamiliar fury grow in her heart. The man wasn't human! She couldn't even fathom the kind of man who could not only turn his back on his own child, but who could casually reject his grandson.

"All right, I'll leave." She spoke with a cold, calmness she didn't feel. "It's your choice, but it's a choice my friend over at the *Examiner* will find interesting in light of your position in this community and your son-in-law's political campaign." Snatching up Joshua's portrait, she turned on her heel, and walked swiftly from the room, head high.

"Mrs. Bingham." The secretary's voice stopped her before she reached the elevator. Her hopes rose that her threat had accomplished the needed result, then plummeted as Ms. Frances continued hesitantly, "Is it true Dana's baby will die without a transplant?"

"Yes." Barbara glanced back.

"If she left the Mormons, he might . . ." Ms. Frances didn't finish the sentence.

"The woman who painted that scene," Barbara indicated the picture behind the secretary, "will never deny her faith." A solid affirmation deep within her told her she spoke the truth. Dana truly would not deny what had come to her at tremendous personal cost.

Turning back to the elevator, Barbara waited for the door to open. When it did, two armed officers stepped into the hall and hurried toward Stephen Dalby's office. Knowing Ms. Frances could point to her at any second, she stepped into the empty cage and breathed a sigh of relief as the doors closed behind her. In less than a minute, she was once more on the sidewalk.

Back in her hotel room, she paced the floor and struggled to control her fury. How dare he treat her that way?! And how dare he ignore Joshua?! Twice she reached for the phone to call her old friend, Eddie Cartwright, who had risen to prominence on the *San Francisco Examiner* staff. But no, she didn't want to antagonize Dana's family further at this point. She still had to meet the mother, and she had no desire to injure Dana's brother-in-law's campaign.

She contemplated calling Warner, then decided against it. He had his hands full with Matt spending so much time at the hospital and with his efforts to secure the Barringer project. She knew there were problems with the project and the break-in had somehow been related to it, but Warner had discussed few details with her. Her heart filled with a kind of sadness. When had she and Warner stopped discussing their business concerns? It had been a long time since they had analyzed a problem together. Even family matters had taken on a superficial level of communication. It pained her to admit there was something lacking in their marriage. Somehow over the years they had managed to lose something bright and precious. Her thoughts did nothing to sooth her frustration or prepare her for the next step she must take.

Too nervous to eat lunch, she downed a soft drink, then called for a cab. During the trip across town she had more than enough time to think. Having developed a preference for blunt honesty in her own life, she now took herself to task for misjudging Dana. Her daughter-in-law obviously had a greater knowledge of the gospel and a deeper commitment to it than she had given the younger woman credit for. How could she have been so wrong about the girl?

Leaning back against the seat behind her, Barbara closed her eyes and pictured the painting in Stephen Dalby's office. She had been wrong to assume that because he'd kept it, he retained some hope of reconciliation with his daughter. So why had the man kept it? Spite? Ignorance of the message so clear to anyone who knew of Lehi's dream? Or might it have a monetary value she couldn't begin to estimate? Deep in thought, she was oblivious to San Francisco's fabled scenery until the cab stopped at its destination.

Linda Dalby's gallery reminded Barbara of a jewelry store. The outside was all black marble, chrome, and glass. Inside it was more spacious than she expected, with deep, lush carpet. She wandered down a long hall and through several rooms where paintings were displayed beneath strategic focal lighting. In one room several landscapes caught her eye and she leaned closer to read the discreet cards bearing prices that made her nearly choke. She stared in dismay at one room filled entirely with nude paintings and sculptures, most of which were such odd perversions of the human form, she couldn't help wondering why the poor models hadn't kept their clothes on. The paintings lining the hall reminded her of the scribbles her granddaughters presented to her whenever they came to visit.

When she wandered back to the front of the gallery, a tall, slender woman in a gold jumpsuit approached her on glittering high-heeled sandals. Her vibrant red hair was piled high with loose tendrils forming a brilliant, but wispy frame about her face. Every long, graceful finger sported a different ring made up of a profusion of gem stones, though the woman's tastes obviously ran to diamonds since there were many more diamonds than any other kind of stone. Gold bracelets jangled at her wrists, and diamonds dangled in splendor from her ear lobes as well. Barbara didn't doubt the gems were real. An intuitive hunch told her this woman wouldn't wear fakes. That same hunch told her she had found Linda Dalby, though it was difficult to imagine this glamorous creature being Dana's mother.

"May I help you with any questions you might have?" the woman asked in a low, cultured voice.

"Yes, I would like to speak with you privately." Barbara forced herself to speak calmly, as though she truly were interested only in a painting.

"Very well. My office is right this way." Mrs. Dalby gestured toward a closed door, then proceeded to lead Barbara to it.

In the confines of the small office, she glanced around, wondering if Dana's mother kept one of her daughter's paintings, as did her husband. She wasn't disappointed, though she found the painting disappointing. It appeared to be a meaningless blur of colors floating like clouds across an endless, dreary gray sky. She'd always equated color with gaiety and frivolity, but something about the little painting left her feeling empty and sad.

"That painting isn't for sale," Linda Dalby pronounced, following her interested gaze. "However we have others of a similar style."

"By the same artist?"

"No, that particular artist only produced a few canvases, then disappeared from the art scene. I don't believe she is still painting."

The look of regret on Linda Dalby's face prompted Barbara to speak. "I know for a fact she still paints a great deal," she said, reaching into her cavernous handbag to produce a small tissue-wrapped package, which she handed to Dana's mother.

Casting Barbara a puzzled look, Mrs. Dalby began carefully removing the layers of tissue until a small, silver picture frame rested in her hands.

"Dana did this?" Linda held the object almost reverently. "But Dana has never done portraits. She seldom includes people in her

paintings at all. The few paintings where she has included people the faces are undefined and emotions are denoted by posture and color."
Barbara couldn't believe what she was hearing. This woman hadn't seen or talked to her daughter for close to four years, but instead of rushing into questions about Dana's well-being, she lectured on style and technique!

"Dana did paint this small portrait," Barbara assured the other woman. "She gave it to me on Mother's Day."

"What are you asking for it?" Barbara was dismayed by the avarice that gleamed in Linda Dalby's eyes. Dana's mother hadn't followed up on any of the openings she'd given her to ask about Dana. Her only concern seemed to be for the painting, and even it appeared to matter only for its monetary value rather than the subject it portrayed.

"I've no wish to sell it," Barbara responded coolly. "I'm surprised you haven't guessed that its value goes way beyond money. The child is my grandchild. In fact, he's my only grandson so far. He's also your grandchild."

"My . . . What are you saying?" Mrs. Dalby's eyes narrowed, though she continued to glance hungrily at the portrait she still held in her hands.

"Dana married my son Matt more than three years ago. Little Joshua is almost two and the delight of our entire family. Recently we learned he has a severe blood disease and will die without a bone marrow transplant." She hurried on while Linda Dalby remained speechless. "He needs a donor whose tissue is almost identical to his own. All of our family have been tested without finding a compatible donor. That's why I've come to you. Close family members are his best chance of a match. Will you agree to be tested?"

"I don't think Stephen will allow that," Linda responded.

"Surely, that's your decision," Barbara inserted smoothly.

Linda was still for several seconds, her eyes vacant as though she looked inward to some picture only she could see.

"Joshua is a beautiful child with a sweet, gentle personality. Already he shows signs of his mother's artistic talent. Coloring books don't interest him; he wants to make his own pictures. Like Dana, he loves bright colors, and like his father he enjoys his world orderly and neat. His Grandpa Bingham brags that one day, when Josh is old enough, the family construction firm will have to expand to include its own architect," Barbara continued to speak of Joshua although the woman seated across the desk from her didn't appear to be a likely candidate for "Grandmother of the Year." It was hard to imagine her wiping up spilled milk or changing a diaper, and the chance that she'd ever get down on the floor and make truck noises with a two-year-old were slim to none. Still she was a mother and Josh's grandmother; there had to be some feeling for the child deep inside her.

"Twenty thousand is as high as I'll go," Linda spoke, her eyes still trained on the small portrait, she held possessively in her hands.

"I told you, the portrait isn't for sale." Barbara was shocked that nothing she'd said seemed to matter to this woman. Her only concern seemed to be for the portrait.

"That's my final offer," the woman continued. "It may take some time to find a buyer, and allowing for a reasonable profit for the gallery must be a consideration."

Struggling to control the words she'd like to fling at this woman, Barbara calmly reached across the desk to reclaim the portrait. She met a slight resistance, but finally Linda's fingers released their grasp.

"Perhaps you should leave," Dana's mother's voice was brittle and contained no warmth Barbara could detect.

"You gave Dana life, and now you have a chance to save her child's life. Doesn't that mean anything to you?" Barbara mustered control to remain calm and pleasant. Too much was at stake to admit defeat at the first obstacle.

"Dana made her choice." A note of bitterness seeped into Linda's voice. "She has a rare talent, which she threw away to become a Mormon. I pulled strings to get her into a prestigious academy in Paris when she was just fourteen. Her father spent a fortune on her education, and she chose to transfer to Berkeley. I could have guided her career and helped her achieve the prominence in the art world her talent deserves, but she allowed herself to be distracted by religious nonsense, then that boy. She's wasting her gift!"

"She didn't stop being your daughter when she made choices you disagreed with," Barbara attempted to reason with her.

"She became an embarrassment." Linda clasped her hands together and leaned forward across her desk, allowing the bitterness she harbored to show briefly on her face. "Your kind have caused nothing but trouble here in San Francisco. I want you to leave."

Carefully Barbara rose to her feet. For a moment she thought her legs might give way as she struggled to control her anger. Looking Linda straight in the eye, she asked, "That's your final word? You care nothing for your daughter and are willing to let your grandson die?"

"It's probably for the best. She'll never paint anything of real significance as long as she allows herself to be sidetracked by an infant or some strange religion."

Feeling sick, Barbara walked from the room. Mechanically she placed one foot in front of the other. Matt had warned her that Dana's family wasn't like other families. She had assumed Matt meant the Dalbys were different like their nonmember neighbors, the Brewsters and the Cohens, were different. Joe Brewster was seldom seen without a beer can in one big fist, and when he had coached the Little League team his son and Hadley played on, Joe could turn the air blue with words Barbara had preferred her youngest son wasn't exposed to. His wife, Betty, spent every Sunday playing golf or shopping at the mall with her teenage daughters. The Cohens, who lived on the other side of the Bingham home, observed different holidays and their lives seemed filled with strange rituals and regulations. But despite their different beliefs, Barbara had never doubted either couple's deep commitment to their children or their basic goodness, and both families had quickly offered to be tested when they learned of Joshua's illness. How naive she'd been, Barbara thought.

She paid little attention to where her footsteps led her until the clanging of a trolley car made her pause. Impulsively, she joined a line of people waiting to board the car. In minutes she found a seat and glanced curiously outside, but not even a fabled trolley, climbing a scenic hill in America's possibly most exotic city, could hold her thoughts at bay.

She'd begun this journey so filled with hope. Her many years in the business world, coupled with a lifetime of church service, had taught her invaluable negotiating skills. She knew how to get her way, how to set and complete goals, even how to work with difficult people. That she might fail hadn't occurred to her.

Failure wasn't something she handled well. She liked winning better, and this failure was harder to accept than any other in her life.

She'd come to terms with her failure to support her husband's business ventures, even her failure to be the feminine, charming wife Warner had every right to expect her to be. She'd realized the futility and stopped years ago; no longer pushing herself to be the perfect cook and homemaker. Today's experience had given her a pretty good idea of how badly she'd failed as Dana's mother-in-law. What she couldn't face was failing Joshua.

Eventually she made her way back to her hotel room. She shed her shoes as she walked through the door and headed straight for the shower. Her feet ached and she felt shrouded in a layer of grime. One corner of her mouth quirked in wry amusement as she thought how she'd visited two elegantly appointed businesses that day and had come away feeling as though she'd wallowed in filth. As the stinging spray wiped away real and imagined dirt, her thoughts once more turned to her grandson, struggling for his life hundreds of miles away in Salt Lake City.

Quietly a truth that had lingered at the edge of her mind all day crystalized in her mind. Should Joshua die, she could comfort herself with the knowledge that there had never been a day in his short life that he had not been loved. The same could not be said of his mother. Had she ever truly been loved for herself, before Matt and Joshua? Barbara knew the answer was no. She'd worried needlessly about Dana's inexperience with the Church, and had doubted that Dana would know how to raise her children in the gospel. Now she knew Dana's lack of church experience wasn't the problem. If she lacked, it was in the area of being loved. She held herself aloof from the Bingham family because she had no idea how families were supposed to interact.

Feelings of guilt swept through her as she caught a glimpse of the harm her suspicions had caused. Because she doubted Dana, she had caused both Warner and Matt to doubt Dana, too. She herself knew something of loneliness and not-quite fitting in. Why hadn't she seen those same qualities in Dana? Once more she found herself remembering that long ago day when Warner's partner had said those cruel things, causing her to doubt Warner's commitment to their marriage, to her. The pain and insecurity had never gone away. Remorse swamped her heart as she acknowledged she'd dealt the same kind of blow to Dana. In her heart she'd never quite forgiven Hal Downey, and it was unlikely that Dana would ever forgive her.

Resolution began to form in her heart. She wasn't finished yet—with her daughter-in-law or with searching for a donor. Rapidly, she pulled on pajama pants and began to button the sleek satin matching shirt. It was time to call Warner.

CHAPTER ELEVEN

Matt unlocked the door to their house and held it for Dana to precede him. She hadn't said much on the ride from the hospital, but the silence hadn't felt stilted or oppressive as had much of the time they'd spent together since Josh had been hospitalized. He'd been surprised Dana had left the hospital without an argument. She'd been angry the one previous time he'd brought her home, when she'd become so exhausted she'd fallen asleep, and he'd given her no choice in the matter. He could only surmise she'd taken Dr. Young's advice to heart and had realized she couldn't spend all her nights at the hospital anymore and be prepared to be a donor for Josh.

He'd returned from their baby's room to find his wife and his father with their heads close together, deep in conversation. To say he'd been surprised would be an understatement. Neither volunteered any information on the subject they'd been discussing. He was curious, but some instinct warned him not to pry. He was simply grateful his wife and his father had parted on what appeared to be friendly terms and that Dana's spirits were better than they'd been for a long time.

As always the house seemed gloomy as he stepped through the door. He'd spent little time in it lately, but even that amount of time had simply added to his fatigue and depression. Suddenly he had a picture of Dana and Josh spending long days here in this dark house while he was at work. The picture was all wrong. Whenever he thought of Dana, she wasn't surrounded by somber colors. Somehow he'd kept a picture of Dana in their California apartment in his mind's eye. He'd refused to see the reality of her world since they'd moved here. How could he have been so blind?

"What do you think?" he asked abruptly. "Should we sell this place and start over with something new, or should we haul all this stuff to the D.I.? I can probably repaint the whole place in a week or two."

"What?" Dana looked confused.

"I hate dark colors. You do too. So let's stop worrying about Mother's feelings, and either get rid of this place, or turn it into something we can live with."

"What made you decide to do that now?"

"I don't know. Yes, I do. I've been here alone a lot of nights while you were at the hospital, and I realized something. When you're here, it doesn't seem so bad, because you are the light and color in my life. But without you, I feel like I'm coming home to an old dark cave. While I was putting in a lot of overtime, you and Josh were here alone. It must have been awful."

"I-I took Josh to the park a lot," she admitted hesitantly.

"It's a wonder you didn't just move over there." He smiled with a bit of self-mockery in his eyes. "When Josh comes home, I want wherever we live to be bright and happy, the way you made our Berkeley apartment."

Her face lit up for just a moment, then shadows of pain moved across her eyes. "Do you think we'll really bring him home again one day?"

"Dana," he said, his arms wrapped around her. "I wish I could promise he would get well, but I don't know. I want him to be strong and healthy, and to see him run and play again. Sometimes I want to yell and scream, maybe pound on something, because I'm so frustrated and frightened. Then I think if my faith were stronger I could give him a blessing so powerful he'd have to get well, but I can't do it. Either my faith isn't that strong, or I feel hesitant to tell God what to do."

Dana looked startled. "I don't think we should tell God he has to make Joshua well. But I can't say 'thy will be done either.'"

"I know what you mean," Matt whispered. "Sometimes I think I spend as much time praying for the strength to accept whatever happens, as I do praying he will get well."

They stood silently for several minutes and Matt allowed himself to hope. It was a small thing, but he sensed a rapport that had been missing for a terribly long time between him and his wife. It wasn't much, but it was a beginning, he told himself as Dana freed herself and wandered toward the kitchen. Matt swallowed a groan. He knew what she would find there. Cereal bowls and glasses filled the sink and were stacked on the drainboard. The nights he'd returned to the house, he hadn't bothered to wash the few dishes he'd gotten dirty. Even when the floors and counter tops gleamed with polish and the window blind was all of the way up, the kitchen was gloomy, but cluttered and dirty the room was definitely oppressive.

She didn't say anything about the mess, only stood tiredly looking around as though she didn't recognize the room. "Is there anything left to eat?" she finally asked.

"Yes, your friend, Mandy, brought over a casserole and a loaf of bread two days ago. There's some of that left. I'll pop it in the microwave. It'll be ready in a couple of minutes." He hurried toward the refrigerator.

He was surprised and relieved that Dana wanted to eat. She hadn't shown much interest in food since this whole ordeal began. By the time the casserole was hot, he had the table cleared and two places set. He found the loaf of bread in the ice box and pulled a couple of slices free to place in the toaster to thaw. Dana hadn't been idly standing by while he prepared a late supper for the two of them. She had filled the sink with hot, soapy water, then set glasses and bowls in the water to soak.

"It's ready," Matt set the casserole dish in the middle of the table. After Dana was seated, he took his place opposite her and mumbled a hasty blessing on their meal. He was surprised when Dana placed two heaping spoonfuls of the casserole on her plate and slowly, methodically ate it all. The casserole contained hamburger and Dana generally picked at anything containing meat, or ignored it completely.

When she caught him watching her, a faint blush tinged her cheek. "Dr. Young said I have to be rested and gain ten pounds before I can donate platelets," she defended her uncharacteristic appetite. "He said he won't consider me for a bone marrow transplant unless Josh's platelet level falls below five and his condition becomes an immediate life-threatening emergency. If that happens, I have to be ready."

That explained a lot, both why she'd left the hospital without a fight and her willingness to eat.

"You're a good mother," he whispered softly. She ducked her head and stared fixedly at her plate. She was probably remembering that just a short time ago he'd suspected her of being the worst possible mother. He must have been out of his mind to even temporarily entertain any doubts about her devotion to Josh.

Dana couldn't speak. Matt's words were a roundabout request for forgiveness, but there was no way to put her feelings into words, because she didn't fully understand them herself. Today when Matt's father spoke with her, she found forgiving him relatively easy. It wasn't hard to accept that his love and fear for Joshua had prompted him to do what he thought was necessary to protect Josh. In a way she actually found it reassuring to know Warner's feelings for her child ran so deep, he'd risk public embarrassment for his grandson's sake.

In an odd way the terrible accusation had released a barrier between her and her father-in-law. She'd known, in an intellectual way, that Warner had never attacked his sons the way her father beat Rick, and that he wouldn't hurt Joshua physically, but he was a large, strong man. Some remnant of fear from her childhood had pushed her to excessive caution. Now she knew with her heart, as well as her mind, that she'd never have to fear for Josh's safety when he was with his grandfather.

The knowledge was freeing in some indefinable way. She had never known her own grandfather and it was satisfying to know that Josh had something she'd secretly longed for and never experienced. It was almost like realizing a hidden fantasy of her own.

She truly didn't resent Warner's expectation that his sons spend long hours with the business either. Her father had devoted endless hours to his career, but there was a difference she could readily see and accept. Her father had kept his business dealings strictly to himself. He'd been secretive and quick to punish if she or Rick were even mildly inquisitive or innocently touched any of his papers. Warner wasn't like that. He discussed every aspect of his business affairs with his sons. They were his partners. He'd allowed Ann, who knew a lot more about horses than furniture, to decorate his office. Today he'd sought Dana's opinion on whether or not he should continue to pursue the Barringer project and openly admitted his uneasiness about dealing with Paul Barringer. He'd listened to her opinions as though they really mattered.

But if forgiving Warner had been so easy, why didn't those same feelings extend to Matt? Matt had also been concerned for Josh, and he hadn't even been the one to call the police. He had apologized and shown her nothing but consideration since that awful night. Still forgiving an overt act such as calling the police was easier than getting past something as intangible as a look in her husband's eyes that told her he didn't trust her.

She wouldn't think about it now. Her feelings were too complex, and she was tired. In spite of her fatigue, she was willing to admit she was glad she hadn't returned to the house alone. She wasn't certain what her feelings for Matt were anymore, but she was glad he was sitting across from her tonight, and that she could lean on him just a little. It was probably unrealistic to expect the kind of trust she thought had existed between Matt and herself in light of the evidence that had appeared so damning. Still she hadn't considered the possibility that Matt had struck Josh for even a second, and she was the one who had first-hand knowledge of abuse and a built-in suspicion of men. The magic they once shared might not ever be there again, but many marriages endured without it. Peace and a comfortable contentment might be all she had a right to expect.

"Did Dad tell you Mother flew to California this morning?" Matt's question startled her, and she suspected he was saying more than his words suggested.

"No, he didn't mention it."

"I thought he probably hadn't." Matt shook his head. "He was afraid telling you might upset you, but I think you have a right to know. She's gone to see your father."

"See Father?" She repeated dumbly, her head whirling. For a minute she thought she might faint. "Why would she do that?"

"She thinks your family is Josh's only chance, and that if they're approached in person, they won't be able to refuse to help him."

"Didn't you warn her?" She spoke from a well of painful memories and a hint of fear. When Barbara had proposed the idea, Dana had thought briefly that perhaps the two deserved each other, but down deep she knew her father would eat her mother-in-law alive. For all of Barbara Bingham's brash, know-it-all air, she was terribly naive when it came to the world her father inhabited.

"I didn't know she'd gone," Matt admitted with a worried air. "Just before we left the hospital, Dad told me. They don't know that I tried to meet him before we were married, or that two of his security people roughed me up for my effort. They know nothing about all the vandalism to our apartment and car, or that someone got into the school's computer system and tampered with our grades right after we were married." He attempted to control the lingering anger, knowing that to express it would only hurt Dana. If only there had been some way to prove Stephen Dalby had been behind those cowardly acts!

"He'll retaliate, you know." She shuddered, remembering leaving the courtroom where she'd testified on Rick's behalf at his sentencing hearing. She'd found her windows and headlights smashed and ugly words spray-painted across her car's interior. Her father had made certain Rick got the heaviest sentence possible and had blocked her brother's first parole hearing two years ago. He had also refused to let her take any of her paintings with her when she left home to join the Church. An ugly suspicion grew in her mind.

"Do you think my father could be behind the problems at your company?" she spoke her thoughts aloud.

Matt looked grim. "It's a possibility I hadn't considered, but I think I'd better have a talk with Dad."

"Perhaps both of us should," Dana spoke from an aching heart but with resigned determination.

"We're both too tired now. Let's get some sleep and discuss this with Dad tomorrow." Matt pushed back his chair and began gathering up dishes. "You go to bed, I'll just clear the table and lock up."

———•———

Warner set his glass on the coaster Barbara kept on his desk to prevent moisture rings from damaging the fine old wood. He liked this desk. Somehow it fit him just right, with its ample surface, multitude of drawers, and warm, rich color. He didn't think he'd ever get accustomed to working at the one Ann had selected for his office. It occupied more space than this old desk, but it only had two drawers. Every time he wanted something, he had to get up and paw through some fancy cabinet halfway across the room or call Robyn to find it for him.

He shifted a few papers and acknowledged, as he often did, that he liked the contrast of rolls of blue prints spread against the dark wood. Even his large, calloused hands—smudged with ink and traces of oil etched deeply into the lines that grew deeper each year—looked right against the desk which he'd inherited from his father-in-law. His father-in-law had been a fine man, a little gruff and a tad too strict, but he'd welcomed Warner as a son even before Barbara made up her mind to have him. He'd be forever grateful for the help and advice the man had given him in starting his business and for being his mentor, especially since he had half a dozen sons of his own to see established in their own careers.

He smiled, remembering his first encounter with Barbara's father. He'd first fallen in love with Barbara in the tenth grade when the solemn eighth grader sat in front of him in algebra class, but he hadn't gotten up the courage to ask her out until he was almost through with college. He'd watched her from a distance for years, and knew some of her brothers quite well, but he'd never actually met her father until shortly after he returned from his mission. It had been at the state fair, of all places. He'd paused to watch various men and boys test their strength against that of a brawny lumberjack who swung an ax to split logs in an incredible show of strength. The contenders' efforts were pitiful compared to that of the lumberjack until one man stepped up to the log pile with a broad grin and shoulders that matched those of the reigning champion. With the blast of a whistle, the race was on. Massive logs were reduced to kindling in minutes, and when the logs were gone, the two giants wrestled to a draw over an ax. When a halt was called, the lumberjack swept up the log lying in a temporary man-made pond used to exhibit his own log rolling skills and flung it across the arena. Rafe Olson calmly walked over to the log and tossed it back. The two men had then embraced each other with a roar of laughter.

"Way to go, Dad!" a voice called and Warner had looked up to see Barbara making her way toward the challenger. Seeing Warner standing nearby, Barbara had beckoned him over to meet her dad in an unexpected gesture of friendship. In time he'd learned the man's integrity matched his mountainous size, and he'd always been a bit in awe of the man he always thought of as a giant among men in every true sense of the word.

He wished she would call. Of course it was still early in California, and he could count on her to telephone as soon as she'd finished the day's business. She'd taken short trips without him before when her business required it, and she always called. Still he felt a restless impatience. This trip wasn't business in the usual sense, and he'd felt uneasy from the moment Barbara announced her intentions. For a strong, savvy woman, she was still naive about men like Dana's father.

He'd never told Barbara or Matt, but before Matt and Dana were married, he'd done a little quiet checking into her father's background. He hadn't learned much except that Dalby was a powerful force in San Francisco civic and political circles, and he had a reputation for hard-nosed ruthlessness in financial affairs. Warren had heard a few unsavory rumors that no one seemed able to substantiate, but if true, the man had ruined more than one individual who had somehow crossed him.

The telephone interrupted his thoughts and he breathed a sigh of relief when Barbara's voice came over the line.

"Are you all right?" he questioned.

"Of course, I'm all right," she responded, but there was something in her voice that troubled Warner.

"How did it go?" he asked as though he hadn't already sensed something wasn't quite the way Barbara felt it should be.

"I don't know how to explain it," she started, in less than her usual confident manner. "Dana's parents didn't welcome news of their daughter. I've never been one to place much importance on abstract impressions when I first meet someone, but Mr. Dalby struck me as . . . I don't know, evil sounds so dramatic, but in his presence I couldn't shake a sense of oppressiveness. I kept expecting something terrible to happen. I don't doubt he was every bit as cruel to his children as Matt told us he was.

"His wife is a glittering fashion statement. I think she's shallow and greedy. Her only interest in her daughter is to see her reach the pinnacle of the art world and accumulate a fortune. Neither one cares anything for Joshua. That sounds terribly harsh and judgmental, but I'm afraid it's the truth."

"Hasty judgements are not always accurate," Warner gently reminded her.

"I know. If nothing else, this trip has convinced me I'm guilty of making hasty judgments where Dana is concerned, but I don't think I'm wrong about her parents. After meeting them, I wonder how she managed to adopt the kind of values that made her receptive to the gospel. And that's another thing—I no longer question her commitment to the gospel." Quickly she told him about the painting in Stephen Dalby's office.

"If he kept one of her paintings, especially that one, he must care something about her," Warner mused.

"That's what I thought, but after meeting the man, I'm convinced he has no idea what the picture represents. He probably only kept it for its monetary value, or to spite Dana."

"He refused to be tested?"

"Refusal is a polite way of expressing his rejection for Josh. He wouldn't even glance at his picture. Linda Dalby was just as bad, only she wanted to keep that little portrait of Josh because she thought she could get a lot of money for it." Barbara went on to describe both visits to Dana's parents, and Warner let her speak without interrupting.

"What time will you arrive back here tomorrow?" he asked when she finished.

"I don't plan to return tomorrow," Barbara answered, then hurried on to explain. "I'm not ready to give up yet. In the morning I'll find Dana's sister. She may be more cooperative than their parents."

"I don't know. From everything I know of Stephen Dalby, he's not a man to displease. It might be best if you come on home and we have our attorney contact her."

"Warner, I can't give up. I researched aplastic anemia on the Internet and found a book about it at the library. The longer it takes to find a donor for Josh, the less likely he is to survive, and if he starts getting platelet transfusions, there's a greater risk he'll reject the transplant if we do find a donor. Other treatments aren't at all promising; they're only meant to buy time, not cure him, and I refuse to give up on a full recovery for him."

"You've tried. Perhaps it's time to leave it in God's hands," Warner spoke with a catch in his voice.

"You know very well how I feel on that score," Barbara huffed. "I think when trials come to us, we should ask God for instruction and support, but He expects us to get off our duffs and do something ourselves. My father always said God answers our prayers after we've done all we can do, and I don't believe I've done all I can yet."

"I don't think it's a good idea to approach the Dalbys again," Warner cautioned.

"No, I won't, but I'm going to find Dana's sister. Her husband is running for the legislature, so they're probably more open and service-minded than the Dalbys. If she's anything like Dana, she won't refuse."

After hanging up the phone, Barbara prowled about the room, feeling optimism and discouragement by turns. She turned out the lights and opened the curtains. The view was disappointing. Thick, dirty fog obscured all but the closest buildings and even the few lights she could see appeared faded and dull. Something about the night and the fog brought an aching, cold emptiness inside the room, and she longed to be home in her own bed with Warner's comfortable bulk beside her.

A light rap on the door sent her scurrying for her robe.

"Delivery!" a voice called out.

Leaving the door on the security chain, she opened it wide enough to peek into the hall. It appeared empty. Glancing down, she spotted a long, gold florist box tied with a shimmering gold ribbon. Obviously the delivery boy had left the box and gone on his way. That was unusual. It was her experience that delivery people, whether they were delivering pizza or documents, always hung around expecting a tip.

Releasing the chain, she picked up the box and carried it inside. She felt a little thrill just looking at the box. It was from Warner, of course. He always had roses delivered to her office on her birthday. Sometimes one of the boys sent her flowers on Mother's Day, most often Robert since he'd married Ann. But she couldn't remember one single occasion when she'd received flowers for no reason at all. Warner must have sensed she needed a little cheering up tonight and called the hotel florist as soon as he hung up from speaking to her earlier.

Her fingers trembled slightly as she reached for the ribbon. She wasn't the kind of woman men sent flowers to. Even as a young woman, the only time she remembered receiving flowers was the time Eddie Cartwright gave her a carnation corsage, sprinkled with glitter, when he escorted her to her high school senior prom. She grimaced inwardly, remembering Eddie. He had been at least three inches shorter than her, and he had sweaty hands and the worst case of acne she'd ever seen. Unfortunately, Eddie was fairly typical of the few dates she'd had before Warner had asked her out.

It wasn't like Warner to send flowers, which made this gift doubly precious. She suddenly smiled, remembering all the blenders, washers, and lawn chairs she'd received over the years on various gift-giving occasions. No one could accuse Warner of being particularly romantic, but at least he never forgot birthdays or anniversaries.

Trying not to act like a silly school girl, she untied the bow and lifted the box lid to stare in astonishment at a smelly heap of black lumps that might have once been flowers. A flashback to an old movie where the heroine received such a gift jumped before her eyes. The girl had screamed and become hysterical with fear. Well, Barbara wasn't about to become hysterical. If this was someone's idea of a joke, it was neither funny nor very original. And she certainly wasn't the kind of woman who became hysterical over something as melo-dramatic as dead flowers.

To her way of thinking, the flowers were more ridiculous than frightening. She knew more than one girl who had gotten second-hand cemetery flowers as Halloween pranks, and even one who received an invitation to the prom in such a silly fashion. She couldn't think of anyone with a warped enough sense of humor to have sent the dismal bouquet. It certainly wasn't something Warner or the boys would think up, and she didn't know anyone in San Francisco except Eddie, who didn't even know she was in town, though she intended to call on him before she left.

Could someone mean to frighten her? The Dalbys hadn't appreci-ated her visit, but surely they were much too sophisticated to perpe-trate a childish stunt like this.

Gathering up the fancy box and its contents, she dumped the entire mess in a trash can, washed her hands, and went to bed. Hours later, unable to sleep, she stared at the dim ceiling and wondered why with all the disappointments of the day, her thoughts kept returning to that box of rotten flowers. She'd been foolish to assume Warner had sent her flowers. Her husband wasn't the romantic, sensitive kind. And she wasn't the giddy, helpless sort that expected that kind of thing. There was no reason to feel this deep, aching hurt.

At last she fell asleep, only to be awakened a short time later by the ringing of the telephone. Groggily she reached for the instrument.

"Hello," she mumbled, just awake enough to feel a surge of fear. Had something happened at home? Was Joshua worse?

"Hello," she repeated, now fully awake. Silence met her ear. "Is someone there?" She spoke sharply. The only response was a soft click, followed by the familiar hum of the dial tone.

CHAPTER TWELVE

Josh was awake when Dana and Matt reached his hospital room. Dr. Young was with him and when the doctor saw them, he motioned for them to put on gowns and join him. They played with Josh for a few minutes and gave him a few of his familiar toys from home that Dana had scrubbed and brought, hoping they would cheer him. He laughed and hugged the patchwork bunny she handed to him, bringing tears to her eyes. Until this illness there had been few nights the little boy had fallen asleep without the bunny, which she'd made for him, in his arms. Too soon Dr. Young informed them it was time to leave.

"He's holding his own," Dr. Young said as they stepped into the hall. "The medication is working for now, buying us a little time."

"But it won't cure him?" Dana asked, already knowing the answer.

"I won't rule out the possibility, nor do I want to give you false hope. The drugs I'm giving him probably won't cure him, though they do sometimes give a weakened system a chance to rest. In a few cases the rest is all that is needed to cause the bone marrow to resume functioning," Dr. Young explained. His tone of voice told her he didn't expect that to happen in Joshua's case.

No one spoke as they continued down the hall until they reached the small waiting room, then Dr. Young turned to Matt, "Yesterday I explained to your wife that I ordered new tests, which indicated this improvement in Joshua's condition doesn't appear to be permanent. It's more like a remission or a leveling out period where he's not getting well, but he's not getting any worse. If he can rebuild some of his strength, and your wife can gain a little weight and become more rested, we should consider her as a donor."

Matt was clearly puzzled. "I thought you told us she wasn't a close enough match."

"The best match is an identical twin or at least an HLA-matched sibling. Occasionally another donor, not necessarily a relative even, will provide a 'perfect' match. When that happens, the patient has an 80% chance of survival. Using a less closely matched donor, such as Dana, sharply reduces the long-term survival rate down to ten to twenty percent." Dr. Young paused when Matt gasped.

"I know those sound like pretty poor odds, but Dana only has a mismatch of two loci. That's not as close a match as I would like, but significantly better than any other alternative." Dr. Young's face was so serious and his words so frightening, Dana had to struggle not to collapse with grief. Matt's hand tightened against her arm to the point of becoming painful, but she didn't pull away.

"I would like to begin the conditioning regimen in a few days if Josh continues to be stable," Dr. Young went on. "If you agree, he'll be given a high dose of cyclophosphamide followed by total body irradiation. This step is necessary to destroy his remaining bone marrow, including his immune system, so we can replace the entire hematopoietic system and reduce the possibility of his body rejecting the graft."

Dana refused to think about the possibility of Josh's little body rejecting the bone marrow she was more than willing to give him. Reading between the lines of Dr. Young's explanation, she understood that without the transplant, hope for Josh's survival was almost nonexistent. But the chance he should suffer so much, then still succumb to graft-versus-host disease, the dreaded GVHD, was unthinkable.

"My mother has flown to California to contact Dana's family. If she has any success, Dana might not be the only possible donor."

Although Matt spoke as though he were thinking aloud, Dana knew he didn't hold out much hope of any humanitarian gesture from her family. He was only grasping for hope of better odds for Joshua's recovery.

"That's good." Dr. Young looked interested. "Though I think we should proceed with the expectation of Dana being our donor. If a better match is found, we'll be ready."

Rain drizzled through the fog when Barbara left the hotel. The city felt cold and unwelcoming as her cab swept through the watery streets, and it was with a great deal of trepidation she left the cab an hour later to approach a large cedar and white brick home tucked back in the trees in an obviously well-to-do neighborhood over-looking the ocean.

"Please wait," she instructed the driver before passing through white wrought-iron gates, which stood wide as though she were expected. Walking purposefully along the curved driveway, she noted that this house like all the others in this remote area was secluded from its neighbors by a small wood of thick trees and tangled shrubs. The fog drifted in wisps like cobwebs clinging to the trees, and in the distance she could hear a roar she couldn't quite place.

She was met at the door by a uniformed maid who politely invited her inside. When she announced she'd come to see Marilyn Vincent, the maid escorted her to a sitting room at the back of the house before disappearing to speak with Mrs. Vincent.

Dominating the room were floor to ceiling windows on three sides. The room perched like an observation platform on a cliff over-looking the water. Through the thinning fog, she caught sight of waves crashing against huge boulders, breaking to spew mist and foam high in the air. She knew now the source of the roar she heard as she approached the house.

Seating herself on a white brocade chair, Barbara looked around the room, noticing the white sofa and chairs. The walls, the filmy sheer curtains, even the thick plush carpet were white. A centerpiece of white porcelain roses with silver leaves was precisely centered on a glass coffee table. Everything in the room was white, with the only contrasts being clear glass or silver.

"It's obvious there are no little boys living in this house," she muttered under her breath.

"Ah, but I wish one did," a melodic voice came from behind her.

Embarrassed, Barbara turned to see a slender woman of about thirty, standing behind her in a loose, gauzy, buttercup-yellow sun dress. Matching high-heeled sandals accentuated her height and poise. She wore her platinum, blond hair in a short, fashionable frizz. She was both beautiful and elegant.

Rising, Barbara held out her hand. "I'm sorry. I certainly didn't mean to criticize, but after raising four sons, I'm acutely aware of what a little boy might do to your lovely things."

"Don't worry about it. The decorator designed this room for its dramatic effect. It's supposed to impress guests. And you're right, it's hardly an appropriate play area for a child. If we ever have a little boy, he'll have his own suite of rooms decorated in all his favorite colors." She smiled widely and indicated Barbara should be seated again.

She seems like a pleasant young woman, Barbara mused as she sank back onto the brocade chair. Marilyn took a similar chair nearby.

"Now, Ms. Bingham," Marilyn smiled again. "Maria gave me your name, but she wasn't certain which paper you represent."

"Oh, I'm not a reporter," Barbara hastened to assure the other woman. "Please, call me Barbara," she added. Now she understood her easy access to the house and to Marilyn Vincent. The woman was expecting a reporter to interview her. She wondered if she'd now be asked to leave. Instead the elegant woman eased back in her chair with a slight smile.

"All right, Barbara," Marilyn emphasized her name slightly. "If you're not a reporter, what is this about?"

"It's about family," Barbara didn't hesitate to explain. As she had the day before, she pulled the small portrait of Joshua from her purse. "I'm your sister, Dana's, mother-in-law. She needs help desperately for her son." Forestalling any possibility that Marilyn might misunderstand, she hurried on. "Money isn't a problem; she doesn't need financial help. Matt and Dana's son, Joshua, has a rare blood disease and will die without a bone marrow transplant." She hurriedly launched into an explanation of blood cells and HLA-matched donors, finishing with a plea for Marilyn to be tested.

Marilyn sat as still as a statue until Barbara finished, and continued to sit for several long minutes afterward. Finally she lifted her eyes to state more than ask, "You've spoken to my father."

"Yes, and your mother," Barbara struggled to keep her voice even.

"They turned you down." Marilyn's voice was flat.

"Yes, that's why I've come to you," she admitted.

Marilyn picked up the picture of Joshua and stared at it for several long minutes. Finally returning it to the table, she stood, and turning her back to Barbara, walked toward the wall of glass. She remained motionless for a long time staring toward the ocean. Barbara suspected the young woman didn't see the waves crashing against the rocky shore nor notice that the fog had almost dissipated, leaving a spectacular vista of white-capped waves rolling relentlessly toward shore. Far in the distance a ship grew larger as it moved into the channel that would carry it safely into the great bay.

Barbara watched Marilyn's slender shoulders shudder and heard her whisper to the glass, "I can't do it."

"I won't lie and say there's nothing to it," Barbara spoke honestly. "But it isn't as bad as you imagine. Donor marrow is obtained from the pelvic bones under general anaesthesia and may require multiple aspirations, but the donor recovers completely in a very short time. You needn't even come to Utah. The bone marrow can be harvested in a hospital here, then flown to Josh in Salt Lake."

"You don't understand." Marilyn turned to face her. "The procedure doesn't matter. Father won't allow it."

"But you're an adult. You don't need your father's permission," Barbara protested.

Marilyn's eyes became bleak. "I'm not as brave or as smart as Dana. I never have been. I've always been the perfect daughter, the perfect wife, and I suppose one day I'll be the perfect mother. Father has always been extremely cruel to those who are not perfect. We had a brother, who was far from perfect, and Father punished him severely." She spoke as though her brother no longer existed.

"It was Dana who sneaked into Rick's room to bandage his

wounds and smuggle food to him. She knew how to become invisible when Father came home, and she found a way to get away to a school in Europe when she turned fourteen. She was always Mother's favorite and Mother protected her, sometimes at Rick's or my expense. By the time Dana returned from Europe, she had enough money of her own from her paintings to choose her own school. She escaped Father completely when she became a Mormon. Obviously she chose her own husband and has a child who loves and adores her."

"She didn't become a Mormon to escape her father." Barbara gently protested.

"Whether she did it on purpose or not, it worked, didn't it?" Marilyn's voice held a tinge of bitterness. "Father didn't choose her husband, pick her house, select her decorator, decide when she should have a child, or choose her child's name."

"No, but she didn't have as much voice as you think in selecting a home or decorating it," Barbara said, feeling a hint of guilty conscience. "You seem to be implying Dana received some kind of preferential treatment in your family. She believes you were your father's favorite, not her."

"Heavens no," Marilyn scoffed. "Father hates all three of us. I think the only reason he didn't insist Mother abort us was because he enjoyed making her suffer. He only tolerates me because I do what I'm told, and because I had the good sense to marry a wealthy, rising politician from one of San Francisco's oldest families. He believes he can catapult Preston into national prominence with his money and connections, then still control him. He doesn't understand that Preston is every bit as ruthless as he is and will cut him out as soon as he has what he wants."

Barbara arched her eyebrows. Once again Marilyn's laughter betrayed a deep bitterness. "It's hard to know who is using whom, but the fact remains, I can't help Dana. I never could, even when she was a little girl and Father would lock her in the wine cellar for feeding a stray cat or for slipping candy under Rick's door. I had to tiptoe around the house and be careful not to make any mistakes, so he wouldn't punish me, too. I was older; it would have been much worse for me, and Mother would have been angry, too. I learned early to never underestimate my mother's temper. She was always afraid I would do something to make Father so angry he would break Dana's fingers, so she'd never become a famous artist who would, in turn, make Mother rich and famous—and independent of Father."

"Your childhood couldn't have been pleasant, but you have a chance to give your nephew, not only a better life, but a chance at life, and it would cost you nothing other than a little time," Barbara tried to persuade the other woman.

"Any hint of a connection with the Mormons might cost Preston the election," Marilyn responded, looking at Barbara directly. "You people have antagonized a lot of people, especially a few powerful leaders, in San Francisco with your fight against gay marriage. Neither Father nor Preston will allow a hint of our connection to Dana to taint Preston's campaign."

"I know a number of people who are quite vocal in their support of gay agendas, but not one of them would condone allowing a child to die because his family's religious or political views differed from theirs." Barbara was equally candid as she rose to her feet and paced toward Marilyn. "Are you telling me that you are refusing to give your own nephew a chance at life because Dana chose to become a Mormon?"

Marilyn turned her back to stare once more out to sea, and Barbara guessed she had no intention of answering her question. She supposed she might as well leave. She returned Joshua's portrait to her bag and turned to move slowly toward the door. Marilyn's voice stopped her.

"I hope I would have the courage to help if I could," she said quietly. "All my life I've blamed my father, then Preston, for turning me into a prisoner, but lately I've begun to think I'm my own jailor. I've wasted years resenting Rick and Dana because they found a means of escape. I denied my own lack of courage. I should leave, go away like Dana did, but ironically, I've discovered I actually love Preston. If he wins the election, we'll live in Washington. I'll have more freedom than I've ever known, and I want that chance to turn our marriage into a normal one. I think Preston wants that, too."

"I don't see—" Barbara began, but Marilyn cut her off.

"It's not merely a lack of courage that prevents me from helping Dana's baby. For eight years I've wanted a baby so badly it's become an obsession, but Father was adamant that children would hold Preston back, and Preston seemed to agree. A few months ago Preston changed his mind. He thinks a large number of potential voters are likely to vote against him because of his stand on gay rights issues, and that he won't win the election if he can't pull in the family values voters, too. He told my father that he believes an obviously pregnant wife will enhance his image with the family issues bloc, without costing him his more liberal supporters. Privately, he told me he'd always planned to have a family and that both he and his mother would be crushed if he didn't produce an heir."

"Are you saying you're pregnant, and that is the reason you can't donate?" Barbara demanded an answer.

"I don't know. I think I am, but I haven't seen a doctor yet, and I'm too scared to buy one of those home pregnancy tests." Barbara noticed the shine of tears in Marilyn's eyes.

"You might be able to donate even if you are pregnant. You could ask your doctor, and I'm sure we could arrange to keep the whole thing quiet so no one would know of your connection to your sister's child."

With tears spilling down her cheeks, Marilyn shook her head. "I won't risk it," she whispered. With chilling certainty, Barbara knew Marilyn would not change her mind.

Barbara's shoulders slumped as she made her way to the door without the maid's help. Concentrating on each step she took, she made her way down the drive, and breathed a sigh of relief to find her cab still waiting. Leaning back against the seat, she struggled with the pain of failure. She'd been so sure she could convince the Dalbys to help Joshua, but she couldn't have been more wrong.

Thinking of Joshua and his total rejection by his mother's family was too painful. Her mind grasped at peripheral thoughts, anything to delay absorbing the enormity of what was happening. Time was running out for Joshua, and she couldn't bear to think about that. Mentally, and to Warner, she'd referred to Dana's family as a dysfunctional family. She'd had no concept of the odd twists that went into that phrase. Surely it had to be the ultimate oxymoron. How could any unit be called a family when it was so utterly dysfunctional?

Warner's face arose in her mind. He'd gained weight over the years, and his face and his hands had a leathery texture from years of exposure to sun and wind. Still he was the most handsome man she'd ever met. How she'd welcome his arms around her right this minute. Her heart swelled with the enormity of the love she felt for him, touched with a twinge of sadness that his feelings for her didn't run as deep as hers for him.

Sudden overwhelming gratitude filled her that he wasn't like Stephen Dalby with his manicured nails, perfect tan, and spa-polished physique. The two men had few traits in common. Of the two, she was glad she was married to the one who valued his family above all else. Thinking of the love and respect between her husband and sons brought a lump to her throat, and the lump expanded to hot tears that stung the backs of her eyes as images of her sons grew to include her daughters-in-law. The small, smiling faces of her grand-children surfaced, causing the tears she fought to suppress to trickle down her cheeks. They were good people, a good family, and good individuals. With this vivid picture of her loved ones before her, she knew. Warner loved her. He loved her as fiercely as she loved him. A man who headed a family like theirs, did so, from love, not duty.

Hal Downey had been wrong. Suddenly she had a clear picture of herself standing in the hall that day, waiting for Hal to get off the phone. He'd known she was there! He'd said those hurtful things deliberately to distract her from the papers she held in her hand, papers that shouted what she hadn't wanted to believe. He'd deliber-ately planted doubts about Warner's integrity in order to ensure her silence. Astutely he'd zeroed in on her personal insecurities, knowing she'd believe him when he suggested there was nothing about her for Warner to love and suggesting that if her husband had lied to her about his feelings for her, he might just as easily lie about his profes-sional ethics. Hurt and insecurity had driven reason from her mind.

Now she knew the truth. Warner's partner had been skimming from the company, systematically draining its assets before striking out on his own. He'd guessed she'd discovered his dishonest tactics and gambled on keeping her silent. Her own vulnerabilities had allowed him to win. She and Warner had paid a far heavier price than just what Hal Downey had stolen from the company.

She sniffed back tears. This wasn't a time for emotional excesses. She wasn't finished yet. No woman who knew what she knew about loving and being loved could give up now. She had a lot to make up to Warner, and it was time to clear up those old questions. She couldn't wait to get home, but that would have to wait just a little longer. There was someone else she still had to see. She wondered how one went about arranging a visit to one of California's state prisons.

CHAPTER THIRTEEN

Matt was walking from his car to the hospital when his cell phone rang. He reached for it, automatically setting his mind to refuse to go to the office. It wasn't his father's voice or even his secretary's that reached him. Instead he was surprised to hear his mother.

"Matt, I'm sorry to call you at the hospital, but I need your help," she said quickly.

"What's happened? Has Stephen Dalby hurt you?" Matt was instantly angry, remembering the beating Dalby's goons had given him.

"No, he was just as rude and unfeeling as you warned me he would be, but he hasn't done anything . . . unless he's responsible for the childish prank that happened last night."

"Mother, what happened?" His grip tightened on the phone. He truly wouldn't put anything past Dalby. In his estimation the man was evil.

"Oh, it was just silly theatrics. Someone sent me a box of moldy, dead flowers last night." Barbara dismissed the incident as a silly prank, but Matt wasn't so sure that was all it was.

"Mother!"

"Don't worry. They certainly didn't hurt me any, but that isn't what I wanted to talk to you about," she went on, all business again. "You were quite young when your father dissolved his partnership with Hal Downey, so you might not remember him well."

"I know he's one of the major contenders for the Barringer project," he rejoined wryly.

"Well, yes. That's what I'm getting to. Before he and your father ended their partnership, he said some things that hurt my feelings. It just occurred to me that he said those cruel things deliberately to create a rift between your father and me to distract us from what he was doing. He was dishonest, and he stole from the company. I discovered what he was doing, but I kept quiet about it for reasons I won't go into. I know now that was a mistake. I should have exposed him for the crook he is. I made a few calls this morning, and discovered his company is facing a major financial and legal crisis at the present time. It occurred to me, that he might be behind the problems at Bingham Construction. I want you to check into that."

"You think he still holds a grudge after ten years?" Matt tried to hide his incredulity.

"I'm not sure it's a grudge exactly," Barbara went on. "But he was extremely angry when he left because I had blocked a project he thought would make him a wealthy man. My interference also precipitated the dissolution of the partnership before he was able to clean out more of the company's assets. Though heaven knows, he got away with plenty!"

"It seems to me he would avoid Dad—and you—like the plague."

"No, not Hal. I think he'll always want to show us up some way, to either cause us to fail or to take something we want. He despises me for thwarting his plans, but I think he hates your father for the simple reason that Warner's personal integrity highlighted his own failures. I think this is just the kind of stunt he'd try to pull."

"I don't know, but if I can figure out a way, I'll look into it," Matt conceded.

"No, I want you to do more than that. When I left Bingham Construction, I turned everything over to Bob Evans, including a file of questionable expenses, invoices, and letters I gleaned from Hal's records before he left. There are a few things in there Bob might not want brought to light, but examine those, too. There's more involved than what first looks apparent. Get that file, read through it, then take it to your father and explain any financial aspects he might not completely understand. When I get back to Salt Lake, I'll tell him what I suspect and why."

"Sure, I'll do it, but I think you're wrong about Downey." Matt agreed to get the papers for his mother and look them over, then went on, "I suspect Stephen Dalby is behind this. I never told you, but right after Dana and I were married, a hacker got into the college's student records and changed our grades. We couldn't prove it, of course, but we always suspected Dana's father hired someone to do the job. Our apartment and cars were vandalized, too. The man is crazy enough to try to get at Dana through me."

"I'm not sure the man is crazy," Barbara responded carefully, "but he certainly is cold. I agree he's a man we shouldn't dismiss as a possible suspect, but it has been four years since Dana joined the Church, and he disowned her. If he'd wanted to cause trouble on this scale, I think he would have done it before now, and certainly not waited until Dana's brother-in-law started running for the legislature."

Matt's laugh wasn't really humorous. "I guess we have two suspects then. When are you returning?" he changed the subject.

"Not for a few days." Her answer surprised him and then she too changed the subject. "How is Josh? Is there any change?" They discussed Josh for several minutes, then she surprised him again by saying, "Give my love to Dana and Josh," just before hanging up the phone.

For several minutes he pondered in his mind the things his mother had said. The idea of Hal Downey trying to sabotage their bid seemed a bit farfetched, but it was possible. He wouldn't dismiss his mother's suspicions altogether. He'd get the papers she wanted him to see, but first he'd have a talk with Dad about his father-in-law.

He still held the phone in his hand. He punched in the number and asked for Bob Evans. The phone went unanswered for long minutes. Finally Josie picked it up. She sounded rushed, and in the background he could hear Robyn arguing with one of his clerks. He asked for Bob.

"He's not here," Josie told him. "He had a doctor's appointment at ten and you just missed him. Do you want him to call you back when he returns?"

"No, just tell him my mother called. She said she left a file with him ten years ago, and she wants me to read it. Tell him to leave it on my desk, and I'll pick it up later tonight."

"Okay," Josie responded. "Is there anything else?"

"No, just leave the daily status report and my phone messages on my desk like you've been doing."

"I will . . . would you mind, that is, after I finish the letters you dictated last night, if I leave a little early? Bart wasn't feeling well this morning, and I'd like to get home in time to fix him a good dinner."

"Sure, go ahead," Matt responded. "Is everything else all right?"

"Yes, we had another one of those mix-ups this morning. Your dad sent Robyn down here to review the procedure for placing orders with Carol and Tony, and they're both a little miffed that Robyn seems to think all of the messed-up orders we've had lately are their fault."

"I've checked their work several times myself and never found anything wrong with the way they place orders. Assure both of them that I'm satisfied with their work."

"Thank you. And, Matt, I want you to know your little boy is in my prayers."

When Matt hung up the phone, he shook his head, marveling at the concern for his son that was expressed at every turn. It went far beyond family. Both his ward and his parents' ward kept them in meals. Both wards checked every day on Josh's condition, and Dana's visiting teacher visited her almost daily. Bingham Construction employees, from truck drivers to secretaries, had voluntarily been tested for donor compatibility, and they never failed to ask about Josh. He especially appreciated the way Josie kept his office running smoothly while he was out so much.

Josie was a good secretary and a better friend. Matt hadn't been thrilled when he'd first learned that his father had given his own secretary, Robyn, the task of training a secretary for him, even before he had arrived to take his place in the company. He thought Robyn sometimes exceeded her authority, and she assumed a superior role he found irritating at times. But he'd never regretted her choice, even if he had been a bit wary at first.

In the time he'd worked with Josie, Matt had gotten the feeling that her husband didn't appreciate her enough. Perhaps that was a common failing of husbands. He certainly hadn't appreciated Dana enough until after he'd made a real mess of things. Josie had hinted that Bart sometimes stayed out all night and that he frequently suffered deep bouts of depression. His doctor had prescribed some kind of medication for the depression, but Bart wasn't consistent about taking it. Matt knew from his own dealings with the man that his moodiness would be difficult to live with, and from bits and pieces he'd gathered, he suspected Josie's husband never lifted a hand to help her around the house.

Thinking of Bart brought a frown to his face. It did seem that he'd been sick an awful lot lately. That could spell even more trouble for the Barringer project if the company won the bid, since Winn would have to depend heavily on the other two foremen, Robert and Bart, as lead men on a project of that magnitude. And why was Bob Evans seeing a doctor in the middle of the week? He was getting old, but he always appeared to be healthy as a horse. Matt hoped it wasn't something serious. He didn't relish the prospect of getting along without Bob, especially now with the Barringer project about to materialize and Josh so critically ill.

He couldn't help feeling torn in two. He was needed at work, but Josh and Dana needed him, too. Both were important, and this juggling act he was caught up in was creating more pressure than he felt capable of dealing with.

———

Barbara felt certain she was being melodramatic, but the same white sedan had been behind her for quite some time. She'd first noticed it when she crossed the Golden Gate Bridge. Now with rain pounding against the little rental car, and the highway edging perilously close to the bluffs overlooking the bay, she couldn't avoid a shiver of apprehension. She decided that it was just her destination that was putting creepy thoughts in her mind. There couldn't be any connection between that nonsensical note she'd received during breakfast and the car just behind her. The car was just traveling the same direction she was, she assured herself. Still, a look in her mirror confirmed that the white sedan had drawn closer.

There was no reason for the car to be following her. Just because she was on her way to the prison at San Quentin to visit Dana's brother was no reason to imagine something sinister about a car that just happened to be behind her. It was probably just getting closer because she had slowed down when the rain began. It had nothing to do with that absurd note warning her to get out of town that she'd received during breakfast. It was just someone's idea of a practical joke. Dead roses in a gold foil box flashed into her mind, and she pressed a little harder on the gas pedal.

The next time she glanced at the mirror, she didn't see any noticeable difference in the space between her compact and the car behind. The rain was growing heavier and thick coils of fog billowed across the highway, leaving her uncertain whether the road followed a cliff, or if it ran close to the beach. There could be acres of subdivisions between her and the bay for all she knew. She blamed the humidity for the slippery dampness of her hands where they clutched the wheel.

Get a grip, she reminded herself. *This isn't exactly an isolated country road.* A reassuring number of headlights moved steadily toward her, telling her she wasn't alone. According to the road map she'd purchased when she rented the car, the exit wasn't far.

With a nervous glance at the mirror once more, she began to slow and moved into the turning lane right after she passed the sign indicating the San Quentin exit. To her horror, she could see the flash of the turn signal on the white sedan. Frantically she considered going on to the junction with Highway 580, but another check of her side mirror revealed a large truck in the lane to her left. She couldn't pull back into the through lane. She was committed to the cut off.

This road was smaller than the freeway she'd left behind and traffic was lighter, though far from nonexistent. But for the rain and the car behind her, she suspected it would offer a spectacular view. Her heart was in her throat each time she caught a glimpse of the bay to her right or approached a curve. The other car maintained a consistent space between them and made no threatening move toward her, and she chided herself for being uncharacteristically fanciful. Still she couldn't quite shake a sense of impending disaster.

Finally she reached San Quentin and began picking her way toward the prison, following directions she'd received at the car rental desk. With the prison in sight, she stopped at an intersection and once more her eyes sought the rearview mirror. To her relief the white car was gone. She hadn't noticed it turn, and its absence now made her feel foolish, though relieved.

An armed guard peered into her car and asked her to open her trunk before directing her to a parking area. Seeing a white sedan parked on the row ahead of her, she found it impossible to suppress a shiver. Though it looked just like the car that had followed her from San Francisco, it probably wasn't. She should have memorized the license plate number, but that would have given her irrational fear too much credence. White sedans of any make or model were common enough; there was no reason to think this was the same car. She passed through another cadre of guards before being admitted to the forbidding building.

She looked around apprehensively as she joined a line of people, mostly women, waiting for admittance to the visiting area. Some had a hard, ruthless look about them, while others appeared lost and confused. An obviously pregnant young woman clutching a two-year-old by the hand stood behind her, and a little way ahead she saw an elderly couple with bent shoulders, holding hands as they shuffled forward a few steps at a time. Too many faces mirrored a bleakness as hopeless as the dingy prison walls.

An overwhelming sadness for the plight of these women assailed her. Once she might have felt a guilty kind of superiority, but now they touched her heart. Surely these women hadn't been blessed with fathers, husbands, and sons who honored their priesthood as she had. Instinctively she knew that most of these women had seen little of the light of Christ in their lives for a very long time. Gratitude for the blessings of the gospel and for the men in her life, all worthy priesthood holders, brought a sting to the backs of her eyes.

Finally she spoke to a bored, middle aged man wearing a

California State Prisons uniform. "I have an appointment to see Richard Dalby," she spoke crisply.

The man's finger moved slowly down a list on the clipboard he held. He paused, then spoke without lifting his eyes. "Canceled, no visitors allowed."

"What? That can't be. I called yesterday and was told I would be allowed to see him today."

"Sorry," the man mumbled. "Next."

"No!" Barbara refused to yield to the next person in line. "I want to know why I can't see Richard Dalby when I was told last night that I could."

"Look, lady. There are a lot of reasons for canceling a prisoner's visiting privileges. All I know is that your visit has been canceled. He might have decided he doesn't want to see you. Now move along."

"Where's your administrative office?" Barbara held her ground.

"Joe!" He motioned toward one of the armed guards, and Barbara wondered if she was about to be arrested. Before the guard reached them, the man with the clipboard was already speaking to the weary, pregnant mother who had waited behind her.

To her surprise, the guard conducted her down a short hall, unlocked a door, and led her to an office area that looked much like any other office. He motioned her to a seat, spoke briefly to a gray-haired woman at a nearby desk, and left.

After a surprisingly brief wait, the woman motioned for her to come closer. After verifying her name and address, the woman stared silently at her computer screen for several minutes before speaking.

"Mrs. Bingham, you stated when you called yesterday that your daughter-in-law is Richard Dalby's sister. Do you know him well?"

"I've never met him," Barbara stated truthfully. "But I have a message from his sister she wants me to give him. She can't leave her baby who is critically ill, so I offered to come for her."

"His sister has never visited him. There's no record any family member has ever visited him," the woman went on.

"Was my appointment canceled simply because he's never had a family visitor before? Or did he refuse to see me because of my connection to his family?" Barbara was still looking for answers.

"Actually the cancellation had nothing to do with you," the

woman's voice became brisk. "He knew of your intended visit and didn't oppose it. He's in the infirmary this morning. His condition is serious, and his doctor recommended no visitors."

"He's ill?" Barbara's hopes plummeted. If Rick were seriously ill, there would be no point to persuading him to be tested. He couldn't be a donor anyway.

"He's not exactly ill," the woman went on. "He was involved in an altercation with another prisoner last night. Even if his injuries weren't of a serious nature, he wouldn't be allowed to have visitors. Fighting results in an automatic loss of privileges."

Making her way slowly to her car following the brief interview, discouragement sat heavy on Barbara's shoulders. She didn't want to give up, but it could be weeks, possibly several months before Rick would be permitted to have a visitor. Time was running out, and she had failed miserably.

"Barbara?" The sound of her name brought her head up. A figure leaned against the side of her car. In the glare of the bright sunlight which had replaced the rain, she couldn't see a face, only the silhouetted shape of a tall man with sloping shoulders. Her heart began to pound, and she considered running, or at the very least screaming, for one of the guards.

"Barbara." The figure stepped forward. Ready to scream, she hesitated. She could see his face now and there was something familiar about it, but she couldn't quite place where she had seen the man before.

"It's Ed Cartwright," he identified himself with the little boy grin she had once considered his one redeeming physical attribute.

She squinted. "Eddie?" she asked incredulously.

"Well, it's been a long time since anyone except my mother has called me Eddie," he laughed. "But, yes, it's me."

"I can't believe it. What are you doing here?" She shook her head as she waved in a broad gesture, encompassing the prison.

Ed's smile disappeared to be replaced by a grimness she'd never imagined on her old friend's face. "I suspect I'm here for much the same reason you are," he admitted freely. "We're both curious about Richard Dalby, and I'd like to suggest we go somewhere quiet where we can compare notes."

—•—

Twenty minutes later they sat across from each other in a quiet restaurant, waiting for their meals to be brought to their table. Barbara leaned her head back against the padded banquette, eyeing her former classmate. He had changed a great deal from the bashful, pimple-faced boy she'd once known. He certainly hadn't magically become handsome, but he was a far cry from homely. And she'd have to be blind not to notice he was neither short nor skinny anymore, either. With a jumble of questions in her mind, she blurted out whatever came first onto her tongue.

"Did you follow me to the prison?" She'd noted, when they had climbed into their separate cars, that he was the owner of the white sedan she had suspected of trailing her from San Francisco. "And how did you know I was interested in Rick?"

"I guess I did follow you, though it wasn't intentional." Ed's smile was back. "My trip was prompted by an old friend, who knew about my interest in Rick Dalby. He's a doctor who works several hours each day at the prison infirmary. He called me at the paper to tell me about the fight that wasn't really a fight. He was disturbed by what was clearly an attack by another inmate being billed as a fight. I noticed we were following the same route this morning, but I didn't recognize you until I heard you arguing with a guard about your appointment to see Dalby."

"I guess that answers both of my questions," she smiled, ruefully remembering her earlier fears. "But what is your interest in Rick?"

Ed rubbed his chin as though debating how much to tell her, then relaxed as the waitress slid two plates onto the table between them. When she left, he picked up where they'd left off.

"My involvement with the Dalbys goes back a few years to when Rick was a teenager. I was hot on the heels of a story about a series of convenience store murders when the Dalby kid was arrested. Everything pointed to him as the murderer, but he was never charged. Enough evidence was introduced at his trial to indicate he might be involved . . . or to taint the jury's minds so that they saw the possibility.

"At first I suspected Rick's old man was using his money and influence to get his son off, but something about the trial smelled funny, and I came away thinking the kid had been railroaded. Dealing drugs is no small offense in my book, and even with a juvenile record a mile long, it seemed he got an unduly harsh sentence. I tried to visit him a couple of times, but he wouldn't see me. None of the family would talk to me either."

"Okay," Barbara hesitated before biting into her hamburger. "But why are you interested now?"

"Politics," he responded candidly around a huge bite of his burger. He wiped his mouth before clarifying. "The city editor assigned me to do some candidate profile pieces. Vincent's campaign makes no secret of the fact his wife was a Dalby. I remembered her refusal to see me earlier about her brother. Something about that story had always bothered me, so I decided to use this new assignment as a means of interviewing her. I had no problem securing her cooperation this time. While doing a little routine checking into her background, I discovered her sister had married one of your sons. I also learned that a few years ago, Dana had been a particularly promising young artist, she hasn't had a show in years, and she seemingly no longer has any contact with her family."

"Her family disowned her when she joined the Church," Barbara bluntly informed him. "She still paints, but she is more focused on her husband and baby at this time." Ed nodded his head as though he'd suspected as much.

"My appointment to interview the candidate's wife was yesterday. But it seems you got there before I did and left the lady so upset she was barely coherent when I attempted to interview her. That piqued my curiosity, of course, and I made up my mind to look you up." He smiled again, leaving no doubt in her mind, he was leading up to some questions of his own.

"You didn't decide to get even by sending me a box of dead roses, by any chance, did you?" she asked, only half teasing.

"Did I what?" She'd managed to shock him. She didn't wait for him to ask the questions she knew he eventually would. As briefly as possible she told him about Josh and the reason she'd come to San Francisco to cajole Dana's family into helping him. She finished with the two odd deliveries she'd received, first the box of dead flowers, then the note with its implicit threat.

"They turned you down flat?" Ed asked with narrowed eyes. She nodded her head.

"Ironically, I threatened Stephen Dalby that if he didn't cooperate I might expose his selfish behavior to the press," Barbara mused. "I really didn't intend to; I have no desire to interfere with Preston Vincent's campaign, but I guess I just did."

"No, not necessarily. I'll use the information you just gave me if it looks like its important for the voters to know about it, but at this point, it only interests me as an indicator of a much bigger story. And that story involves Stephen Dalby, not Preston Vincent. I think I'd like to know why you've been given an invitation to leave town, and why an easy-going guy like Rick Dalby suddenly got beat up, just when he was about to finally talk to someone."

"There's something else I should perhaps tell you, though I don't want it in your paper." Barbara met his eyes, and she knew he saw the warning there, but likely wouldn't heed it.

"I don't generally make promises of that nature." Ed made his position clear. "If I know something, and I think it improves my story or is something the public has a right to know, it goes in."

Remembering the blunt honesty of the boy she'd once known, she said, "You haven't really changed all that much, have you?"

"No, the world is still black and white, although I no longer believe that because something is true, it's automatically the whole world's business." He smiled in that disarming way of his. "Something tells me you haven't changed too much either. You still charge in, defending truth and justice, with little regard for the fallout."

Barbara laughed. "I think we've just told each other we were a pair of self-righteous, little prigs, and there's a good possibility we still are."

"Only now I would use a kinder term," his mouth quirked. "My fundamental beliefs haven't changed, but I have learned a modicum of tact. So how about it?"

Barbara cocked her head to one side and observed him for a few long moments before relenting. "Very well, I won't demand any promises." Quickly she sketched the story of the harassment directed at Matt and Dana shortly after their marriage, then related the series of problems plaguing Bingham Construction. "What are the odds those things are related to Stephen Dalby?" she concluded.

"He'd be foolish to harass his daughter through your family's business at this time," Ed mused. "He wants his son-in-law, Preston Vincent, elected and I suspect he isn't above cheating to achieve that goal. I can't see him jeopardizing the election for a bit of personal vengeance, but I wouldn't rule it out either. My instincts tell me he was behind that beating Rick took. For some reason he didn't want him talking to you."

"Do you think there's any chance I'll still be able to tell Rick about Joshua and ask him to be tested?" Barbara's heart felt heavy as she once more faced the futility of the project she'd set herself.

"Go back to Salt Lake," Ed advised her with a sympathetic smile. "And leave it to me. I'll have a talk with my friend at the prison, and see what he thinks. If it can be worked out, I'll have him get in touch with your grandson's doctor."

From the gleam in his eyes, Barbara knew getting help for Josh and assisting an old friend weren't all Eddie Cartwright expected to gain.

CHAPTER FOURTEEN

"I need to stop by the office for a few minutes," Matt said as he set his phone in the cup holder on the console between them before reaching for the car's ignition. It was barely becoming dark, but they were leaving the hospital once more to sleep at home. "If you'd rather, I can run you home first."

"No, I'll go with you. There's no need to go home, then drive all of the way back if you're only going to be a few minutes," Dana responded as she leaned her head back against the headrest and closed her eyes. He knew she was exhausted. Even though she had to have slept better the past few nights—being home in their bed instead of curled up on one of the gray sofas at the hospital—making the decision to begin chemotherapy for Joshua had drained all her resources. He felt wiped out too, he admitted. He wanted this nightmare to end, yet he feared the end. It might mean losing Josh, and he wasn't prepared for that. Over and over he prayed he wouldn't have to face losing Josh.

He drove carefully, trying not to think too much. Several times he glanced over at Dana. She seemed to be asleep, but he couldn't be sure. She hadn't wanted to leave the hospital tonight, but the head nurse had insisted that even though Josh had been given his first dose of cyclophosphamide and could become very ill before morning, Dana should go home and get a full night's sleep. He suspected she'd have difficulty sleeping wherever she might be. She never seemed to sleep in anything other than short snatches anymore, and she was particularly keyed up tonight.

A button on his key ring opened the gate and he pulled into his usual parking spot.

"I'll just be a minute," he said as he shut off the car and turned to Dana. "Do you want to go inside with me or wait here?" She didn't respond, and he realized she was asleep. Light spilling from one of the nearby security pole lamps lit her face, and he watched her breathe slowly in and out. The soft light concealed the lines placed there by worry and fatigue. He wasn't usually fanciful, but he thought she looked like the sleeping princess in one of Joshua's story books, and he toyed with the idea of waking her with a kiss. But no, she was tired and needed all the sleep she could get. Besides, he feared she might not consider him her Prince Charming anymore. He eased the door open, and took care to keep it from making any noise as he closed it once more.

The night watchman, Scott Lewis, met him at the door to the building.

"Good evening," the older man greeted him. "How's the little feller doing?"

"He got his first chemo treatment tonight. So far he isn't sick, just sleepy."

"Darn shame, a little guy like that havin' to go through that chemo business. Me and the missus went to the temple this morning. We put his name on the prayer roll."

"I appreciate your concern. It means a lot to me," Matt responded, truly touched by the man's words. "I won't be long. I just have to pick up some papers." He hurried inside the building, taking the stairs two at a time to reach his office.

He found the folder precisely where Bob said he'd leave it for him. Hastily he picked it up, slid it into an oversize manilla envelope, and turned to leave, closing and locking his office door behind him. Less than a minute later, he reached for the light switch in the outer office and the room was plunged into sudden darkness. That was odd. Wasn't there a security light that stayed on at night? He seemed to remember one. He toggled the switch, but the light didn't come back on. Standing still for several moments, his eyes adjusted to the dark until he could make out the shapes of desks and office equipment.

He didn't remember the outer office being quite so dark when he'd come in a few minutes ago, but if the blinds on the north end and both his and Bob's office doors were closed, there couldn't be much light. Come to think of it, most of the light had come from the hall, but those lights seemed to be out now. There should be an exit sign over the door to the stairs that stayed on even during a power failure he remembered, but evidently it had burned out. He'd speak to maintenance tomorrow about getting the light replaced.

Moving into the hall, he realized there was more wrong than a burned-out light bulb. Not one security light could be seen the entire length of the corridor. A small generator in the basement should have kicked on power for them when the regular power source failed. Taking a step back, he decided to make his way to his secretary's desk. He was pretty certain Josie kept a flashlight there along with a small emergency kit.

He retreated further into the office and tried another switch. Again nothing. As he'd suspected, the power had gone out. He fumbled his way to Josie's desk, where he searched by feel alone for her flashlight. Moments later, deciding the search was futile, he straightened. He'd have to feel his way to the stairs. It stood to reason that if the power was out, the elevator wouldn't work either.

It was strange how different time and space felt without light. He sniffed, imagining he smelled smoke. His brothers would get a good laugh out of his disorientation and near panic over a power failure. They'd teased him plenty when as kids they'd discovered he was afraid of the dark. He was an adult now, and he knew better than to panic because he couldn't see, or to imagine monsters—or smoke—lurking in the darkness. This was one little adventure he didn't plan to tell his brothers about.

Keeping in physical contact with the wall, he moved toward the stairwell, counting doors as he passed to keep his bearings.

Remembering the huge window in his father's office, he pushed against his door hoping a little light would escape into the totally black hall. To his surprise he found the door locked. He and his brothers locked their offices each night, but Dad never had before. Since the break in, they'd all become more security conscious, and he supposed that accounted for the locked door. It appeared to him they also needed to become a whole lot more maintenance conscious. It was bad enough to have a power failure. That wasn't any of their fault, but faulty exit signs meant it had been too long since batteries had been changed. He'd insist first thing in the morning that both the security lighting and the fire alarms be tested.

He should be almost to the stairs, he surmised just before his hand slid over the knob. As he bent to grasp it tightly, he discovered he was a bit lightheaded, and he could feel his eyes watering. Giving the handle a tug, he was surprised when the door didn't move. He tugged again with the same result. Puzzled he stood still, wondering if he'd become disoriented and was trying to open a closet instead of the stairwell door. The door couldn't be locked. There wasn't a lock on the staircase doors, top or bottom!

He coughed and panic ripped through him. He wasn't imagining smoke; it was real! The hall was slowly filling with it! He'd been ignoring an acrid odor for some time, not associating it with anything burning. It didn't smell at all like wood smoke, which meant it was probably electrical or chemical. Whatever it was, he had to get out quickly or he'd be overcome by the strong fumes in the air that were steadily becoming thicker.

Please, God, he prayed as he stumbled back down the hall, seeking a spot where he could breathe. *Don't let me die. Dana and Josh need me, and I have so much to make up to them both.* He had to find a way out. Surely Lewis or his dog would notice and come after him. They'd call the fire department. He just needed to get back to his office and wait for help to arrive.

His mind felt groggy, and he stumbled as he tried the various doors. He'd lost track of doors and had no idea whether he was close to his own office or not. At last his key fit a door, the door knob twisted beneath his hand, and he staggered into what had to be his office. He shoved the door closed, and took in several deep breaths.

The air was better, but he knew it wouldn't take long for the smoke-laden air to creep under the door and through the vents into this space also. It was at best only a temporary haven.

Wait! The telephone. He scrambled for the telephone on the nearest desk. There was no dial tone. Somehow he wasn't really surprised. There was still his cell phone. But no, he'd left it in his car.

Several times he cracked his shins as he hurried past the desks toward the window at the end of the room. Frantically he clawed at the blind covering the window until it fell at his feet. But the tall pole lamps that should have illuminated the parking lot and construction yard were dark, and there was no moon. His eyes adjusted to the dim illumination of distant stars and the glow of the city, finally giving form to the objects around him. He knew without searching that the window wouldn't open. He'd have to break the glass, but how? The tempered glass was designed to withstand tremendous force. It was meant to withstand fierce winds, even bullets. Even if he did manage to break it, then what? He'd kill himself if he jumped three stories to the concrete parking lot below.

"Dana," his heart whispered. "Will you ever know how much I love you?"

He leaned against the glass and made out the shape of his car. He imagined Dana sleeping inside, not knowing of his plight. His mind filled with pictures of her in the car below and of Josh fighting for his life inside his plastic bubble. Fear filled his heart as he noticed something dark like an insidious cloud surrounding his car, slowly hiding it from his limited view. He'd parked in front of an air vent! He imagined the noxious fumes that chased him down the hall, escaping from the building to seep inside the car. Would Dana wake in time to save herself?

"Dana!" he screamed. "Dana!" Over and over he screamed her name. He hammered his fists against the unyielding window. Frantically he searched for a weapon, something strong enough to break the glass. He slammed a chair against the window, a three-hole punch followed, and every item he could find of any weight. It was no use. The smoke was creeping into the room, filling his lungs, making him dizzy.

Crawling on the floor, he made his way to a washroom where he turned on every tap and soaked his clothing. As he pulled at the towel it ripped from its roller, and he drenched it before wrapping it around his face and turning toward the stairs once more. There had to be a way to get that door open. He reached back for the rod that had held the towel. It wasn't much, but it was all his confused, groggy mind could grasp.

Slowly Dana came awake. Her head ached. She coughed several times and her eyes watered. Suddenly she was wide awake. Smoke was coming from the huge vent in front of the car. She grabbed for the door handle and staggered out onto the concrete. Anxiously she looked around. Where was Matt?

With awful certainty she knew he was still inside the building. Her first impulse was to make a dash for the door. She halted half way there to hurry back to the car, holding her breath as she returned to the cloud surrounding it. Snatching the cell phone from the cup holder, she retreated to a safe distance to hurriedly punch in 911. Tears streamed down her face as she reported a fire at Bingham Construction and told the dispatcher that her husband was inside the building.

"Fire trucks are on their way," the dispatcher assured her. "You should hear the sirens within a couple of minutes," the voice tried to reassure her that help would arrive shortly. "Please remain on the line until fire personnel arrive."

"No," she refused. "I have to help him." She threw the phone aside when the dispatcher attempted to talk her out of entering the building. Rushing toward the front door, she tried to remember the building's layout. She'd only been there a few times, but her artist's eye for detail recalled that the stairway opened from double doors to the left of the foyer.

Sufficient light entered the open area from the glass doors and windows to enable her to reach the stairs. Crouching low to conserve air, she moved as quickly as possible upward. Twice she stopped to call Matt's name. If he hadn't already been overcome by smoke, she knew he would make his way to the stairs. She didn't want to even

"There's one more thing," Warner spoke to Matt this time as he loosened his hold on Dana, and she settled back on the sofa. "I've decided to withdraw our bid for the Barringer project."

"Withdraw?" he gaped at his father. "Because of the fire and Downey?"

Shaking his head, Warner denied he'd been driven to the decision by the frightening events of the past few days. "Not in the way you think anyway," he added. "I'm not one to be driven off by scare tactics or cut-throat competition. The truth is, I've missed Barbara the past few days, and I've been thinking about what happened to the two of you, and about little Josh, and it struck me that life is precious. I haven't appreciated that enough. None of us know how much time we'll have together. I decided not to waste whatever I've got left. Knowing I could build the Barringer Complex is enough; I don't actually have to do it. A long time ago Barbara and I had some dreams we shared about places we wanted to see and things we wanted to do. I think it's time we held a little summit meeting to decide which of those dreams are worth resurrecting."

CHAPTER SEVENTEEN

"We should have done this years ago." Warner wiped butter from his fingers and leaned back in his chair, a satisfied smile hovering at the edge of his mouth.

"It hasn't been that long since we've had lobster," Barbara smiled back. She knew the lobster was only a small part of the mood that surrounded them both. Warner had arrived two days ago, and it seemed they'd been in constant motion ever since. They'd ridden the cable cars, visited Telegraph Hill, checked out the museum and the new library, driven past the old Candlestick Park, and ate a picnic lunch on a grassy hill with a wonderful view of the Golden Gate Bridge. And they had talked for hours. A candlelight lobster dinner at Fisherman's Wharf was the culmination of an unexpected mini-vacation she would never forget.

Warner let one eye relax in a slow, lazy wink, and Barbara felt a girlish flutter in the pit of her stomach.

"Shall we go back to the hotel?" There was a mischievous glint in his eyes.

"I thought you wanted to see a movie?"

"I think I prefer 'live action' tonight." His smile widened to an incorrigible grin, and she felt a flush creep across her skin.

"I think you're flirting," she tried to tease back, but a lump caught in her throat. She didn't care if she was acting like an infatuated young girl falling in love with her first beau. She'd wasted so much time. She must have spoken her thoughts aloud because Warner reached across the table and took her hand.

"I know," he whispered back. "We both wasted a lot of time. We let the business of living take over our lives. Somewhere along the way, we let pride and hurt feelings get in the way of our relationship with each other."

"I thought because we didn't fight with each other, and we're both active in the church, that was all we needed to have a good marriage, but sometimes I missed what I thought we had at the beginning of our marriage," Barbara spoke with lingering wistfulness.

"We did start out right," Warner added firmly, "and I don't think we ever stopped loving each other. We just got so caught up in work and family, we put being together on a back burner. We let little things like other people's opinions and our own insecurities become obstacles."

"I can't believe I ever doubted you," Barbara added with a hint of regret. "I'm so sorry. It really is true that we never stopped loving each other, but sometimes we let the light grow dim."

"Perhaps that isn't all bad either." Warner's smile was back. "Now we get to fall in love all over again without all the trouble of falling out first."

Barbara laughed and rose to her feet. "I think you mentioned going back to the hotel." She held out her hand, but Warner was already ahead of her, picking up her jacket.

When they reached the hotel, Warner helped her out of the taxi, then stepped to the window of the cab to pay the driver. Barbara took a few steps toward the hotel, then turned back to watch Warner. They were neither one particularly impulsive— in fact Warner's last impulsive act had done nothing but cause trouble—but she was glad for whatever had prompted him to join her in San Francisco. She was also glad that for once she hadn't followed her own impulse. She'd come very close to telling him not to come, that she wanted to see

Matt and Dana after the ordeal they'd gone through, and that they could talk once she got home. She'd almost told him she didn't particularly like San Francisco, and that she had no interest in staying a couple more days. She smiled, recalling the past two days. Warner had certainly shown her the city in an entirely different light.

He'd just turned toward her, when a slight tug at her side caught her unaware. She whirled about to see a thief sprinting down the street with her purse.

"Stop that man!" she screamed and took a few staggering steps in the thief's direction, stopping only to jerk her high-heeled shoes off her feet.

"Call the police!" Warner shouted. He passed her and was rapidly closing in on the thief, who seemed headed for a flashy sports car parked at the curb. She glanced around wildly as though expecting a telephone to suddenly materialize before her. To her surprise, one did.

"Here, lady! I dialed 911." A teenager thrust a cell phone into her hand.

"I already called the cops!" The cab driver called, as he pulled away from the curb, then stopped abruptly in front of the sports car, so it couldn't get out if the thief reached it.

She was scarcely aware of the phone in her hand as she watched Warner launch into a tackle like she hadn't seen since their college days. She was running before Warner and the thief hit the side walk. *Look out for a gun*! she wanted to scream. They should have let the thief go. Nothing in her purse was worth having Warner injured or killed!

She arrived beside a jumble of arms and legs and barely grasped that Warner was on top before she became aware of a voice coming from the phone she still held. Gasping for breath and struggling to calm her racing heart, she spoke into the phone, and was quickly assured that help was on the way.

Slowly Warner struggled to his feet. The smaller figure lay still. Warner, too, was out of breath, and he stood for several seconds, breathing heavily, before he reached back down to pick up Barbara's purse. With a flourish, he handed it to her. She was vaguely aware that a crowd had gathered, and a police car with flashing lights was screeching to a halt beside them. Warner was all that mattered.

Instead of reaching for her handbag, her arms flew around his neck, and her joy was complete as he held her in a crushing embrace.

"It's a female!" she heard someone say. Warner released her, and they both turned to watch a policeman bending over the body still lying on the ground.

"Is she hurt?" someone else asked, and Barbara and Warner moved closer.

"A woman?" Warner appeared staggered. "I didn't know . . ."

"She's still a thief, ain't she?" The teenager reached out to reclaim her cell phone, and Barbara noticed for the first time the girl's spiked hair and bare midriff. Earrings decorated more exposed skin than Barbara cared to note.

"Thank you," Barbara attempted to be gracious. She really was grateful for the girl's generosity.

"Sure!" The girl waved before disappearing into the crowd.

She turned back to see Warner kneeling with one of the officers beside the woman on the ground. She stepped closer. The thief was sitting up now, glaring angrily at Warner. The words coming from her mouth made Barbara wince. Her eyes widened, and she felt a growing sense of disbelief. The woman wasn't some anonymous stranger, down on her luck. Barbara knew her.

"Linda Dalby!" she gasped. Hate-filled eyes turned her way, and Barbara fought an urge to cringe in shock. She must be wrong. Why would a wealthy, fashionable woman like Linda Dalby stoop to petty theft? Or was it petty theft? With sudden certainty she knew. Mrs. Dalby cared nothing for the small amount of money or credit cards she might have found in Barbara's purse.

"Josh's portrait!"she breathed the words, but loud enough that the woman struggling to free herself heard.

"It's mine!" Linda screamed. "You stole it, just like you stole Dana. She was the only one with any talent. I sacrificed everything for her. I protected her. I sent her to Paris so he couldn't hurt her hands. She was going to make us rich. That stupid boy ruined everything!" She lunged toward Barbara, but the officer restrained her before she could reach her target.

Linda continued a stream of threats and obscenities as the officers escorted her to their squad car. One turned to advise the Binghams of directions to the precinct station where they could press charges.

Troubled, Barbara turned to Warner, and he read the question in her eyes.

"We have to," he assured her. "She needs help, and she won't get it if we ignore what she did. Besides I'd like to know what else she's done to get revenge on Matt and secure Dana's talent for herself."

At the police station they were given papers to sign, then told to return the next day. Wearily they returned to their hotel. Barbara felt an aching sadness as she pulled on her nightgown. Linda Dalby had managed to wipe out the light-hearted mood that had existed a few hours earlier.

When they returned to the police station the following day, they were surprised to find Ed Cartwright waiting for them. "Do you have a minute?" he asked.

"Hello, Ed." Warner shook Ed's hand, and it pleased her that her husband held her hand as they strolled down a long hall with the other man. The two men had known each other back at East High, though probably not well since Warner was a few years older than Ed. Barbara knew Warner was aware she had gone out with Ed a few times back then, so she found it kind of nice that he betrayed a hint of possessiveness now. Ed pushed open a door and they found themselves in a neglected garden area. A picnic table sat beside an overflowing trash can. Ed led the way to a bench nearby.

"You heard what happened last night." Barbara said, assuming the thwarted purse snatching was his reason for meeting them this morning.

"I heard, but only in a round-about way," he admitted. "I learned from a source, who will remain unnamed, that candidate Preston Vincent's mother-in-law was committed to a private sanitarium early this morning."

"What?!" Warner stopped to stare incredulously at Ed.

"Yes." Ed shook his head with disbelief. "She was really cool about it. Instead of calling her husband last night, she contacted Vincent's attorney, who got Judge Roper and assistant D.A. Williams out of bed and cut a deal with them. She confessed to hiring some thugs to beat up Matt several years ago, damaging Matt and Dana's cars, as well as sending a threatening note and dead flowers to you."

He nodded toward Barbara. "She also confessed to attempting to steal a portrait from you. In exchange for her guilty plea, she committed herself to the sanitarium by claiming she was intoxicated when she did all those things, although I noticed she was sober enough to obtain a restraining order against her husband. He won't be allowed to see her or receive any information about her condition. She plans to file for divorce under California's community property laws, and the information she gave the D.A. about some of her husband's business dealings should keep him too busy defending himself to contest the action."

"But why?" Warner shook his head in disbelief.

"Hate, revenge, greed, all of the above. She says her husband only married her because he wanted a son, and that he has abused her since the day they got married. When Marilyn was born he punished her severely because the baby was a girl. She had several miscarriages after that, and each time the punishment became more intense. By the time Rick was born, she wanted revenge, so she told Stephen the baby wasn't his. It was the only time he beat her badly enough to break bones and put her in the hospital. But she received some kind of malicious satisfaction in seeing him mistreat the son he'd wanted so badly, but didn't believe was his."

"But he's her son, too," Barbara protested.

"Evidently she saw him only as Stephen's son," Ed explained sadly.

"Was she responsible for someone beating Rick at the prison?" The thought made Barbara sick.

"She said no. That was entirely Stephen's doing. Stephen wanted to keep Rick from talking to you and possibly tainting Preston's campaign," Ed explained. "She's pretty indifferent to anything concerning Rick. She just wants Stephen to suffer the way she claims he made her suffer all these years, and she wants as much of his money as she can get. She obviously doesn't care about Marilyn or her husband's campaign either."

"What about all this?" Barbara asked anxiously. "Won't your story destroy Preston's chances?"

"Do you want him to win?" Warner voiced his surprise.

"I don't know. I don't know anything about his stand on most issues, but I feel sorry for his wife. I'd like for her to be able to leave here."

"None of this was Preston's fault. I can try to keep it quiet for a while, but eventually it will come out. His attorney plans to recommend to Vincent's people that they back away from the Dalby connection. If they announce Marilyn's pregnancy right away, and use it as an excuse for her to keep a low profile, they can probably weather the scandal without a lot of damage," Ed pointed out. "I won't push it. I'm after bigger fish, as you've no doubt guessed."

"It's Dalby himself you want," Warner speculated.

Ed grinned, but neither confirmed nor denied the angle he intended to pursue.

When Warner and Barbara left the police station it was too late to catch a flight for Salt Lake that night. They returned to their hotel room to get a good night's sleep before their early morning flight.

"Poor Dana. She'll have to be told everything," Barbara mused as she tossed her handbag on the bed. "I don't think it ever occurred to her that her mother treated her better than the others, or that in a sick kind of way Linda actually tried to protect her."

"Only because she spotted Dana's talent at an early age and saw it as a means of bettering her own life." Warner made no attempt to conceal his contempt for the woman.

"I feel sorry for Linda in a way," Barbara confessed, though she could see her husband didn't exactly share her view.

Warner set the room key on a small table before sinking into a chair. "I can't believe she calmly confessed everything."

"What can't you believe?" Barbara sat down on the side of the bed and bent forward to pull off her shoes. As she wiggled her toes, she turned to look at Warner. "You can't believe she would confess, or you can't accept the fact that it was a woman who did all those awful things?"

"Oh, I learned some time ago to never underestimate a woman," he chuckled. "Especially this one." He reached across the short gap between them to pull her onto his lap.

"Warner!" Her voice was sharp, but a giggle spoiled the severity. "I'm too heavy. Let me go."

"Never," he growled and nuzzled the side of her neck, sending shivers all the way to her toes.

"Don't you think we should call the kids?" Barbara was surprised by the breathless quality of her voice.

"Later," Warner mumbled and she felt her zipper sneak down the back of her dress.

"Do you think Linda will be safe in that sanitarium?" Barbara asked, but she was finding it difficult to concentrate.

"Who?" Warner didn't sound very interested in an answer to his question.

"Linda Dalby," Barbara answered in a distracted voice.

"Let's forget Linda Dalby," Warner suggested. "That woman spoiled some very good plans last night. Let's not let her do it again."

"M-m-m-m," Barbara murmured her agreement.

As Dana and Matt left Josh's room, Dana looked back at her little boy, lying helpless in his hospital crib. Weakly he reached out for her, crying and begging her to stay. Her steps slowed, and only Matt's hand on her arm kept her moving. Once outside the room, she leaned against the wall and yielded to the tears which had been threatening for so long.

"He's so sick," she sobbed.

"I know." Matt's voice wobbled, and she knew he was barely managing to hold back his own tears. "It's just so unfair!"

"Matt. Dana." A tentative voice reached them. Brushing back the tears with the back of her hand, she looked up to see Matt's older brothers and their wives facing them.

"We didn't mean to intrude," Robert spoke.

"Mom and Dad called. They're coming back this morning," Winn added. He shifted, looking uncomfortable.

"Oh, Dana." Ann impulsively put her arms around her sister-in-law. "They said a lot has happened while they were gone, and they have a great deal to tell you, but I think that can wait. You look like you need to get away for a few minutes. There are some benches outside on the lawn and the sun is shining, so it isn't too cold. I think the two of you should go find one of those benches and spend a few minutes alone. We'll stay right here in case Joshua needs anything."

Dana was too emotionally spent to argue. She let Matt put his arm around her and lead her out of the building. They made their way to a bench, half hidden by a large pine tree. At first they didn't speak, and though the view of the city spread below them was breathtaking, they scarcely noticed.

"I don't see how he can take anymore," Dana spoke at last. "This treatment is so much worse than the first one, and Dr. Young says there will be more."

Matt gripped her hands tighter without speaking.

"Are we being selfish, Matt?" Dana asked in a tentative whisper. "Are all our prayers and this horrible chemotherapy merely extending his suffering? If God meant him to get well, wouldn't our prayers be enough, without putting him through all this nausea and pain?"

"I don't know." Matt shook his head in a helpless gesture. "Last night I read something Brigham Young wrote about healing. It gave me some comfort. He said that expecting healing to happen merely because we prayed for it is like expecting crops to grow without plowing the ground or casting the seed. He said that in addition to fasting and prayer, we should apply every remedy we have knowledge of. He also seemed to suggest that only when no medical care is possible should we rely on faith alone."

"In my heart I know that's true," Dana agreed, "But sometimes it's just so hard to see the treatment cause him more suffering than the illness does. Lately I've wondered if he would be happier in heaven where he'd no longer be weak or in pain, then I think no, I can't let him go. I need him too much."

"I don't think that's selfishness," Matt tried to comfort her. "I think that's the way parents, who love their children were meant to feel, and I admit I've thought those same things." Silently he thought of all the times he'd begged God on his knees, his voice choking with tears, to spare this child he loved so much. He knew Dana had done the same. "At this point I guess, we're both asking ourselves if we want him to live if his life is to be filled with pain and unhappiness. Can we let him go, if going will free him of suffering and speed him to work he may have been called to on the other side? Is our faith great enough to let him go without bitterness?"

Dana buried her face in her hands and her shoulders shook. Matt held her until her tears were spent. Slowly she looked up at him.

"If he dies, it won't be forever." She searched his face for confirmation that they would be together again. Something deep in his eyes gave her the assurance she sought. "We'll be together again, and he'll still be our little boy."

"Yes, that's what being an eternal family is all about." Matt's words rasped through a layer of deep emotion. "Without that hope, how could we ever say 'thy will be done'?"

The words touched her soul with soothing comfort. She wasn't giving up on this life, or the next. With sudden clarity she saw that was exactly what she had done. She'd given up on this life, not for Joshua, but for herself. Matt had hurt her, betrayed a bond of trust she had thought symbolized their unity, and thus ceased to be her fantasy hero. There's nothing wrong with dreams she told herself. They had carried her through a lot of years of misery. The hope in her heart told her that reality could be better than all of her adolescent dreams. She was no longer a girl who needed to live on dreams. She was a woman in love with a man—a real man, and real men had flaws. They made mistakes, just as women did. She didn't need a knight in shining armor to make her world perfect, she needed Matt to walk beside her, sometimes stumbling a bit, sometimes leaning on her, but always there to catch her when she fell, help her find the way, and firmly keep them both pointed toward that eternal goal of being a family forever.

"I love you." The words were simple, but she meant them with all her heart. Matt's eyes mirrored his surprise and a joy he didn't seem quite ready to accept.

"Does that mean you've forgiven me?" He choked on the words.

"Yes, but only if you'll forgive me for the times I wasn't mature enough to be there for you." He held her close, and she thought of a silly statement she'd read a long time ago. *Love means you never have to say you're sorry.* Whoever said that was wrong. Love meant forgiving, and asking forgiveness. It meant being quick to say "I'm sorry" in order to keep a gulf from growing between two hearts that cared. Love is built on recognizing wrong in yourself and your partner, and never giving up on making the wrongs right.

As Matt held her and their tears mingled, another truth eased into her heart. Their marriage was stronger now. The trouble they'd faced and were still facing hadn't weakened, but had strengthened their bond. An obstacle which could have destroyed their marriage had strengthened it.

"Matt," she stroked his cheek as she spoke. "We've asked God for a great deal lately, but right now, I think we should thank him for Josh and for each other."

He agreed and clasping hands, they bowed their heads. Warmth filled her heart, assuring her that gratitude was part of love, too.

———•———

When they returned to the hospital, it was to hear themselves being paged. Hurrying to the fourth floor they found Dr. Young waiting for them.

"Good news!" he almost shouted as they approached the desk where he stood. "I just got off the phone with that California doctor. Rick Dalby's tests show he only mismatches at one locus."

"And he'll donate?" Matt stammered.

"Yes!"

Dana's legs suddenly felt too weak to hold her, and she clung to Matt to keep from falling. Her prayers, not only for Josh, but for Rick, hadn't fallen on deaf ears. In that awful place, God had touched Rick's heart. He held out hope that not only might she keep her son, it was possible she might also regain her brother.

CHAPTER EIGHTEEN

Matt felt Dana tremble as he led her to the waiting room where the rest of the family was assembled. Dr. Young had assured them the doctor performing the transplant was one of the best in the country and that he too would be with Josh through the entire procedure. The two doctors had carefully explained that the procedure wasn't really surgery. Rick's bone marrow had been mixed with heparin and a tissue culture medium, then passed through a stainless steel screen to break up any particles which might have been in the mixture. It was now being administered to Josh through an intravenous route. The marrow stem cells would pass through Josh's lungs before going to the marrow cavity prepared for it. Because of Josh's vulnerability to infection, he would be allowed no visitors during this critical time.

They stepped into the room to see the same combination of hope and fear on every face that they felt in their own hearts.

"He'll be all right," Ann tried to assure them, her fervent words almost a prayer.

"Next time you write to that brother of yours," Winn's voice was gruff with emotion, "tell him he's got a job on my crew."

Matt saw Dana bite her lip to keep from crying. She'd been in touch with Rick many times since he'd agreed to be Josh's donor, and she'd been told his next parole hearing was coming up in a few weeks. She also knew he must have a firm job awaiting him in order to be considered for parole. Stephen Dalby had promised his son employment, but Rick wanted nothing to do with his father, and Matt couldn't fault him for that. To his credit, the elder Dalby had attempted to visit his son after he learned he really was Rick's father, but he was turned away. He did assure Rick's new attorney that he wouldn't object to parole this time nor interfere in any of his son's plans. At any rate, Stephen Dalby was facing so many legal problems of his own at the moment, he might not be in a position to offer anyone employment for long.

"You saw Josh?" Warner walked over to grasp his son's hand, then envelope Dana in a huge embrace.

"Yes, he was smiling a little bit and terribly interested in what was going on. He's so thin and without his curls or eyebrows, he looks more like a baby than a little boy. I-I had a hard time leaving him," Dana admitted with a tremulous smile.

"Well, of course you did," Barbara smiled encouragingly at her daughter-in-law. "We mothers tend to take our children's ills very seriously."

Gradually the whole group settled onto the couches and talk drifted to other matters, though Matt noticed he wasn't the only one who checked his watch at frequent intervals, and who jumped every time anyone approached the waiting room door. Dana was sandwiched between him and his father, and though she tried to appear calm, if the transplant took as long as they'd been told to expect, she wouldn't have a fingernail left at the rate she was chewing them off.

"Did you discover what caused the cave-in at the new excavation?" Warner asked Winn.

Winn answered with one word. "Dynamite!"

"And no one heard it?" Barbara asked in surprise.

Robert shook his head. "This project is west of Tooele in a pretty remote area," he explained.

"We've eliminated both Downey and Dalby as suspects. Who else could it be?" Matt asked the question that had been asked over and over without answer since they had seen that the sabotage had continued even after Downey filed for bankruptcy and both of the Dalbys had been cleared of suspicion. Canceling the Barringer bid had also failed to bring an end to the costly sabotage.

"Let's talk about something else," Sandra put an end to business talk. "How's your barn coming?" She turned to Ann, and Matt noted a flicker of annoyance before Ann responded. She hated having her new riding stable referred to as a "barn."

"It's doing great," she answered with a smile. "We should be ready for a couple of boarders by March, and it looks like we're right on schedule to start classes in late April." She looked hesitantly at Robert, then when he smiled and nodded, she went on. "Riding classes aren't the only classes we're thinking of starting. We talked with a counselor from LDS Social Services yesterday, and she said we could start parenting classes even before our adoption application is complete."

"That's wonderful," Barbara beamed and patted Ann's shoulder. "You'll make a wonderful mother. I just hope you get your baby before . . ." She trailed off with a look of dismay.

Warren winked at her and Matt nearly broke into a chuckle. His parents had been different since that trip to San Francisco. He couldn't exactly say what was different, but he liked it.

"I suppose we might as well tell them," Warner drawled with a definite twinkle in his eyes. "We were going to wait until the transplant was over and Josh was on the mend, but perhaps this is as good a time as any." His smile disappeared, and he looked terribly solemn, perhaps even a little nervous. He stood and held out his hand to Barbara.

"We've been called on a mission," he announced gravely. "It won't be right away," he added before anyone could interrupt or congratulate them. "We've been called downtown a couple of times in the past few weeks, and we accepted the call when it was issued a few days ago. We don't know where we're going yet, but all the new mission presidents get some training in July before we begin our assignment."

"You'll be great, Dad." Winn stepped to his dad's side to give him a fierce hug, and the room erupted in a round of laughter and congratulations along with a few tears. Dana was last to hug her father-in-law, and he continued to stand with her by his side as he talked to the others.

"I wish Hadley were here." Barbara wiped at her eyes, and Matt stared in astonishment. He couldn't ever remember his mother being carried away with emotion enough to cry.

"Oh, Matt, get me a tissue." She turned toward him, and he rushed to a table near the door to snatch a handful.

"Well, Dad, you're getting pretty good at this surprise business," Winn remarked. "First you dropped that Barringer bid and left us scrambling for jobs to take its place, now this. Do you think we can keep the business afloat while you're gone?"

"I've no doubts whatsoever," Warner responded confidently. "You're more than ready to take my place, and with a couple of V.P.'s like your brothers to keep you in line, you'll do fine. Besides there's plenty of time to work out the details."

"I don't think so," a voice came from the open doorway a few feet away. "The only detail left to work out is which one of you is going to die first."

Matt swivelled his head toward the door just as the speaker stepped inside. He held a gun, which he pointed directly at Matt's father. A cold sweat broke out on Matt's face as he observed Dana standing beside his father, snuggled closely against his left side.

No! This can't be happening! echoed through his mind, and though he knew he hadn't actually screamed, someone must have made some sound because the man looked around and moved the gun back and forth, slowly panning the room. Matt caught a glimpse of the gunman's face and froze with shock. Bart Adams! No! How could the man holding a gun on his family be one of the company's foremen and his own secretary's husband?

"Don't try to play the hero," Bart sneered. "I'm very good with this little beauty, and I can take care of all of you before you could even get close. Then I can take my time picking off your wives."

Feeling sick, Matt looked toward Dana. She appeared completely calm and unafraid, but she was purposely avoiding looking at him. That hurt. If these were to be their last moments on earth, he wanted to look into her eyes and say good-by. But the shock only lasted a moment before he understood. She wasn't ignoring him because she didn't love him, nor was she trying to protect him. She had quickly realized that the gunman hadn't yet seen him. Although Matt was only a few feet from Bart, he stood behind the gunman, partially hidden by the door and the table where he'd gone to get his mother a tissue. Dana's calmness was an avowal of her faith and confidence in him. She believed he could, and would, rescue them all. Her trust astounded him, sending a surge of adrenalin through his veins. He'd die before he'd let her down.

But there wasn't room to slip behind Bart, besides any movement on his part would alert Bart to his presence. Somehow he'd have to disarm Bart. A sharp blow from beneath the extended gun hand would divert the gun upward, and though the gun might discharge, the bullets would hopefully land in the ceiling. Bart was bigger than him, but he didn't doubt he could hold him until his brothers reached them. He'd have to get closer. A trickle of sweat began creeping down his back.

"Fifteen years! I sweated fifteen years for you," Bart was yelling. "But you don't care. I had the experience, but the best jobs were always for your precious sons. You wanted to build the Barringer Complex, but who did you pick for foreman? Not the man with experience! You were going to make your kid my boss!"

"Bart, put the gun down, and we'll talk—" Warner tried to reason with him, but Bart cut him off.

"No, I'm through taking orders from you or anyone. Ten years ago, when Hal was here, he told me what to do. He showed me how to switch orders without getting caught, but when he left, he didn't want me around anymore. He said I wasn't good enough. So I stayed with you, and I worked hard, but it was never good enough for you. I was never good enough for Josie, either. All she ever talked about was how wonderful you all were.

"She found that envelope I took from her desk. I only took it because I thought Hal might have put something in it about me. But Josie didn't believe me; she took your side like she always does. She said I needed a doctor," Bart fumed, waving his gun. "Now she's gone. She left me. But I'll show her. I'll show all of you. I'm the one in charge now." As Bart lifted the gun slightly and took a step closer to Warner, Winn and Robert stepped forward also, but Bart swung the gun toward them.

"Don't even think it," he snarled at them.

It was obvious that Bart had gone over the edge, Matt thought. There would be no reasoning with him. Matt eyed the slightly larger opening between Bart and the door. He could run for help, but Bart would undoubtedly hear him and begin shooting. Everyone would be dead by the time he could get help. Somehow Matt had to disarm Bart. Holding his breath, he inched closer to him. He took a deep breath, prepared to strike.

"Dana!" A swirl of color flashed into the room and streaked toward Dana. "You haven't been to see the baby all week, so I brought her to you!" It was all the distraction he needed. He leaped toward Bart and with both fists shoved the gun upward. It barked sharply, and he continued the upward cut to land his clenched fists under Bart's jaw. Before he could disentangle himself to strike again, he went down under a tangle of bodies as his brothers, followed closely by his father, dived on top of him and their assailant.

He didn't know which one of his brothers yanked the gun out of Bart's hand, but the fight was over almost as quickly as it had begun. He rolled away and struggled to his feet with Dana's help. For several minutes he simply held her and thanked God that she was safe.

Gradually he became aware of Sandra returning to the room with a couple of security guards on her heels. His mother was shouting orders into the white phone, probably ordering the police to hurry. Mandy's baby was screaming, and Mandy seemed to be suffering from shock. She stood in the middle of the room. Her eyes looked glazed, and little whimpering sounds came from her trembling mouth.

Robert's wife, Ann, tried to comfort her. "It's all right," she said as she lifted the screaming baby from Mandy's arms. She began to rock the baby as she whispered soothing nonsense in her tiny ear. "Everyone is safe now."

"I think that's the bravest thing I ever saw anyone do." Warner hugged Mandy as though she were family, when in fact they were total strangers.

"I was so scared he would shoot you, and you didn't give me a chance to warn you." Dana left Matt's side to hurry to her friend.

"I wasn't brave; I was stupid!" Mandy wailed. "I didn't know! I didn't even see him! He might have killed Victoria."

"Oh, Mandy, Victoria's fine. We're all safe thanks to you and Matt." Dana burrowed her way into Warner's arms to hug her friend. "I knew Matt would save us somehow. He just needed a distraction to keep Bart from turning his head far enough to see him. I prayed, and you were the answer to my prayers!"

Barbara produced a roll of adhesive tape from somewhere and Robert wrapped the whole roll around Bart's arms and legs before Winn would release his hold on the man. Finally Winn stood and walked straight to where Matt was standing.

"Good job, little brother." Winn wrapped an arm, bigger than their father's, around Matt. "Wouldn't you know, the one time we needed a little muscle, it would be the runt who came through for us! We would have taken state, if you'd been on the team back at East."

"That was brains, man, not brawn." Robert joined them to rub his knuckles across his shorter brother's head. "I taught the kid everything he knows," he teased.

The police arrived to take Bart away, and the head nurse poked her nose in the room several times to remind them they were in a hospital and they were expected to be quiet. When Dr. Young stepped into the room, they were all instantly silent. Matt came to stand beside Dana, and she reached for his hand.

"Everything went well," the doctor spoke softly. "As I explained earlier, we really won't have any indication of how successful the transplant will be for two or three weeks. And it will be several months after that before we can say conclusively that it worked, and that the transplant has not been rejected."

"May we see him?" Dana asked.

"Only through the window I showed you earlier. He has no immune system at all now and must be kept in isolation."

"I understand." Dana nodded her head, then she and Matt followed the doctor from the room. None of the family spoke, but Dana had the feeling they were somehow sending love and concern down the hall with her with each step she took. Gone were all the resentment and misunderstandings that had marked her relationship with Matt's family for so long. She still found her mother-in-law intimidating, but that relationship was improving. She was conscious of how hard Barbara was working to develop a positive understanding between the two of them, and this time Dana was determined to meet her half way, or better. She would never forget that it was Barbara who found Rick and gave both Josh and Rick a chance at life.

In minutes Dana and Matt stood together at a window separating them from their son in the next room. He was asleep and her heart ached at the sight of blue shadows beneath his eyes. His thin, fragile body, still covered with bruises, appeared much too weak to support his hairless head, and the tubes and wires connecting him to bags on poles and sophisticated looking monitors lent a grotesque air to the scene.

"He's going to get well," Matt said and this time there was real conviction in his voice. Warmth started in her chest and swelled until it filled her entirely. A sensation of stepping from a dark and clinging mist into a meadow of bright sunlight spread through her.

"Yes, I know it, too." Her arm went around her husband's waist, and she leaned her head against his shoulder. The battle wasn't over. The next few months would be long and painful, but the Spirit whispered to her soul that they would make it; all three of them. God had heard their prayers. He'd pulled them from the slippery rocks and safely placed their feet on a firm path.

"I love you and Josh with all my heart," Matt whispered against her ear. "I'll thank God all the days of eternity for giving us this second chance."

Placing her hand against the glass, she gazed longingly at her baby. Against her ear she heard the steady beat of Matt's heart. It was enough. She had hope and love.

ABOUT THE AUTHOR

Jennie Hansen is a well-recognized name in LDS romantic fiction, with several successful best-sellers to her credit, including *Run Away Home* and *Some Sweet Day*. A circulation specialist at the Salt Lake City Library, Jennie has also worked as a librarian, newspaper reporter, and editor. She has served in all the auxiliaries as well as stake and ward Primary presidencies. Most recently she has served as the education counselor in her ward Relief Society and is currently the ward Teacher Improvement Coordinator.

She and her husband, Boyd, make their home in Salt Lake County. They are the parents of four daughters and a son.

Jennie writes from a firm belief in our Savior's love for all of his children. She believes that love is an integral part of relationships between a man and a woman, between family members, and in lasting friendships.

Jennie welcomes readers' comments. You can write to her in care of Covenant Communications, P.O. Box 416, American Fork, Utah 84003-0416.

ALL I HOLD DEAR

Icy prickles ran up the back of his neck, warning him he was being followed. His eyes went to the rearview mirror searching for any sign of his pursuer. Nothing but a wall of white met his eyes. Still he knew. Whoever was following had moved closer.

A slight loss of traction and a tug to the right reminded him to keep his attention focused on the twisting mountain road. The road was paved, but it wasn't maintained like the freeway he'd left an hour ago, and it had been some time since he'd passed another vehicle. If he had an accident or became stranded, he was on his own.

The big four-wheel-drive Grand Cherokee Jeep he drove wasn't immune to icy roads, but it improved the odds he'd make it. Carefully he steered into the skid and his breath resumed a more normal cadence as he felt the tires once more grip the pavement. The higher he climbed, the heavier the snowfall became. Soon it would be accumulating on the road and he'd have to stop to put on chains.

Once more his eyes darted nervously to his side mirror. The gloom of dusk had given way to night, making travel on the mountain impossible without lights. Still nothing behind him, but they were out there. The absence of traffic warned him the locals were expecting heavy snow and were staying put.

He couldn't say how he knew he was being followed. Perhaps it was paranoia, brought on by torture and starvation during the long months of his mistaken incarceration in South America—that was how the shrink back in Dallas had explained it—but he couldn't shake the feeling. Someone was out there and whoever he was, that someone had hovered nearby, playing some kind of waiting game while he'd been recuperating in the hospital. And when he'd checked himself out and begun his journey north, he'd felt a sinister presence following. Since the snow began falling an hour ago, he'd sensed his relentless shadow drawing closer.

He hadn't once caught a glimpse of anyone following, and he'd tried several times, to shake or expose whoever was behind him, without any luck, but the feeling persisted. He couldn't even say how he knew he was being followed. He just knew. He laughed mirthlessly at his own expense. He didn't know how he could be so sure someone who meant him harm was following him when he certainly didn't know much else. Not even his name.

The shrink back at the hospital had told him he was Nicholas Mascaro, but the name didn't feel right. The only name that really stuck in his head was Sam. He didn't know if that was his own name or the name of the person he had to find. He wished he had more than a shadowy impression that he had to find someone. Some force deep inside himself wouldn't let him rest or even try to trace his own past until he found this mysterious person.

His grip tightened on the steering wheel as he strained to see between the intermittent swipes of the windshield wipers, and the urgency gnawing at the back of his mind grew sharper. He sensed time was running out. He had to be there. He wasn't even sure exactly where he had to be and he didn't have a clue why, but from the moment he'd awakened in that hospital in Dallas, some powerful premonition had warned him he wasn't safe and that he had to reach Colorado. Once he reached Colorado, something had drawn him on. He'd stopped at a truck stop to pick up a road map, and the moment his eyes found a tiny dot high in the Rockies, he'd known his destination was a wide spot in the road called Isadora, named for some prospector's mule. He didn't know how he knew the story of the town's name, but he did.

He couldn't have lived in Isadora unless the shrink had lied to him, and he couldn't see any reason why he would have done that. Supposedly he had grown up on his grandfather's farm in Vermont. As far as he knew, he'd never been to Colorado.

By the time he reached the summit, the snow had obliterated the road. He could only divine where to drive by following the wide space devoid of trees that lay between two towering banks of snow which had been pushed there by state road crews after the last storm. He'd have to stop soon to chain his tires. The all-season tires on his Cherokee were good, but not good enough to begin the downward journey without the extra traction of chains.

At the top, the plowed area widened, allowing him space to pull over. Before leaving the vehicle, he pulled the hood of his heavy sweatshirt over his head and zipped up the windbreaker he wore over the shirt. He'd wanted to purchase a heavy parka before he began this trip, but the store in Texas didn't carry anything heavier than the lined windbreaker, and his reluctance to stop any longer than necessary to purchase gas and food had prevented him from seeking out a clothing store as he drove north. Before reaching for the door handle, he flexed his fingers inside the leather driving gloves he'd purchased back at the truck stop along with the chains and a coil of thin nylon rope.

The wind stole his breath as he stepped into the storm. Some ingrained habit had him scanning the slope of the mountain he had so recently traversed. Visibility was poor and he could see little else but snow and the dark shapes of trees, but *he* was still out there, still coming closer.

Quickly he spread out the chains and though he didn't consciously remember performing the task before, that portion of his brain that continued to elude him took over and swiftly completed the task. Before stepping back inside the utility, he once again scanned the road behind him.

The tiniest flash of light caught his eye and his heartbeat accelerated. He watched the faint prick of light appear and disappear as the driver of an unseen vehicle maneuvered his way up the steep switchbacks. Indecision swept through him. He could get back in his car and continue on, hoping to evade his pursuer once he reached a lower elevation, or he could conceal himself and wait until the other vehicle reached the summit. Surprise would be on his side and he'd know at last who was persistently trailing him.

Red showed briefly, then again. The driver of the approaching car was applying his brakes at increasingly frequent intervals. A quick mental recap of the road told him as he watched through the snowy whiteness that the other driver was approaching a particularly bad curve. It was difficult to tell much from the glimpses he caught of moving lights, but he suspected that neither the driver nor the vehicle were prepared for the Colorado Rockies in a snowstorm.

Even as the thought ran through his mind that the other vehicle was moving too fast for the conditions, he saw the red flush of brake lights magnified by the snow, then watched as the lights wavered back and forth before forming a graceful arc plummeting down the mountainside.

For several seconds he stared uncomprehending at the spot where the light had disappeared. Slowly silence settled around him. Even the roar of the wind-driven snow took on a hush. He was alone. For the first time in a very long time no one was watching him. Pursuit had ended with that arc of light.

He climbed back in the Cherokee with every intention of continuing his journey, but as he shifted gears he knew he couldn't do it. On the off-chance that someone had survived the crash, he had to go back down the mountain. Maybe, just maybe, he consoled himself, he'd recognize his pursuer and discover why he was being followed.

Slowly he backed and turned until he could begin to retrace his route. As he edged his way carefully down the steep descent, he considered the possibility he might be walking into a trap. He wondered what it was inside him that wouldn't allow him to take advantage of this short reprieve and simply disappear over the mountain. He didn't question how he knew that his pursuit had only been temporarily interrupted. The rapid swipe of wiper blades mocked the inner voice that told him he couldn't leave without making certain the occupant of that car wasn't suffering and in need of help.

When he reached the curve where the other vehicle had left the road, he parked and peered over the side where a shattered guardrail testified that he hadn't imagined the car's hapless flight. He didn't waste time wondering what to do, but quickly returned to his Jeep for the spool of nylon cord he'd purchased along with groceries and chains early this morning. Securing one end of the cord to the trailer hitch on his bumper and wrapping the other end around his waist and one shoulder to form a kind of harness, he began the laborious trip down the steep mountainside.

The snow was light and powdery, like Utah snow; otherwise he would have been soaked to the skin before he traveled twenty feet. Fleetingly he wondered how he knew about Utah snow. He dismissed the question; there were too many things a Vermont schoolboy who grew up to become a Dallas businessman couldn't explain.

Even powder turns wet in time and he could feel cold and wetness along his legs as he struggled through the knee-deep snow. More than once he stumbled over unseen rocks and shrubs and fell to his knees. Sometimes he rolled or skidded a considerable distance before regaining his feet. Each time, he struggled to become upright again and resume his trek down the mountainside.

He nearly tripped over the wreckage before he actually saw it. Raising one hand he wiped the snow from his face and eyelashes and stared at the twisted white sedan lying tilted to one side and tightly wedged between two tall spruces. Inanely he noticed the tires first, top-of-the-line touring tires, excellent for speed, but not meant for climbing the Rockies in a Colorado blizzard.

A caution that seemed to be instinctive had him moving slowly along the side of the vehicle as he approached the driver's crumpled door. The glass was gone from the window and he peered inside. At first the vehicle appeared to be empty and it took several seconds to recognize the snow-mounded shape lying across the seat and partially tucked beneath the dash as a human form.

Opening the door proved impossible, so he reached through the broken window to brush away the snow obscuring the man's face. The face meant nothing to him. Removing a glove, he moved his fingers along the side of the man's neck, searching for a pulse he knew he wouldn't find.

Withdrawing his head from the car window, he stood with both hands braced against the side of the wreck. What now? he questioned. Had this man been following him? How could he be certain?

There was only one answer and he grimaced in distaste; he'd have to search the body and the vehicle. He felt like a vulture as he circled the trees and car to approach from the lower side. Brushing snow from the mangled license plate he confirmed that the car had come from Texas, though he couldn't decipher all of the numbers.

He'd noticed the windows were both missing from the passenger side and the caved-in roof left a little more clearance on that side than over the driver's seat. He dropped to his knees, and after considerable struggle he pulled his six-foot frame through the narrow opening.

Gasping for breath, either from exertion or high altitude, he needed several minutes to orient himself to the task at hand. At least the blowing snow was less forceful inside the wreck, though it continued to sift a dusting of powder throughout the interior of the car.

With meticulous care he brushed snow from the body in the front seat and checked each pocket. He noted without surprise that the dead man had bled very little. Either his more serious injuries had been internal or the cold had inhibited the blood flow. He found a wallet with plenty of cash, but no identification. A small cell phone on the man's belt had been crushed beyond any possibility of salvaging. Next he turned to the glove compartment that had popped open due to the force with which the car had struck some object in its tumble down the mountain.

His hand closed around cold steel in its search for registration papers. Slowly he withdrew the gun and recognized its familiar weight and shape. Somewhere in his own murky past he'd had more than a passing familiarity with a semi-automatic Smith & Wesson like this one. Automatically he checked the load and removed one cartridge before tucking the gun in the back of his belt, beneath his jacket. Even if the gun were accidentally fired, the hammer would first strike an empty chamber.

Continuing his search, he placed a plastic box of shells and a sheaf of papers in his jacket pocket. He'd read the papers later. Even though the falling snow provided a kind of light, he couldn't see well enough to read. The gun and the driver's lack of I.D. verified his hunch that this man had been following him, but it wasn't conclusive evidence. He turned his head to where keys dangled from the ignition, but he knew an attempt to open the trunk would be futile. He'd already noticed how tightly the rear end of the car was lodged against one of the spruces, completely pinning the crushed trunk closed. Now that he was no longer moving, cold seeped through his wet clothes, reminding him he'd better get back to his own vehicle and get warm.

Sudden pain struck the back of his head. Convulsively his hands gripped the mangled dashboard and his body stiffened, expecting a second blow. When it didn't come, he slowly relaxed and looked around. Grimacing, he recognized his mistake. He'd been too hasty in his attempt to extricate his head and shoulders from the cramped space where he'd been conducting his search, and he'd bumped his head against an overhead piece of steel.

Lowering his head, he once more began to move backward. As he told his hands to release their death grip on the dashboard, something in the back of his mind began to scream an alert. His eyes flew to his hands. His left hand was gripping more than a twisted dashboard. Carefully he brushed away the remaining snow covering the object. He recognized it at once. No amount of wishful thinking could convince him the strange box with a small readout screen and several dials was a simple laptop or even a fuzzbuster. He had his answer; he was being followed all right, and he'd never spotted the car because it could stay miles behind and easily follow him with a tracking device like this one. In a flash of memory, he could see himself using a similar device on a fast-moving speed boat. A man with long black hair stood at the helm. Then, as quickly as the memory came, it was gone.

Cold sweat broke out down his back. Now he knew for sure someone was following him, but he still had no idea why. Panic surged through him. He had to get out; he had to get away; he had to reach Isadora. But first . . . he reached behind him and withdrew the gun. The accident had probably disabled the tracking device, but two or three sharp blows made certain it would tell no more tales.

By the time he worked his way out of the wreckage and re-coiled the end of the nylon cord around himself, he knew there was no need to try to cover his tracks. The wind had increased to an eerie howl and the snow swirled in dizzying waves. The storm would hide any evidence he'd been there. It might be days before someone discovered the broken guardrail and searched the slope below. The car would remain invisible from the road until spring.

The cord wasn't as helpful as a climbing rope would have been, but it kept him moving in the right direction and prevented his sliding back down the mountain as he stumbled steadily upward. Fatigue and cold took their toll, and he speculated whether adrenaline had the same power as antifreeze to keep a moving object from freezing. A hysterical laugh broke free and that sobered him enough to keep him climbing for several more minutes.

When he finally bumped into the guardrail, he stood stupidly trying to remember something for several seconds before he connected the rail with the Cherokee and stumbled forward the remaining few steps. His hands wouldn't work properly, and it took several agonizing minutes to open the door and collapse inside.

His teeth chattered and his movements were slow and clumsy as he fumbled to wrap himself in the car blanket he'd left on the back seat. He should remove his wet clothes and get into something dry, but his awkward fingers were beyond struggling with zippers and buttons. He just wanted to sleep, but an angry voice in the back of his head shouted he'd come too far to stop now. Sleep was death.

He had to reach Isadora; he had to find Sam. With a groan he pulled himself to a sitting position and fumbled with the key. It took several tries before the engine roared to life. Slumping forward, he pressed his aching head against the steering wheel until life-giving warmth revived him enough to make him realize he couldn't just sit there. He had to keep moving; he had to get away.

Before shifting into gear, he pulled a small brown bottle from a bag on the seat. One of the painkillers would take care of his headache, but he hesitated in the act of reaching for the thermos bottle that sat between the seats. He'd experienced this same reluctance before, almost as though he were violating some taboo. His hands shook as he poured coffee into the lid and brought the cup to his mouth. He swallowed the tablet, drained the cup, and shuddered. He didn't like the taste any better now than he had when they'd brought a cup of the hot brew to him in the hospital, but at least it was warm and perhaps the caffeine would help him fight off the lethargy that threatened to lull him to sleep.

Even with chains, the return trip to the summit was slow and arduous. Twice he had to back up to gain a running start to force the Jeep through monstrous drifts. The descent on the other side passed in a haze. He was only vaguely aware of driving through rolling foothills and crossing wide meadows.

Toward morning the snow began to subside and in the distance he could see a few lights indicating a small town. He anticipated getting breakfast and a room where he could sleep for a few hours before going on. He didn't know how much time he had. Common sense told him that whoever had invested in a sophisticated tracking device to follow him hadn't acted alone. Someone else was out there, and when he found his tracker had disappeared, he'd take up the chase.

Two things happened at once. A road appeared to the right and his foggy mind made a connection it should have made hours ago. The only way that the tracking device could have followed him all the way from Texas was if a signaling device was attached to his own vehicle. He didn't doubt for a minute someone else would pick up the signal and resume the chase. Without consciously planning his action, he swerved to the right. He could see steep mountains in that direction. He'd find an isolated area and go over the Cherokee with a fine-tooth comb until he found that device, then he'd destroy it. If he couldn't find the transmitter, he'd have to abandon the truck.

Thirty miles up the sadly deteriorating road, the choice was made for him when the engine sputtered and died. As he grabbed for the emergency brake to keep from rolling backward down the steep mountain road and off the side, he berated himself for his own folly. He should have continued on to the small town he'd seen just before dawn and bought gas. How could something so important have completely slipped his mind?

Closing his eyes, he shook his head and wondered if he might be insane. It wasn't the first time he'd questioned his mental condition. Two weeks ago he'd awakened in a private room in a Dallas hospital with almost no memory of who he was and how he'd gotten there. He'd been plagued by horrifying dreams that made no sense. Vague memories of a jungle cell and indescribable pain haunted his waking hours. There was also something he mustn't tell anyone. A doctor had assured him that physically he was fine, though he was seriously malnourished. The good doctor had continued to provide him with bits and pieces of his life, though nothing but the agonizing months he'd spent in a foreign jail felt real. The doctor had given him a prescription for pain medication for his persistent headaches and encouraged him to talk about a past he couldn't remember.

Someone from Washington—he never had gotten it straight whether the man was C.I.A., military, or some kind of lawyer—had told him his imprisonment had been a mistake and his rescue was an accident. He'd been on a business trip to South America when guerrillas in the war-torn country had mistaken him for a gunrunner who had double-crossed them. They'd held him until government soldiers had stormed the insurgents' stronghold, freed him, and turned him over to the U.S. consulate. Some American politician had flown him back to Texas aboard his private jet.

The government man had told him to put it all behind him, return to his condo and his healthy bank account, and get on with his life. Only he couldn't do it. His unreliable mind warned him not to confide in anyone, that he was still in danger, and urged him to flee.

Crazy or not, he couldn't continue to sit here and wait for the snow to bury him. He opened his eyes and felt something strange as he surveyed the mountainous splendor all around him. He had no idea where he might be, but he'd been here before. The mountain peaks, even shrouded in white and trailing lingering clouds, were the first familiar sight he'd recognized since he'd awakened in the hospital. He knew, too, that a small cabin lay nestled in a side canyon approximately six miles further up the road. Excitement gripped him and his mind filled with purpose.

He reached behind him for his duffle bag, then decided not to take it with him. The hike would be difficult in knee-high snow, and the bag would be too much to carry. Instead he unzipped the bag and drew out two pairs of heavy socks and an old pair of sweat pants someone had loaned him while he'd been in the hospital. Without removing the jeans that had dried and stiffened against his legs, he pulled the sweat pants over them. He removed his running shoes and replaced his damp pair of socks with new ones, then struggled back into the shoes. Reaching into his bag once more, he grabbed a couple of t-shirts, a sweater, and a fresh hooded sweatshirt. After donning them, he rezipped his jacket, then hesitated before reaching for the small brown plastic bottle. He shoved it into his jacket pocket with the box of shells and the papers he'd taken from the wreck. He drained the last of the coffee and shoved an apple and a package of cookies into the other pocket of his windbreaker.

Taking a deep breath, he opened his door, then reaching sideways, he released the emergency brake. As the Jeep Cherokee began rolling backward, he jumped to the ground. At first it moved sluggishly and he wondered if the deep snow would force it to a halt, but slowly it gained momentum. When the Jeep reached a curve a hundred yards away, unlike the road, it failed to turn. In seconds it left the road, appeared to teeter at the edge of the cliff, then tumbled over the edge. When the sound of tearing metal pounding against rocks far below caught his ears, he turned his back and began walking.